With a swift movement Marcus kissed Antonia full on the lips.

Momentarily Antonia was too stunned to resist, then she broke away from the heat of his mouth, bringing up her right hand to slap his cheek.

Marcus straightened, ruefully rubbing his face. 'I suppose I deserved that, but I must confess, Miss Dane, that your. . .eccentricity quite robbed me of my good sense.'

'I think not, sir! I believe that your overweening arrogance leads you to believe you can take whatever you want! Do not trouble to ring for the butler, my lord—I can see myself out!'

Francesca Shaw is not one but two authors, working together under the same name. Both are librarians by profession, working in Hertfordshire but living within distance of each other in Bedfordshire. They first began writing ten years ago under a tree in a Burgundian vineyard, but although they have published other romances they have only recently come to historical novels. Their shared interests include travel, good food, reading and, of course, writing.

Recent titles by the same author:

A COMPROMISED LADY

THE UNCONVENTIONAL MISS DANE

Francesca Shaw

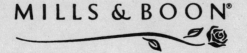

MILLS & BOON®

MILLS & BOON and MILLS & BOON with the Rose Device are registered trademarks of the publisher.

First published in Great Britain 1997
Harlequin Mills & Boon Limited,
Eton House, 18-24 Paradise Road, Richmond, Surrey TW9 1SR

© Francesca Shaw 1997

ISBN 0 263 80436 4

Set in Times 10 on 12 pt. by
Rowland Phototypesetting Limited
Bury St Edmunds, Suffolk

04-9711-73842

Printed and bound in Great Britain

Chapter One

The stagecoach lurched, then with infinite slowness toppled on to its right-hand side, precipitating Miss Antonia Dane into the lap of the portly bank clerk next to her. Wildly clutching at his lapels only served to take both of them on to the floor of the coach, where they were shortly joined by a curate, a basket of apples and a small child who promptly set up a piercing wail.

'Donna!' Antonia looked round anxiously for her companion as she attempted to lever herself upright from the mass of tumbled humanity. 'Oh, I do beg your pardon, sir,' she apologised, removing her elbow from the clerk's midriff. 'Donna, there you are! Are you unhurt?'

'A little shaken, my dear, but otherwise unhurt, I believe.' Miss Maria Donaldson came into Antonia's view over the heap of bodies, patting her neatly coiled hair into place, her pince-nez already firmly back in position on the tip of her nose. 'But I think we should alight as soon as may be.' She turned to the red-faced farmer wedged next to her. 'If you could force open the door, sir, I believe I could climb through.'

After considerable upheavals, the farmer managed to

assist Donna's slight frame through the door and on to the sloping side of the coach. Sensing escape, the small child set up a fresh wail and to Antonia's relief was handed up to his mother who followed Miss Donaldson into the spring sunshine.

It was a shaken but unhurt group of passengers who eventually assembled on the rutted road to view the wreck of their conveyance. The driver and guard unhitched and calmed the horses, but further useful activity then seemed beyond them. The driver removed a filthy hat the better to scratch his equally dirty hair, the guard helpfully kicked the nearest wheel and the men amongst the passengers stood around sucking their teeth in contemplation of the depth of the ditch into which the coach had fallen.

'Really, my dear Antonia,' Miss Donaldson murmured gently. 'I have never been able to understand why men feel that giving something a sharp kick will restore it to working order.'

Antonia's lips quirked in amusement. 'It never works, but I think it must make them feel better. Come, let us see if our luggage is still safely strapped on behind.'

'Your elbow has come through the sleeve of your gown,' Miss Donaldson observed as they turned from their scrutiny of the large luggage basket at the rear of the stagecoach. 'Is your pelisse still in the coach?'

'It must be,' Antonia responded indifferently, her fingers twitching together the hole in the threadbare linen sleeve. 'It proves I was right to wear this old gown for the journey—I have too few good dresses to damage like this.'

She set her straw bonnet straight on her head, tucking in a straggling brown curl and retying the ribbons under her chin. 'I think we will achieve little by waiting here until the coachman finally realises he must send for help. The last fingerpost said Rybury was only three miles; if we take our pelisses and handbags from the coach, we can walk and at least wait for our luggage in comfort at the inn.'

The curate, who was more than happy to assist the ladies, was just handing out their things from inside the coach when, with a thud of hooves on the wet chalk, two horsemen rounded the bend and reined in at the sight of the shambles in their path.

'My lord!' exclaimed the curate with delighted recognition of the man who sat astride the tall chestnut gelding. 'This is Providence indeed, if you would be so kind as to instruct your groom to get help to right the coach.'

The nobleman thus addressed dismounted, tossing his reins to his groom before striding over to regard the wreck. 'Has anyone been hurt, Mr Todd?' he enquired of the curate, his glance keenly surveying the ill-assorted group of passengers.

Antonia encountered the brief scrutiny of a pair of dark brown eyes before they moved on to as swiftly peruse and dismiss the small birdlike figure of her companion. She found herself colouring, with what had to be indignation, at such a cursory survey. For although shabbily dressed, and undoubtedly not at her best after a long coach journey, Miss Antonia Dane with her tall figure and striking dark looks was accustomed to attracting more attention than this man had afforded her!

Her eyes followed the tall, carelessly elegant figure as he stood, hands on hips, regarding the stage coach and the ditch. Bareheaded, the light breeze ruffled his dark blond hair which was, Miss Dane decided, in sore need of his barber's attention. He might appear careless of his dress, but cut and cloth were of the finest and the burnished leather of his long boots spoke of a man who need not, unlike Miss Dane, watch every penny.

Mr Todd the curate trailed after him, explaining to his lordship the circumstances of the accident and the fortunate fact that no one had been injured. The groom nudged his own hack forward. 'Shall I ride to the village for help, my lord?'

'No need, Saye. We passed Shoebridge and Otterly hedging the Long Meadow back around the bend; fetch them and we will have enough men to right the thing.'

As the groom cantered off, his lordship turned to the coachman and guard who shuffled to attention, recognising authority when they saw it. 'You—hitch the horses up on long traces, and you two, fetch cut poles from that pile there. . .'

Antonia watched him take command, organising and ordering until the male passengers were marshalled into an obedient team, some levering up the wheel, others with their shoulders to the rear of the vehicle. With the addition of two sturdy hedgers and with Saye at the horses' heads, the stranded coach began to teeter upright, then stuck again in the soft soil of the bank top.

'I fear we cannot do it, Lord Allington,' Mr Todd gasped, his clerical black besmirched by mud. 'We must summon more help from the village.'

Without reply, his lordship stripped off his buff coat, rolled up his sleeves, and applied his shoulder to the coach. Thus encouraged, the men exerted themselves to the utmost and heaved. Seconds later, with a shuddering crash, the vehicle once more stood on four wheels.

The coachman and groom rehitched the team, the grateful passengers picked up their luggage and began to climb aboard and Lord Allington, fending off the flustered attempts of the curate to brush down his coat, remounted and rode off.

'How very gratifying,' Miss Dane remarked waspishly, pausing on the step of the coach to regard Lord Allington's retreating back, 'to have the leisure to ride round the countryside setting we lesser mortals to rights.'

Miss Donaldson cast a sideways glance at her former pupil, noting the pinkness of her cheeks and the brightness of her dark hazel eyes. Antonia always exhibited an independence of spirit, more to be expected of a fashionable matron than an unmarried lady of four-and-twenty, but even so, Lord Allington seemed to have ruffled her out of her habitual well-bred composure.

'He is a local gentleman, by all accounts,' Miss Donaldson observed calmly. 'And even you must concede, Miss Dane, that it was fortunate that he had the leisure to rescue us today.'

Mr Todd, catching the reference to their rescuer as he handed her into the coach, added, 'That was Marcus, Lord Allington, from Brightshill. He is of an old Hertfordshire family and owns all the land on this side of Berkhamsted to the crest of the Downs.'

Antonia settled in her place before remarking, with a deceptively gentle smile, 'Not quite all, Mr Todd. You forget, do you not, the Rye End Hall lands?'

'One hardly regards those any longer,' the curate responded dismissively. 'The lands and Hall are sadly neglected, as one might expect after the scandalous behaviour of the last owner—but I shall say no more of that in front of ladies. It will be a good thing if the rumours are correct and Lord Allington does intend to add them all to his own extensive estate. They will then be subject to the good husbandry which characterises the Brightshill lands—and the tenants will be employed. There is too much want in Rybury.'

Antonia opened her mouth as if to speak, then closed it, staring out of the window with furrowed brow. Miss Donaldson, seeing the look of worry, said low-voiced, 'Did you never meet Marcus Allington when you still lived at Rye End Hall?'

'You forget, Donna, in the ten years since I left home to live with Great Aunt in London, I have never been back to Rye End Hall. It must have been this man's father who was at Brightshill when I was a child, and he would have been away at school and university, I suppose. I would not know if my father or brother knew them well.'

Miss Donaldson reflected that, from what she had heard of the late and unlamented Sir Humphrey Dane, normal social intercourse with his neighbours would not have figured large either for himself, or for Antonia's late brother Howard.

The coach was finally rumbling into Rybury and pulling up before the only inn the village boasted. The host of the Bell walked out to greet the passengers, all of whom were only too pleased at the chance to sit in comfort and drink his ale while exclaiming loudly over their recent misadventure.

The coachman and guard lifted down the ladies' luggage and Antonia and Donna stood looking round. Rybury, neat rather than picturesque, looked at its best in the spring sunshine with primroses on the green and children fishing for tiddlers in the Rye Brook. The pike road cut across the green and a by-road led over a bridge to a straggle of cottages, on the edge of a fine stand of woodland already touched with new green.

'Would you ladies be requiring the use of a cart?' the landlord enquired, wiping his hands on his apron as he approached.

'Yes, thank you, landlord. We will need these trunks taking to Rye End Hall; is there a carter who can help?'

'Our Jem can do that for you, ma'am, just as soon as he's finished serving the coach passengers. It's a nice clean cart for you ladies, better than that old thing.' He nodded towards the stagecoach. 'Would you care to step into the private parlour and take some refreshment while you wait, ma'am?'

As he ushered them into a rather dingy front room, he chatted on. 'Going to be staying at the Hall, then? That's been empty this last six months since Sir Humphrey and Master Howard were both carried off within a fortnight of each other.' He shook his head. 'Sometimes I wonder if it weren't a judgement on them both and the wicked life they led. . .'

Miss Donaldson cleared her throat reprovingly and he darted a quick glance at her frosty profile. 'Begging your pardon, ladies, you did know what had occurred. . .?'

'Sir Humphrey was my father, Mr Howard Dane was my only brother,' Antonia supplied quietly.

'Oh. . .ah! Sorry, ma'am, if I've spoken out of turn. The coach is just leaving now, I'll get young Jem out directly.' He hurried away, clearly realising he had over-stepped the mark.

'I can see the local people held my father and brother in as high regard as we, Donna,' Antonia remarked bitterly, pacing up and down the rather lurid Turkey rug before the fire. 'The lord knows what we will find when we finally get to Rye End Hall!'

Young Jem, a skinny version of his father the landlord, soon appeared with the cart, drawn by a neat cob, and set to loading the baggage and trunks before fetching his passengers.

Miss Donaldson, regarding the narrow seat, began to climb into the back, saying, 'I can sit here on the trunk, my dear.'

'I shall not hear of it Donna!' Antonia protested. 'You sit up here in the front with Jem—I will walk through the woods. I have a headache coming on, and it is less than a mile by the footpath,' she added as Donna still looked unsure.

She followed the cart across the green and past the cottages, pleased to find, after a few yards, the beginning of the footpath she remembered. As she picked up the hem of her skirts and hopped over the frequent muddy patches in her stout boots, Antonia reflected that it must be a full ten years since she had last trodden this path.

Then her mother had just died and her father had not yet embarked on the course of drinking, gambling and philandering which had ruined the family fortunes and corrupted her brother. As soon as rumours of his conduct began to reach polite Society, her great aunt, Lady Honoria Granger, had descended and borne her off to Town. Honoria had expected some opposition from her niece's husband, but Sir Humphrey had been only too pleased to be spared the trouble of bringing up a daughter.

It had been fortunate that Lady Honoria had been left well provided for by her late husband and had been able to afford to educate and then bring out Antonia, for Sir Humphrey, with the girl off his hands, had shown every sign of forgetting he had ever had a daughter.

Antonia stopped every now and again to pick primroses, feeling more at ease now she was out of that wretched public conveyance. How right she had been to wear her old gown, she thought, seeing the chalky mud spatters around the hem.

Whilst she had lived with her great aunt, she had wanted for nothing, but when the old lady had finally succumbed to increasing old age and had gone to live under her grandson's roof, her cousin, mindful of his own inheritance, had wasted no time in pointing out to Antonia that she could expect no more support from that quarter.

Antonia had been under the misapprehension that she had been living on income from her mother's legacy to her, but Cousin Hewitt had soon, and with smug satisfaction, put her right. Not only would she now have to manage without great aunt Honoria's beneficence, but Hewitt Granger had also made it pretty plain that she and her companion, Miss Donaldson, must find alternative accommodation.

Slowly following the winding path, Antonia found herself in a clearing full of sunlight. Shedding her bonnet and pelisse, she perched on a fallen tree and held her face up to the warmth, grateful to be in the clear air and out of London.

In the midst of the upheavals of her aunt's infirmity and removal, the death in a driving accident of a brother who had been almost unknown to her and the sudden demise of her father from an apoplexy a mere two weeks afterwards had passed as though they had been no concern of hers. The family solicitor had dealt with everything. After a precarious half-year in lodgings whilst the lawyer sold all he could find to settle Sir Humphrey's debts, Antonia had finally received word that only the house and land remained.

She was just reflecting, and not for the first time, on how fortunate she was that Donna, her old governess, had offered to accompany her to Rye End Hall, when she heard a boy's voice raised in a yelp of pain. Heedless of her discarded bonnet and cloak, Antonia ran across the clearing, pushed through a straggle of branches and found herself in the company of two urchins, neither of them a day over ten years of age.

One, a wiry redhead, was disentangling himself from the bramble bush into which he had tripped. His companion, an even grubbier child, was holding by the feet four limp-necked, and very dead, cock pheasants.

There was a long moment while the children stared at her, round-eyed with terror, then, as she took a step towards them, they dropped the birds and took to their heels.

Well! The local poachers certainly started young hereabouts, Antonia thought, stooping to pick up the still-warm pheasants. No doubt they were encouraged by a lack of keepering, for in the depths of debt Sir Humphrey had discharged all his servants but for a slatternly housekeeper. Still, the birds were hers, snared on her own land, and they would at least serve as supper tonight!

'Caught red-handed!' a triumphant, rough voice said behind her. Antonia spun round to find two burly individuals in decent homespuns, shotguns under their arms and a couple of terriers at their heels, confronting her. 'Did you ever see the like, Nat? A female poacher, as I live and breathe. You give us those birds, my pretty, and come along of us quiet-like.'

Antonia opened her mouth to protest that she had just picked up the birds; then the thought of those two skinny, frightened children, and what would happen to them if these men caught them, kept her silent.

The two keepers advanced towards her, one taking the birds from her limp grasp, the other seizing her roughly by the arm, tearing the old gown even more. Shocked by the contact, Antonia gasped and pulled away.

'Let me go!' she demanded breathlessly.

'Let you go? Oh dear, no! After we've caught you on his lordship's land, with his lordship's pheasants?' He grinned, exposing stained teeth. 'It's your lucky day, my pretty, you won't have to cool your heels in the village lock-up. Oh, no, his lordship's at home, and him being a Justice of the Peace, he likes to see a poacher whenever we catch one. And he'll like to see this one, won't he, Nat?'

Both men eyed Antonia slyly. She was suddenly very aware that she was without bonnet or pelisse, that her old linen gown clung around her limbs and she was quite unchaperoned.

Who could they mean by 'his lordship'? This was Rye End Hall land—her land—but the humiliation of arguing about her identity with these two was more than she could countenance. No, better to go along with it and get out of this wood as quickly as possible. Whoever this magistrate was, at least he would be a gentleman and she could make her explanations to him in decent privacy.

The keeper's fingers were moving suggestively on her bare skin through the tear in her gown. Antonia turned such a look of glacial fury on him that he let go of her elbow, then, recalling himself, seized her painfully by the wrist instead.

The walk back through the woods was mercifully short, but by the time they reached the stable block of a big house she did not recognise Antonia was flushed and breathless, her hair tumbling about her face and her skirts torn and bedraggled.

Her captors marched her through the servants' quarters, up the backstairs, through a green baize door and into a hallway that seemed vaguely familiar to Antonia. The butler, alerted by the commotion, emerged from the dining room to hear the gamekeeper's explanations. He looked her up and down with utter disdain, before departing to inform his master of the arrival of a felon for his attention.

Antonia stood, inwardly shuddering with mortification, forcing herself not to struggle and thus appear even more undignified and unladylike than she already must. After all, when in the presence of this gentleman, she could explain the circumstances of this unfortunate incident. And what was more, she fumed, she expected an apology for the behaviour of his keepers for their overzealousness in straying onto her land and their insulting familiarity with her person!

When the butler finally reappeared to usher them in, she straightened her back, raised her chin and stalked with as much hauteur as she could manage in the circumstances, into the study.

The magistrate into whose presence she had been hauled was sitting behind a wide mahogany desk, his fingers drumming impatiently on the leather surface beside a pile of papers which had been pushed to one side.

Antonia stared in horrified recognition at the man she

had seen only hours before. Lord Allington, for it was indeed he, returned her stare without the slightest sign he had ever set eyes on her before.

Raising one tawny brow, he remarked, 'Well done, Sparrow: you have enlivened what was proving to be a thoroughly dull day. I was hoping for a diversion from this tedious correspondence—' his long fingers flicked the pile of papers dismissively '—but a female poacher is more than I could have looked for. Thank you, Sparrow, you and Carling may go.'

'What, and just leave her, my lord?' The senior game-keeper was surprised.

'Well, I hardly feel she is likely to prove more than I can handle; or do you think she has a dangerous weapon concealed somewhere?' The dark brown eyes were warm as he surveyed the clinging, bedraggled gown that did nothing to hide the form beneath. Antonia flushed angrily, but gritted her teeth, determined not to bandy words with him in front of the keepers.

With barely concealed reluctance the two men shuffled out, closing the door behind them. Antonia put up a hand to push the hair off her face and realised she had succeeded in spreading dirt, and what felt horribly like pheasant's blood, all over her forehead.

Marcus Allington got up and came round the desk to look at her more closely. 'You are certainly a novelty, my dear, and a considerable improvement on the usual crew who plunder my birds. At least, if you were cleaned up, you might be. . .' He continued to stroll round her.

Antonia felt the blood burning up her throat and cheeks at the insolence of the scrutiny.

'Now, what shall we do with you, I wonder?' He came back round to face her. 'I suppose you realise I could sentence you to hard labour for this—your fingers would not be so ready for setting snares after that.'

He lifted Antonia's right hand, turning it over caressingly between strong fingers whilst holding her furious gaze with his eyes. Even in the midst of her anger, she saw the sudden surprise as his touch registered the soft skin where he had expected work-hardened roughness.

Seizing her advantage, Antonia snatched her hand away and, in a swirl of muddy skirts, put a heavy chair between herself and Lord Allington.

'You are no village wench, not with hands like that! So...who the devil are you? And what are you doing with my birds?' he demanded, voice suddenly hard.

Antonia found her tongue at last, and spoke with all the hauteur at her command. 'A lady, sir, and one who does not relish being manhandled by either you or your men.'

'Damn it, woman, do you expect me to believe that? Look at yourself!' His scornful stare swept from the top of her disordered hair to her boots emerging from beneath her muddy hem.

'Kindly mind your language, my lord,' Antonia said frostily, sinking on to the chair with as much grace as if she were at Almack's, and not in danger of having her knees give way beneath her.

Marcus Allington sketched her an ironic bow before leaning indolently against the edge of the desk. 'My humble apologies, madam. I should have realised, from the moment I set eyes upon you, that I was dealing with a member of the Quality.'

Flushing, Antonia looked down at herself. Mud-caked walking boots were all too obvious below a torn and besmirched hemline. Her old and faded gown was ripped, there were bloodstains where the birds had touched the skirts and her elbow protruded through the hopelessly threadbare sleeve. Without her bonnet, her dark brown curls, always hard to manage, now cascaded about her shoulders and she could feel her face was filthy.

She glared at him, resenting his easy elegance, even in the riding apparel he still wore. Marcus Allington's broad shoulders and long, muscular legs were set off to perfection by the country clothes. . . Antonia recollected herself, annoyed at the spark of attraction she had felt for an instant.

'If I present a disordered appearance, it is no wonder,' she retorted sharply. 'Having been set upon, dragged through the mire and brambles—is it any wonder? And,' she pursued, before he had a chance to reply, 'all I was doing was walking in the woods.'

'Trespassing on my land, in possession of my game.' His voice was flat, his face hard. 'I expect my keepers to earn their wages. Madam,' he added sarcastically.

'Your land? I hardly think so, my lord. Those woods are Rye End Hall land.'

'Not for these past five years.' He regarded her with sudden interest. 'What do you know of Rye End Hall?'

'I own it,' Antonia informed him coldly. With an effort she tried to hide her dismay at the discovery that her father had sold off land. How much more had gone without her knowing? It had never occurred to her to scrutinise the estate maps when the solicitor had handed them back to her: she knew the extent of Rye End Hall lands too well. If Sir Humphrey had sold off woods so close to the house, what else might have gone?

'You appear surprised, madam?' It was a question, but his voice held more sympathy than previously. 'Surely you have not been sold short in your purchase of Rye End Hall?'

'I have not purchased it, my lord; it came to me on the death of my father.'

'Your father?' Now it was Marcus Allington's turn to be taken aback. 'You cannot be Sir Humphrey Dane's daughter!'

'And why not?' Antonia's chin came up defiantly. Whatever her father and her brother had become, the Danes were an old and proud family, and all her instincts and her great aunt's training were evident in her bearing now.

Despite her ludicrous appearance, Marcus could not now doubt she was telling the truth. The more he looked at her, the more he saw a family resemblance. He remembered her grandfather, white-haired and patrician, visiting his own grandparents; how as a young boy he had been overawed by the bearing he now saw traces of in this woman.

'You have to admit, Miss Dane, that your appearance, and the circumstances in which we meet, are much against you.' He straightened, crossing to the bellpull beside the fireplace. 'Let me order you some refreshment, and then you must tell me how I may help you.'

Antonia realised just how hungry she was: they had set forth from the Golden Fleece in Holborn before dawn and a hastily snatched meal of bacon and bread at Abbots Langley was hours in the past.

The footman was hard put to disguise his amazement at being sent for sherry and biscuits for the female who had just been dragged through the servants' quarters as a common criminal.

She fell to hungrily when the refreshment arrived, then

recollected herself and nibbled delicately at the almond wafer. 'You are very kind, my lord, but I am in no need of assistance.'

Marcus Allington possessed the irritating ability to raise one eyebrow. He said nothing, but the quirked brow and the ironic twist to his lips, spoke volumes.

Antonia flushed, goaded into an explanation she did not want to make. 'I can see you wonder at my gown, sir, but if one travels on the public stage, naturally one does not don one's best attire for the journey.' His eyes were resting thoughtfully on the torn sleeve and Antonia hurried on, 'Your men tore my garment when they apprehended me!'

'No. . .' Amused recollection lit the brown eyes. 'It was already torn after the accident to the stagecoach.'

Antonia, scarcely acknowledging to herself that she had been piqued by his lack of recognition, blurted out, 'When I was dragged into your presence, you made no sign you had seen me before.'

'You must forgive me,' he said smoothly, sipping his sherry. 'I remembered the tear, but not, I regret, you. Although, now I come to think of it, you were, were you not, wearing a bonnet and pelisse?'

'I had laid them aside in the woods, just before your men came upon me.'

'All the better to catch my pheasants, no doubt,' he said drily.

'I have already told you, I did not know they were yours. And of course I did not catch them—I. . .I found them upon the footpath.' She had no intention of betraying the two urchins.

'Tsk, tsk, Miss Dane,' Lord Allington admonished. 'You really are a very poor liar.' His voice hardened.

'Let us stop playing games. I believe neither that you caught those birds nor that you found them. Describe the culprit you had them of, madam, for you do yourself no favours in my eyes in protecting him.'

'Liar? How dare you, sir! Being in or out of your favour counts as nothing to me. If I prevaricated, it was simply because I have no intention of delivering up to your tender mercies one of your unfortunate tenants, forced into poaching merely to stay alive!' She was upright and quivering with fury in the chair.

'It is not my tenants who are starving, Miss Dane.' Marcus strode over to where she sat. When he put one hand on each arm of her chair, she had to will herself not to shrink back from his cold regard. 'When you reach your inheritance, madam, look around you and see the state in which your departed father left his people, before you come preaching to me of mine.'

Antonia stared back into his hard face, appalled at what he had told her. She did not know how to respond: he was too close, too overpoweringly male. . .

With a swift movement he bent his tawny head and kissed her full on the lips with a hard, possessive, sensuality. Momentarily she was too stunned to resist, then she broke away from the heat of his mouth, bringing up her right hand to slap his cheek.

Marcus straightened, ruefully rubbing his face. 'I suppose I deserved that, but I must confess, Miss Dane, that your. . .eccentricity quite robbed me of my good sense.'

Antonia sprang from the chair in a swirl of skirts. 'I think not, sir! I believe that your overweening arrogance leads you to believe you can take whatever you want! Do not trouble to ring for the butler, my lord—I can see myself out!'

Her hand was on the doorknob when he said softly, 'Miss Dane.'

Hating herself for responding, Antonia turned to look at him. 'Well?'

'Feed your tenants, Miss Dane, then at least they will not have to steal my property to survive.'

Chapter Two

Antonia swept past a startled footman, who leapt to open the front door for her, down the shallow flight of stone steps and halfway down the gravelled drive before her anger calmed enough for her to slow to a stop. As consumed by anger as she was, there was no point in storming off into the Hertfordshire countryside without getting her bearings first.

Now she could see the front of the house, she realised that she could recall it from rare visits as a small child with her grandfather. But her memories were of a far less elegant effect: it was obvious that Marcus Allington had applied both an admirable taste and considerable amounts of money to Brightshill.

The pleasure grounds were beautifully kept, with close-scythed lawns sweeping to stands of specimen trees. Through the trees she could see the glimmer of water where she could have sworn none had been before and the drive was bordered by classical statuary, each pedestal nestling in a group of flowering shrubs.

'Insufferable man!' Antonia fumed aloud. She felt even more down at heel and grimy in this setting, the only discordant note in a perfect landscape. 'Well, I am glad of it!' she exclaimed. 'Serve him right if I lower the tone!' She realised she was scuffing the perfectly raked gravel with her boot, to the betterment of neither. She was in danger of forgetting who she was, although after being mauled like a loose woman by that. . .that. . . man, it was little wonder.

She shot a fulminating glance in the direction of the study window and was startled to see Marcus Allington standing at the casement, regarding her. Antonia straightened her shoulders, gathered up her frightful skirts in one hand and swept an elaborate curtsy to the semi-clad deity on the nearest pedestal. Looking closer, she saw he bore a quite remarkable resemblance to the Prince Regent—although without the corsets—a thought that brought back her natural sense of the ridiculous.

Giggling faintly, and without a second backward glance, Antonia walked down the drive as though she owned it. Once through the gates she began to hurry, half-running, conscious that it must be a good two hours since she had parted from her companion and that Donna would be becoming anxious.

The wind through the bare hedges was turning sharp as the afternoon drew in and she was reminded that, however pleasant the day had been, it was still only March and she was without her pelisse and bonnet.

Suddenly the neatly cut and laid hedges and sharply defined ditches gave way to a raggle-taggle of overgrown bushes and choked muddy puddles. Through one of many gaps in the boundary, Antonia could see an ill-drained field with clumps of dead thistles here and there. There was no doubt she was now on Rye End Hall land. The fruits of her father's and brother's neglect were only too evident: Antonia remembered uneasily Lord Allington's comment about her tenants.

She turned into the entrance of the Hall, between rusted gates hanging crazily from the tall posts. The lodge houses were empty; their neat little gardens, which she remembered from her childhood, were now lost under brambles and nettles.

Hurrying up the drive, Antonia formulated a light-hearted version of her adventures to tell Donna, carefully omitting all references to that insolent, exciting kiss. Miss Donaldson might be small in stature and a gentlewoman to her backbone, but she would have no compunction in marching round to Brightshill and telling his lordship precisely what she thought of his outrageously forward behaviour!

The front door opened as she approached and there was Donna, her anxious expression lifting in relief. 'There you are, my dear! I was just trying to decide whether I should go in search of you.' She broke off as her eyes took in the full awfulness of Antonia's appearance.

'What have you been doing? There is blood on your face—are you hurt? Have you fallen in the woods?' She ushered Antonia in as she spoke, hurrying her through the hall and into the kitchens at the rear of the house.

'No, no,' Antonia hastened to reassure her. 'It is pheasant blood, not my own. I have had quite an adventure, Donna—and another encounter with Lord Allington, our infuriating neighbour.'

'Infuriating, dear? Oh, bother this fire, it will never get the water warm if I cannot induce it to draw better.' She raked at the smouldering logs in the grate but to little effect.

Antonia sank wearily on to a settle and stared round at the dereliction that was the kitchens. The walls she had always remembered as lime-washed twice a year were begrimed with smoke and hung with cobwebs. The chimney crane and jacks were rusted and the wide shelves and dressers were either empty or heaped with filthy piles of chipped crockery. Miss Donaldson had obviously found a broom, for the flags in front of the hearth and settle had been swept, only to reveal the ingrained grime of the floor beneath.

'It cannot have become so squalid in a mere six months,' Antonia said despairingly. 'No wonder the lawyer advised against our returning here! Well, perhaps this is the worst room. If Father hired some slattern of a cook. . .' Her voice trailed away as she saw Donna's face. 'Are they all as bad as this?' she asked despairingly.

Donna came and sat next to her on the settle, taking her hand in hers as if to give the younger woman strength. 'I have not looked into all of the rooms—perhaps the kitchen seems worse because you remember it as a place of bustling activity, bright and clean in your dear mama's day—but all seem filthy and there is hardly any furniture remaining.'

Antonia took a deep breath, ruthlessly quashing the strong desire to burst into tears and run pell-mell down the drive to take refuge in the inn. This was their home now, and they were going to have to make the best of it. 'Well, it is getting dark and we must find some candles, heat some water and have something to eat before we go to bed. It is too late now to try and improve matters.'

Faint steam was at last rising off the kettle. Antonia poured a little into a bowl and washed her face and hands while Donna fastidiously brushed off the surface of the table, spread a cloth she had brought in the food hamper upon it and began to unpack their provisions.

Their simple supper was soon spread out: some potted ham, cheese, apples, bread and butter and a fruit cake. Donna made tea, after scouring a cracked teapot she found on a shelf, and they drank it, grateful for its warmth. As they ate, Donna prompted Antonia to recount the tale of her afternoon's adventure. Even the heavily censored version she received was enough to make her shudder, and exclaim at intervals.

Replete, Antonia sat back and pushed out her feet towards the faint heat from the range. 'Let us simply leave everything as it is until the morning. We cannot see to do anything, and we have had a long and wearisome day.' Even as she spoke, there was a rustling and a scuttling from behind the dresser. 'Oh, no! Mice!'

'If we are fortunate,' Donna replied grimly, packing the food back into the wicker hamper as she spoke. 'I did not like to tell you, my dear, but when I first entered the kitchen I fear I saw a rat.'

'Urgh! Well, that is tomorrow's first task—to find a ratcatcher and a large cat. Let us see if we can find a bedroom fit to sleep in.'

A dispiriting survey by candlelight revealed a series of filthy chambers, only three of which contained beds. They finally decided on the room that evidently had been occupied by the housekeeper, before she had finally been driven out by Sir Humphrey's outrageous behaviour and total unwillingness to pay wages.

Made up with their own linen, the bed was at least clean, if not particularly comfortable. But even the pervading smell of damp was not enough to keep the ladies awake; both were asleep almost as soon as their heads touched the pillows.

By seven o'clock the next morning, they were already breakfasted and holding a council of war in the kitchen. Antonia was attempting to make a list on a piece of paper retrieved from Sir Humphrey's study, along with a blunt quill pen and a pot of thick brown ink. 'I will put down some ink on the list first of all!'

Miss Donaldson watched her young companion's bent head with a worried frown in her eyes. The candlelight struck burnished lights from her hair and her pleasant voice was light and amused. Really, Miss Donaldson mused, any other young lady of her acquaintance would be having a fit of the vapours by now.

In the years Donna had known Antonia, she had come to respect her spirit, the courage that allowed her to rise above all the misfortunes that had come her way. She would cope with this disaster of a house, that was certain: but she did not deserve the burden.

'Donna. . . Donna?' Antonia tapped her hand with the quill. 'You have not been listening to a word I have said! We need to make a list of provisions and one of us must walk into Rybury and see what we may purchase there. No doubt young Jem from the inn would be willing to fetch the rest from Berkhamsted for a small consideration. He seems a reliable lad, do you not agree?'

A furtive scratching in the wainscot reminded them of another pressing need. 'And send up the ratcatcher,' said Donna with a shudder. 'There must be a woman in the village who will come up to scrub. . .'

'Let us hire two if we can,' Antonia interrupted. 'It

will take more than one woman and our own efforts to set this place to rights!'

The light from a fresh, sunny morning was struggling through the begrimed windows. Donna blew out the candles and crossed the kitchen floor to throw open the back door, letting in a flood of spring sunshine and the smell of damp earth. It also admitted young Jem, cap in hand and pink with the importance of his message.

'Good morning, and begging your pardon, ladies, but my ma says, do you need some things fetching, or any help, like?'

'Jem, you are a godsend,' Antonia beamed at him, deepening his confusion. 'Come in and sit down while we finish this list of provisions. And tell me, Jem, are there any women in the village who would come and clean for us?'

'Oh yes, ma'am.' Then a look of doubt came over his face. 'Well, that is. . .er. . .'

'For a regular weekly wage, of course,' Miss Donaldson supplied firmly. She knew enough of Sir Humphrey to realise why Jem was doubtful. 'And a rat-catcher.'

'That'll be Walter Armitage, so long as he's over his rheum,' Jem said helpfully. 'And what about a cat, ma'am?'

'That would be perfect, Jem, if you can find one. Now, here is the list. Do you remember everything we need?'

'Provisions, ratcatcher, cat, charwomen,' Jem recited confidently. 'And would you be needing a boy, ma'am— for odd jobs, like?' He stood twisting his cap in his hands and looking hopeful.

'We will,' said Antonia, regarding his cheerful open face, which was as clean as one could reasonably expect of a fourteen-year-old. 'But will your father not be requiring you to help around the inn?'

'I can do all my chores by ten, ma'am, and then be up here directly.'

'Very well, Jem.' Antonia settled on a daily wage which, although very modest, made the boy's eyes gleam, then he shot off through the back door, clutching the list tightly.

'That was fortuitous,' Donna announced. 'And the first thing I am going to do when that boy gets back is to send him up the kitchen chimney to get rid of the birds' nests.' She unfurled a vast white apron, wrapped a cloth around her neat coiffure and, hands on hips, regarded the kitchen.

'If you begin here,' Antonia suggested, 'I will attack the bedroom, then at least we can eat and sleep in comparative comfort.'

Pausing only to drop yesterday's wrecked dress into a tub of cold water in the hope that, once clean, some of the cloth could be saved, Antonia too swathed herself in an apron and marched upstairs.

She scrubbed at the misted glass hanging on the bedroom wall until she could see her own reflection in it and twisted up her hair under a turban like Donna's. Really, her coiffure was a disgrace, she thought. The unruly curls needed the attention of a hairdresser regularly if she were not to look a complete romp, but just now she had neither time nor resources for such fripperies.

She was wearing a sprig muslin dress that, although faded, at least had no rips or tears. Antonia rolled up the sleeves, flung open the casement and set to with a duster on a stick to knock down the cobwebs that swathed the walls. As one large spider after another was dislodged from its eyrie and scuttled for the open door, Antonia reflected how glad she was that the light the night before had been so poor. She chased a particularly hairy specimen out with a broom and began to take down the curtains.

By midmorning the room was swept, dusted and aired. The hangings were in a heap on the floor for the washerwoman; only the bed remained to be attacked. Pulling off the sheets they had put on the previous night, Antonia was relieved to find the mattress not as fusty as she had feared. Even so, it, and the pillows, needed a thorough shake and air. She dragged it to the window and hung it out to refresh the flattened goosefeathers. It was too heavy to shake, so Antonia hung over the sill and pummelled it vigorously with her hands.

There was an indignant shout from the side path beneath as a shower of dust and stray feathers rained down. Startled, red-faced and still folded in two across the sill, Antonia raised her head to find Marcus Allington beating the dust from his jacket with his gloves.

'Lord Allington! I am so sorry. . .' Antonia looked down into his upturned face, noticing he seemed amused rather than annoyed. She bit her lip, regretting the instinctive apology to a man who had treated her in such a cavalier fashion only the day before. It was bad enough to be manhandled by his keepers, but to have him force his attentions upon her and then arrive at her house unannounced was the outside of enough! 'Were we expecting you, my lord?' she enquired coldly. 'Perhaps you are missing a pheasant or two?'

'I would not know, Miss Dane: I leave counting my

birds to my keepers. And after your very convincing explanation of the circumstances yesterday, I would not dream of looking for them here in any case.' He seemed very cheerful this morning, and quite unperturbed both by her coldness and the unconventional circumstances. Antonia was visited by the sudden insight that, beneath his conventional exterior, Marcus Allington was a man who enjoyed the unexpected.

A strangely comfortable silence ensued. Then she realised his gaze was resting appreciatively on the quite indecorous amount of cleavage she was displaying in her upside-down position.

Hastily she scrambled back over the sill, pulled the gown up at the neck then, with as much dignity as she could muster, looked out again. 'If you follow the path round to the back of the house you will find my companion, Miss Donaldson, in the kitchen, my lord.'

Marcus Allington bowed rather ironically before sauntering off round the corner. Antonia watched him, the blond hair on which he had not replaced his hat ruffled by the breeze, the breadth of his shoulders even more impressive seen from above. Recalling herself sharply, Antonia put up her hands to remove her turban, then stilled the action. No! Why should she titivate herself for him when he had coolly arrived without a word of warning or a by-your-leave?

She shook out her skirts and apron and sailed down the stairs, only to discover as she reached the hall that her heart was beating uncomfortably fast. Well, he had caught her at a disadvantage, hanging out of the window in an unseemly manner, entirely inappropriate to her status as a gentlewoman. Anyone would be flustered in such circumstances. Why, she would have felt just the same if it had been the vicar's wife. . .

Thus reassured, Antonia entered the kitchen with a calm smile and the firm intention of treating Marcus Allington as if yesterday—that kiss—had never occurred.

She found Miss Donaldson uncharacteristically discommoded by being discovered, duster in hand, standing on a chair. 'Do allow me to hand you down, ma'am,' Marcus was saying in a tone that suggested he was used to assisting middle-aged gentlewomen down off kitchen chairs every day of his life.

'Thank you, Lord Allington, I am most grateful.' Donna's cheeks were pink as she hastily tossed the duster behind the settle. 'Will you not take a cup of tea. . . oh, dear, I do wish I could suggest you took it in the drawing-room, but really, it is not. . .'

'. . .fit for habitation,' supplied Antonia, entering behind them. 'Good morning, Lord Allington. How kind of you to call, I do trust you have had a pleasant ride over from Brightshill. I regret to say there is at least one dead pigeon—ours, I hasten to add—in the drawing-room, so I feel you would be more comfortable here on the settle.'

'Good morning, Miss Dane,' he returned easily. 'I felt I should look in on you and assure myself you had recovered from yesterday's excitements.' His eyes met hers with a mischievous gleam in their dark brown depths. 'You will, I know, forgive me for the informality of not leaving my card first.'

'Allow me to introduce my companion, Miss Donaldson. Please sit down, my lord,' Antonia said repressively as she went to help Donna with the tea things.

His lordship, unwilling to sit whilst the ladies stood, glanced round the kitchen. 'Have your servants not yet arrived, Miss Dane? Allow me.' He took the cups from Donna and set them on the now clean table.

'We have. . .' The word 'none' was on the tip of her tongue, but then she broke off, remembering his great house and the quantity of servants therein. To admit that she and Donna were of such limited means that employing a maid and one or two charwomen was the only prudent course open to them was suddenly insupportable.

'The London house is still being closed down,' she said airily, implying that a multitude of menservants and maids were busy with dustcovers and the packing of trunks. 'And with this house being in such a state, I thought it best to leave it a while before deciding how many to engage.' Beyond him, she caught a glimpse of the look of pained shock on Miss Donaldson's face at this barefaced deceit.

'Meanwhile, young Jem from the inn has gone to hire us some charwomen in the village. London servants would take one look at Rye End Hall at present and turn tail immediately.' Antonia managed a light social laugh. 'You know what servants are—or perhaps not? Perhaps Lady Allington deals with all such matters?'

Marcus's lips quirked in acknowledgement of such a blatant piece of fishing and Miss Donaldson cast up her eyes to the cobwebbed beams. 'I very much regret to inform you, Miss Dane, that I find myself without a wife at present.' He crossed his booted legs, quite at ease on the hard settle, his eyes twinkling with amusement, his tone totally lacking in the regret he professed to feel.

Antonia had the grace to colour at her own boldness.

'That is a pity, Lord Allington, for I had hoped to find a congenial neighbour. More tea?'

'I hope you will find me a congenial neighbour, Miss Dane—I am generally reckoned so to be.'

'But women are different,' Antonia remarked without thinking.

'How very true, ma'am. I have often observed that to be the case. As to more tea, I must decline. I am on my way to see Mr Todd; I believe you are acquainted with our curate?'

'Yes, indeed, we were travelling together yesterday.' Antonia was blushing in earnest now. 'Good morning, my lord.'

As soon as the door had closed behind his lordship, Miss Donaldson protested. 'Antonia! I had never dreamed you capable of such gaucheness! And such dissembling about our supposed servants. . .I do not wonder you blush so! What will his lordship think when he discovers the true state of our affairs?'

'I suspect he already knows,' Antonia replied ruefully. 'There is not much escapes Lord Allington's sharp eye. I know I behaved badly, Donna, but he aggravates me so! And he wants Rye End Hall to add to the land he bought from my father: he will be asking to buy more land soon and, if he realises just how badly things stand with us, the offer will be very small.'

'You just say no,' Miss Donaldson replied robustly.

'But I suspect I may have to sell some land to raise the money to repair the fabric of the house—and we have not even seen it properly in daylight. If he realises how desperate I am I will have lost all my bargaining advantage.'

'How dreadful to think of a young lady having to

understand such matters,' her companion murmured, her eyes glittering behind her pince-nez. 'But I do take your meaning. However, it is not the only reason you have behaved so—shall we say—out of character, is it, my dear?'

Antonia returned the shrewd glance with a guilty smile. 'I know, Donna; it is pride, I am afraid, the pride of the Danes. I cannot bear to have people know to what straits we have been reduced. And after that humiliating encounter yesterday. . .'

Miss Donaldson was too wise a woman to pursue the topic, but as she gathered up the teacups, she thought that there must have been more to yesterday's events than had been recounted to her. There was a tension that was almost palpable between that man and her young friend.

'At least we now have two rooms that are habitable and we can eat and sleep in cleanliness and relative comfort.' Antonia replaced the tea cups on the freshly scrubbed oak dresser. 'Let us undertake a complete survey of the house and see what we have in the way of furniture and linen.'

It took them until three in the afternoon to complete their tour. Antonia was sitting at the kitchen table, sorting the disappointingly short lists of furniture remaining, while Donna sliced bread and butter for their belated luncheon.

'Father must have either sold a great deal or it has had to go to satisfy the creditors,' she sighed sadly. 'All the lovely French pieces from my mother's chamber and the blue drawing-room have gone. By the time we have thrown away the pieces that are too full of worm to keep, we will be rattling around like two peas in a drum.'

Miss Donaldson laid down a platter and paused on her way to fetch the butter to con the lists. 'You know, my dear, this list would be quite adequate if only we were in a modest house. I do not say that everything is of the first height of elegance, but it will be passable with polishing and some repairs. The linen needs darning, but it is of good quality.'

'If wishes were horses, Donna. . . We are in a mansion with twenty-two rooms, to say nothing of the servants' quarters. Unless we move into the stables, there is no smaller accommodation.' Antonia cut a piece of bread and butter, her brow furrowing in thought.

'The one saving grace is that, with the exception of those few slates off on the west wing, the fabric of the house appears remarkably sound. It needs cleaning and many minor repairs, but nothing beyond the skill of the village craftsmen. We must fashion ourselves a small suite of rooms and close up the rest of the house.'

Further conversation was interrupted by the arrival of young Jem looking mightily pleased with himself. He was laden with two wicker baskets, one of which was brimful of provisions, the other spilling over with kittens.

'Good heavens, Jem! I asked for one cat, not every stray in the village!'

The boy extracted a fine tabby from the centre of the basket. 'But she's just had kittens, miss, and she's a good mouser. With all the kittens she'll work even harder, miss, and when they grow up, they'll be catching, too.'

'Well done, Jem, that is a sensible thought,' Antonia praised him. 'There are certainly enough mice in this house to feed such a hopeful family. Put the basket in the scullery and find her a saucer of water.'

Donna inspected the shopping while the cat was settled

into her new home. 'This is excellent, Jem.' As she sorted through she asked, 'Did you manage to engage the char-women for us? And the ratcatcher?'

'Widow Brown and her daughter will be coming up first light tomorrow. The ratcatcher can't come until Wednesday, but he's bringing his dogs and a boy, so they'll do the house and the stables and all. And my dad says, I ought to do the chimneys for you.'

The lad gratefully accepted a platter of bread and cheese from Donna and set to with a will, talking with his mouth full. 'I got the provisions from Berkhamsted, my mum saying I should, you being Quality, like. Every-one is pleased to hear the Hall is occupied again, I 'spec you'll have lots of tradesmen calling. . .'

Antonia left Donna pinning old sacking over the fire-places while Jem readied a motley collection of brushes and sticks to attack the chimneys. The sunshine was warm on her shoulders as she found the gate into the kitchen garden. The warm brick walls still retained their trained fruit trees, and the shape of the beds could be descried despite the rank growth of weeds and dead vegetables.

She walked up and down the brick paths, looking hope-fully for anything edible, but could recognise nothing except some mint and thyme. The fruit trees needed prun-ing, but the new growth on the fans was vigorous and were promising for later in the year. That exhausted her sum of horticultural knowledge, which was worrying, for a flourishing kitchen garden would make all the differ-ence to the degree of comfort they could expect.

Jem had just emerged sootily from the kitchen chimney when Antonia returned to the house. 'Is there anyone in the village who would tend the kitchen garden for us, Jem?'

He stood fidgeting on the piece of sackcloth to which Donna had banished him whilst she swept up his sooty footprints. 'Old Walter Johnson, who used to do the gardens here, is still alive, miss. He's got the rheumatics something awful, but he knows what he's doing right enough, and he could bring a lad with him for the heavy digging.'

'That sounds excellent, if you think the old man can manage.'

'He'll do right enough, and be glad of the money. You could have had his eldest son, but he's in Hertford gaol.'

'Goodness!' Miss Donaldson exclaimed. 'I do not think we would want to employ someone of that kind.'

'Was only poaching, miss. Caught red-handed, he was, and his lordship at Brightshill sent him down. He's devilish hard on poachers, is his lordship.'

'Lord Allington, you mean?' Antonia enquired, flushing at the recollection of her own experience of his lordship's treatment of poachers. When Jem nodded, she asked, 'Is poaching much of a problem around here, then, for him to be so strict?'

'It has been—folks have got to eat, when all's said and done, but it'll be all right now you are here, miss,' said Jem confidently. 'There'll be work again on the land and the grounds and in the house, I'll be bound. But all your tenants have had it hard the last few years. A lot of families would have starved if it hadn't been for the odd pheasant or rabbit off your land or his lordship's.'

Antonia was suddenly consumed by a great blaze of anger against her father and brother for their negligence and profligate behaviour. She had been aware of the effect their ruinous ways had had on the family fortune and name and on her own prospects. Now she was reminded how they had betrayed their responsibility to their tenants, who seemed to be starving at the very gates of the Hall.

And as for Lord Allington, how could one defend a man who was willing to imprison breadwinners for putting food into the mouths of their children? It was iniquitous! The man was inhumane, there was no other word for him, she fumed inwardly. She knew that all landowners took a hard line over poaching, as they did over any offence against property, but surely a rational man could show some leniency where people were starving?

Looking uncharacteristically grim, she found Jem some coppers from her reticule for his day's labours and sent him off home with an apple to munch and an injunction to approach the old gardener in the morning.

After supper, Donna sat placidly cutting up hopelessly worn sheets to make pillowcases while Antonia remained at the table with a pile of papers and a quill pen.

After an hour Donna, tired of hearing her heavy sighs, enquired, 'What are you doing, my dear? It cannot be good for your eyes and it certainly seems to be giving you no satisfaction.'

'I am reviewing our financial position. You recall we agreed that we should be able to afford to engage a maid, a footman and a cook?'

'Indeed. Were we mistaken? Do we have less money than we thought?'

'No, we were accurate in our calculations. But, Donna, how can we in all conscience bring in smart town servants

to look after our comfort and consequence when the
people on the estate are in such straits? We must spend
the money on charwomen and gardeners and men to do
the repairs; then, at least, the money will be going to as
many families as possible. You and I must look after our
own clothes and do the light cleaning and the cooking.'

There was a short silence after this outburst while
Miss Donaldson removed and polished her pince-nez. 'I
applaud the sentiment, my dear, but I do at least think
you should have a maid to lend you some consequence
and to answer the door. It is going to make receiving
guests most difficult and what any prospective suitor
would think. . .'

'It will give any prospective suitors a very clear idea
of my true position!' Antonia responded briskly. 'I hardly
feel, in view of my father's reputation locally, that the
local gentry will be beating a path to my door.' She left
unsaid the thought that, at her age and in her financial
position, the sooner she resigned herself to spinsterhood,
the better.

'How true,' agreed Donna. 'It is such a pity that Lord
Allington is unmarried. His wife would be just the person
to introduce you to local society.'

'I agree; and if his lordship were married, I am certain
his disposition would be considerably more conciliatory.'

It was on the tip of Miss Donaldson's tongue to reply
that she found Lord Allington quite agreeable as he was,
but a glance at Antonia's stubborn face persuaded her
that this was best left unsaid. She folded her sewing away
and rose from her seat by the fire. 'I think we should
retire, my dear; we have yet another long day before us.'

Chapter Three

'Antonia, what are those chimneys over there through the trees?' Donna's voice floated faintly down the stairs from the servants' attics.

'Which chimneys? And what are you doing up there?' Antonia responded, puzzled. She pushed back a wayward strand of hair behind her ear, put down the polishing cloth with which she had been attempting to restore some lustre to the newel posts of the main stair, and climbed towards the sound of her companion's voice.

Miss Donaldson was leaning on the sill of one of the dormer windows that looked out across the leads to the woods lying to the west of the house. 'How verdant the countryside has become in the three weeks we have been here! I feel spring has come at last—it quite fills one with hope for the future.'

Antonia looked at Donna's thin cheeks, usually so sallow, now touched with colour, and realised her friend was flourishing in the face of this new challenge. The daughter of an impoverished India army officer, she had had no choice after his death, when she was in her early twenties, but to become a governess.

Although she had spoken little of her previous employers, Antonia knew she had not found the role a congenial one. Becoming companion-governess to the fourteen-year-old Antonia had better suited her temperament and the two had soon become fast friends.

'Yes, it is lovely.' Antonia came to lean on the ledge next to Donna, and for a moment neither spoke as they breathed in the fresh smell of the breeze wafting softly across the beechwoods from the Downs. 'What brought you up here?'

'It occurred to me that we gave these rooms only the most scant scrutiny that first day; I wanted to see if we had missed anything, but there is only a chair with a broken leg—and another damp spot we had failed to notice. But then I noticed those chimney stacks—see?'

Antonia followed the pointing finger to where ancient twisting brick stacks just broke the tree-line. 'Good heavens! The Dower House! I had quite forgot it. The last time I was there, I must almost have been a babe in arms: my father's elderly cousin Anne lived there for years but, since they had quarrelled violently long ago, we never visited. She is long dead now.'

'Will the house be yours, then?' Donna enquired, the germ of an idea growing in her mind.

'Well. . .yes, it must be, for it is part of the estate.' She met Donna's eye and they thought and spoke as one. 'Furniture!'

'Of course, it may have been cleared out by your father and sold when his cousin died,' Donna said with the practical air of someone who was determined not to be disappointed.

'Perhaps not.' Antonia thought out loud. 'They were

on such bad terms and he had other things to occupy him. . .'

'Such as his wine cellar,' Miss Donaldson supplied waspishly. 'Well, we must go and have a look, and the sooner the better. Just let me look in at the kitchen first, I left Widow Brown preparing the vegetables for dinner.'

A scene of chaos greeted them as they stood on the threshold. The charwoman was chasing the tabby cat round the kitchen with a broom, a badly mauled, skinned rabbit was bleeding damply on the hearthrug and a pot of giblet stock boiled over on the range.

'Mrs Brown, whatever is the matter?' Donna demanded.

The charwoman grounded the broom and stood panting, red in the face. 'Dratted cat, miss! It's the rats it's meant to be eating, not what's in the pantry!' The cat, seizing its opportunity, dragged the rabbit off into the scullery and Antonia darted across to save the stock pot before it boiled dry.

'Oh, dear,' lamented Donna. 'I fear that rabbit was all that is left of our dinner. Did the boys leave any other game this morning, Mrs Brown?'

Shortly after they had arrived, Antonia had had the notion of encouraging her tenants to 'poach' the plentiful game that infested her neglected lands. She had struck a bargain: she would take a cut of the animals they snared or shot; in return, they could keep the rest to feed their families. She had laid down the strict condition that they did not stray by so much as a toe into Brightshill or any other estate in the neighbourhood.

The scheme was already starting to work well. Her tenants would be better fed and she felt confident that they were now safely removed from all temptation to run foul of the law—or Lord Allington's gamekeepers. In return, she and Donna dined well on rabbit, pheasant, pigeons, and on one occasion, venison. They had become adept at plucking, skinning and stewing to the great benefit of the housekeeping account and, perhaps more importantly, had begun to heal the rift between landlord and tenant that her father's dissolute and neglectful behaviour had opened. Whenever she met any of her tenants, Antonia had been warmed by their obvious gratitude.

And there was still the river and the lake to consider; Antonia had looked at her late brother's fishing rods, but after becoming entangled in hook and line when removing them from the cupboard, had regretfully decided she needed lessons before threatening the local pike and perch.

'I believe there is still a brace of wood pigeons.' Donna peered into the larder. 'But I had better stay here and see what I can retrieve; will you go on to the Dower House without me, Antonia? Now, Mrs Brown, let us see what we can do here. . .'

Antonia, glad to escape from the smell of burnt stock, slipped out of the back door with relief. Rain earlier that day had given way to sunshine, although she had to watch her step with the mud as she picked her way across the freshly gravelled paths through the walled vegetable gardens.

Old Johnson was hoeing between lines of seedling vegetables, grumbling without bothering to straighten up at the skinny lad who was putting in pea sticks along newly dug trenches. Knowing full well that the gardener could—and would—hold forth at length with incomprehensible gardening questions if she gave him the opportunity, Antonia gave them a cheery wave and went out through a wicket gate into the ruins of the pleasure grounds beyond.

She negotiated clumps of brambles and nettles, remembering with sadness the smooth sweep of lawn and well-tended shrubberies that had once occupied the area. Her mother had loved to stroll in the cool of the evening in the formal rose garden she had created: now Antonia could not even recognise where they had walked together arm in arm.

She swallowed hard against the almost physical pain of remembering and resolutely walked on to the belt of trees that fringed the pleasure grounds, separating them from the gardens of the Dower House and the pastures beyond.

A small group of fallow deer started away, almost under her feet, reminding her that the fences must be in disrepair. The animals were lovely to watch, but would swiftly lay to waste any efforts to civilise the gardens. Gloomily Antonia walked on, attempting to calculate how much fencing would cost, not only for the grounds but, more importantly, the fields and pasture land.

The Dower House was hidden behind a rampant hedge of briar and thorn, taller than her head. Approaching as she was the rear of the house, Antonia came first to the garden gate, which hung crazily from one hinge, the wood quite rotten and covered in lichens. Antonia lifted it aside gingerly and walked through, finding herself in a paved yard with a well in the middle.

The house had been the original farm on the estate. Built in the reign of the first James, it was a two-storey building of two wings constructed of local red brick, under a tiled roof capped by the twisting chimney stacks

Donna had espied from the attic that morning.

The yard in which she now stood had once been the farmyard, but when the house had become the Dower House and the new Home Farm was built, the outbuildings were demolished and the yard became part of the gardens.

The small mullioned windows reflected only dully, despite the bright sunshine; as Antonia approached, she saw the leaded panes were thick with grime and festooned with cobwebs. There was a low back door under a heavy porch; she tried it and found it, not surprisingly, locked. She hesitated, realising she would probably have to ask young Jem to break in, for they had found no keys that could belong to this house up at the Hall.

Disappointed, for by now she was quite excited at the prospect of exploring, she was turning away when she saw a key hanging on a hook on a beam in the porch. It was red with rust and obviously not, judging by its size, the key to this door. Antonia turned it in her hand, staining her fingers with the rust. It could be the front-door key: it was worth trying. Gathering up her skirts, she took the drive that led round the side to the front of the house, facing across overgrown lawns to the main gates beyond.

Antonia could still remember the only occasion she had visited the house. She had been with her mother and they had driven in the carriage the short distance down the lanes from the Hall; the strange old house and the crabby old lady in her old-fashioned clothes were a vivid memory, even twenty years on.

Not expecting it to work, Antonia tried the key in the front-door lock. It grated and resisted, then suddenly turned with a loud click and the panelled oak swung open.

The hall beyond was dark and gloomy with shadowed recesses and the black gaping holes of opened doors. Antonia hesitated, unwelcome memories of every Gothick tale she had ever read welling up in her mind. She stood, one hand on the door frame, her toes safely on the outside of the threshold, poised to run at the first ominous creak.

Then the ridiculousness of her position struck her: a grown woman frightened to enter her own property in broad daylight! What would she say to Donna—that she was too afraid to look for the furniture they so badly needed? Boldly Antonia stepped into the hall—but left the door wide open behind her.

As she moved from room to room, her skirts raised puffs of dust. But, to her amazement, everything was completely dry: there were no damp stains or musty smells, only dry dust and airlessness shrouding the contents of the house, left just as they had been when Cousin Anne had died nine years before. Relations between Sir Humphrey and his querulous relative had been so poor her father must have ordered the place shut up and had never troubled himself to investigate further.

The ancient brick and oak had stood the test of time and the elements in a way more recent buildings had not. Quite at her ease now, for the old house had a homely, safe feeling to it, Antonia roamed from room to room, lifting dust sheets, peering at hangings in the gloom, running her fingers along the dark wood of the sturdy old furniture. The stairs were wide and shallow and led her up to a gallery and a suite of bedrooms.

Antonia was just inside the door of what must have been Cousin Anne's chamber when she heard the floorboards creaking in the hall below. Her hand flew to her throat and she froze, all the tales of ghosts alive again in her mind. Panic gripped her and with it a blind urge to get out into the sunlight. Whoever—or whatever it was—had reached the foot of the stairs; she could hear the boards groaning.

There must be back stairs. . . Antonia picked up her skirts and flew down the landing on tip-toe, down a passageway, through a doorway and found herself at the head of a flight of narrow, winding stairs. She stumbled down, the very act of running feeding her panic, round a dark bend and crashed into something large, solid and alive.

'Got you!' Strong hands seized her roughly by the shoulders and shook her. Muffled against woollen cloth, Antonia turned her head frantically and screamed. She could see nothing in the gloom. The man holding her was clenching her upper arms in a vice-like grip that brought tears to her eyes and her heart was leaping in her chest till she felt quite sick.

There was no one within earshot to come to her aid: Antonia held back her screams and saved her breath for struggling. She began to kick with a vengeance, stubbing her toes against unyielding leather boots. Suddenly released, Antonia stumbled back against the wall, but before she could open her mouth the man seized her by the wrist and dragged her down the last few stairs into the kitchen.

'Come on, wench, let me have a look at you in the light. . .out to see what you could steal, were you?' The light from the casements fell on Antonia's dust-stained face and her captor released her with an oath. 'Hell's teeth! You again!'

Shaking and furious, Antonia glared into the hard face

of Marcus Allington. She found her voice. 'How dare you assault me in my own house!' But although she was angry, she was also shaking with relief that it was he.

'I thought you were a housebreaker—the front door was wide open, I could hear somebody moving about upstairs.' He glared back. 'What do you expect me to do? Pass by and let the place be ransacked?'

Antonia's knees sagged and she let the kitchen table take her weight as she rubbed her stinging wrists. 'I thought you. . .I thought you. . .'

'You thought I was the vagrant, someone who was going to attack you?' He took a step forward, seeing how white her face was under the dust, noticing a cobweb caught up in her dark curls, seeing with a pang of guilt a bruise forming on her wrist where his unyielding grip had held her fast.

'No. . .' Her voice quavered, then broke. 'I thought you were a headless ghoul!'

'A ghoul! Really, Miss Dane!' Marcus began to smile then, seeing her tears, softened. 'Antonia. . .I am sorry, come here.' Antonia found herself pulled gently against his broad chest and held. The ridiculous tears of fright kept welling up and she gave in to them, sobbing in earnest as he stroked her hair and quietly murmured reassurance. It had been so long since anyone had held her, offered her the comfort of their arms. Miss Donaldson's brisk sympathy and sensible friendship were not the same.

The tears dried in a few minutes, but Antonia stayed in the shelter of Marcus's arms, her cheek nestled against his waistcoat, his heart beating steadily under her ear. Indeed, he seemed quite content to hold her and stroke her hair as though gentling a startled foal.

Antonia stirred against him as a realisation of the situation overcame her instinctive need to be held. As though her movement had triggered something in him, his hand stopped stroking and moved to caress her nape and the hand holding her against him came up to tip up her face.

'Lord Allington. . .'

'You look adorable with cobwebs in your hair, like a kitten that has been exploring.' His voice was husky and amused.

'I d-do not t-think this is. . .' Antonia knew she was stammering, knew this was neither wise nor proper, but she had no will to break free from his encircling arms.

'Then do not think at all,' he murmured softly, his mouth coming down on hers with infinite gentleness. She clung to him as his mouth moved insinuatingly on hers, drawing her deeper into the kiss. Dizzily Antonia clung to him, drowning in unfamiliar sensation, overwhelmed by the feeling of security his strong arms gave her. From deep within her came a little moan of longing as she clung to him more fiercely.

Marcus lifted his mouth from hers and looked down into her innocent eyes. 'I think I had better take you home.'

'Home?' she quavered, suddenly overcome by a desire to be carried in his arms to Brightshill.

'Yes, your companion will be wondering what has become of you,' he said almost briskly, holding open the door for her to pass through. 'Where is your horse?'

His abrupt return to conventional manners underscored just how improper her behaviour had been. Antonia's face flamed. 'I walked over. My lord. . .you must disregard, I beg you, my behaviour just now. I was frightened, driven by relief after such a scare. Normally I would never. . .'

'I quite understand,' he responded coolly. 'You are not normally in fear of headless ghouls.'

They were now on the other side of the front door. Marcus twisted the key in the lock, then handed it to her, his fingers brushing hers momentarily as he did so. His horse was cropping the grass, its reins thrown over the branch of a tree.

'I will walk back with you to Rye End Hall,' he announced, taking the reins in his hand.

She flushed again at the coolness in his voice, confused by the welter of emotions she was feeling. Yes, she supposed she had offended him by implying that the only reason she had returned his kiss was relief that he was not some vagabond, but he should never have kissed her in the first place! She had no intention of trying to make amends—after all, it was the second occasion on which he had taken liberties with her.

'It will not be necessary for you to accompany me, Lord Allington,' she said with equal coolness.

'I think it is.' He fell into step beside her. 'Even if there are no ghouls, there may well be undesirables in the woods. With no keepering on your lands, anyone could be roaming.'

Stung, Antonia snapped back, 'Do not keep harping on my foolishness, my lord! Have you never read a Gothick tale and then wondered at a creak in the night?'

'No, I have no time for such nonsense.'

In the face of such a comprehensive snub, Antonia fell silent and they walked without speaking along the rutted lane until they reached the gates of the Hall.

'Goodbye, Lord Allington, thank you for your concern

for my property,' she said politely but dismissively, holding out her hand to him.

He accepted neither her hand, nor his dismissal. 'If you have recovered your composure, Miss Dane, there is something I wished to speak of to you.'

'Any loss of composure I may have suffered, my lord, is entirely attributable to you,' Antonia said frostily, then realised what a double-edged remark that was.

Marcus smiled thinly. 'None the less, if you could spare me a moment of your time?'

'Very well, Lord Allington, we are still some minutes from the house.'

'I do wish you would call me Marcus. After all, we are near neighbours: if, that is, you are intending to stay here.'

Antonia raised her brows, 'There is no question of my leaving, my lord. . . Marcus. This is my family home and I intend to stay here.'

Marcus allowed his eyes to stray over the ruins of the pleasure grounds where one deer could be seen nibbling delicately at the remains of a rose bush. 'It must be a powerful attachment you feel that overcomes the many disadvantages of the situation,' he remarked.

'What disadvantages?' Antonia demanded hotly.

'To find yourself without friends, in a property that is tumbling around your ears, set amid derelict lands which can be bringing you no income—forgive me for speaking frankly, but that appears to constitute not one but several disadvantages.'

'The house is not tumbling about my ears: there is merely a little damp; that can soon be rectified.'

Marcus nodded sagely, 'Then no doubt it is the damp that prevents you from furnishing Rye End Hall?'

'And how would you know in what condition my furnishings are, sir?' Antonia demanded, her colour rising.

'It is difficult to keep secrets in the country. Let us be frank, Miss Dane: financially, you are at a standstill. If you have any concern for your tenants, or indeed yourself, you must look to raise income.'

'This is being frank, indeed!' Antonia stopped abruptly and faced him. 'I believe, sir, you cross beyond frankness! What concern can you have with my private affairs?'

Marcus's dark brown eyes looked at her measuringly. 'I am, after all, a neighbour, but more than that, I am in a position to alleviate your situation.'

Antonia stared at him in wild surmise. Marcus Allington, offering her marriage? Surely there was no other interpretation to put on his words, especially after that kiss just now. . .?

'M-Marcus,' she stammered, 'this is so sudden! I scarcely k-know you. . .' She broke off at the look of astonishment dawning on his face. He had it under control in a second, but not before she realised the apalling error she had fallen into. Burning with a humiliation she struggled to conceal, she blundered on, 'That is to say, it is very kind of you to offer help to someone you scarcely know. . .'

'Our families have been neighbours for centuries.' He spoke smoothly, but she could see a trace of colour on his cheekbones. His attempts at tact were as humiliating to her as her original error had been. 'Your father sold me some land several years ago: I would give you a fair price for the farmlands and the woods. It would leave you the pleasure grounds; with the house restored you would be able to sell it easily, perhaps to a London merchant seeking a country retreat. There are many such these days.'

Humiliation turned to anger as his words sank in. So, Marcus Allington had only kissed her, been so sympathetic, in order to gain her confidence as a prelude to snapping up her lands. His impression of her as an empty-headed female must have been compounded by her falling into his arms not once, but twice! To be arrested as a poacher, to be found in a twitter over ghosts and then to so misinterpret his intentions on the flimsiest of evidence—he must think her so foolish she would accept his offer without hesitation or calculation.

'The day will never come when I am prepared to sell so much as one yard of my land, my lord—to you or anyone else!' She gathered up her skirts and swept off, turning as a further thought struck her. 'And your protestations of neighbourly concern would ring more true, sir, if you conducted yourself as a gentleman and did not manhandle me at every opportunity!'

He had swung up into the saddle. Her words obviously stung, for the horse tossed its head in protest as his hand tightened on the reins. 'I am not in the habit of manhandling unwilling ladies, ma'am; I would suggest you look to your own behaviour before you criticise mine. I would hardly characterise you as unwilling just now.'

Before Antonia could do more than gasp at this attack, he had dug his heels into the horse's flank and cantered off down the track. She was still angry when she re-entered the kitchen, now mercifully restored to its habitual order. Miss Donaldson was placidly brewing a pot of tea, the stock was simmering fragrantly on the range, mixing with the delicious odour of roasting pigeon, Mrs Brown had gone and the cats were sleeping off an excess of rabbit in the scullery.

'My dear, whatever is the matter?' Donna put down the teapot at the sight of Antonia's flushed cheeks and furious expression.

'That insufferable man!'

'Which man?' Donna asked, not unreasonably.

'Well, there is only one in the neighbourhood determined to interfere in my life at every turn—Marcus Allington, of course!' She plumped down in a chair and began to fiddle irritably with a folded paper which lay on the table.

'Lord Allington? Why, what has he done to discommode you so, Antonia? Drink this tea and calm yourself.' Donna pushed the cup of tea across and waited anxiously, her eyes fixed on her young friend's stormy countenance.

Antonia took a deep breath. 'I was in the Dower House, exploring; it was very dark and gloomy in there, and in truth, rather frightening. He saw the front door standing open and followed me in; I have never been so scared in my life! And then he. . .then he. . .I was agitated and naturally. . .er. . .clung to him. He. . .' She found herself unable to say the words to finish the sentence.

'Are you trying to tell me he kissed you?' Miss Donaldson seemed inclined to be amused rather than shocked, which only fuelled Antonia's annoyance.

'Really, Donna, I am surprised at you! I would not have thought you would regard such unseemly behaviour so lightly.'

'Well, if you had cast yourself into his arms. . .he is but a man, after all, my dear. And,' she added, musingly, 'a most eligible one at that.'

This was too palpable a hit. Antonia sank her head

into her hands, much to Miss Donaldson's alarm. 'Antonia, my dear! Are you telling me he offered you some insult?'

'No! Oh, Donna, I made such an abject fool of myself. I thought he was making a declaration of marriage, but he was only offering to buy the land!'

'If he misled you in any way,' her companion began hotly, 'he must do the honourable thing and. . .'

Antonia cut across her. 'No, no, it was entirely my own stupidity, and I said nothing which could not be explained away. But I know he knew what assumption I had made—it is so humiliating.'

'But when you came in just now you seemed angry, not embarrassed. Did you quarrel?'

'I told him I would never sell Rye End Hall lands to him.'

There was a short silence, then Miss Donaldson said gently, 'I fear you may have to sell some of them to someone; that paper under your hand is the bill of estimate from Mr Watts the builder from Berkhamsted, who came last week. It seems there are more roof timbers to replace than we had realised and, of course, we had not allowed for the cost of lead. . .' Her voice trailed off as Antonia spread open the paper.

'It seems a reasonable and honest estimate,' she said blankly when she had read it carefully, 'but quite beyond our means.' The two women stared at each other across the table, the tea cooling between them.

The gloomy silence was broken by the arrival of young Jem, whistling cheerily. 'Good day! Is there anything you'd like me to do, miss? Ma's sent the eggs you wanted, and Pa thought you might like a look at the Lunnon paper, it got left behind yesterday at the inn.'

Donna pulled herself together with a little shake, thanked Jem for the eggs and paper and hustled him outside to sweep all the paths around the house.

Drearily Antonia unfolded the newsheet which proved to be *The Times*. For want of a better occupation, she began to scan the advertisements.

She read aloud: 'To be let for six or twelve months certain, a genteel FAMILY HOUSE, handsomely furnished... A young PERSON about twenty years of age, of respectable connections, wishes for a situation in a ladies' school... A GENTLEMAN, late returned from the East Indies, seeks to LEASE a small country estate within fifty miles of the Capital, comprising both UNFURNISHED HOUSE and PLEASURE GROUNDS. Apply to Rumbold and Gardiner, Solicitors...'

Antonia laid the paper aside with a sigh. That would be one solution, if only she could bear to see strangers at Rye End Hall. Or, of course, if it were in any condition to be leased.

Donna reappeared from the garden, saying, 'That Jem is a good, willing boy! Show him any task and he sets to with a will. Is there anything of interest in the paper, my dear?'

'I have not yet looked at the news, I was simply running my eye over the advertisements. Listen to this one.' She read aloud the item concerning the country house required for lease.

'But that is the very solution to our problem!' cried Donna. 'If you let the house, it would remain in your possession and the rental would allow you to have the repairs done and the grounds set to order.' She talked on, warming to her theme. 'If it were a repairing lease, it would free you from those costs and you could set the

fences and land and the tenants' cottages in order. Then
there would be a steady income from those lands as
well. . .'

Perversely, as Donna's enthusiasm waxed, Antonia's
waned and she began to see all the disadvantages of the
situation. 'How would it appear if I let the house? It
would be a clear indication of my penury. And to see
strangers in my home? And all the repairs to be done,
and the grounds in such disorder—who would look at
it? And,' she added with finality, 'where would we live?'

Donna was prevented from answering by a commotion
at the back door. Jem's voice could be heard plaintively
protesting, 'But, my lord, I'd better tell the mistress
you're here. . .'

'I will announce myself,' Marcus Allington replied
coldly, stalking into the kitchen as he did so. He was
followed closely by his head keeper, Sparrow, who in
his turn was holding a man by the collar.

Antonia leapt to her feet, startled by this unexpected
eruption of men into her kitchen. 'My lord! What is the
meaning of this intrusion?'

'I do apologise for disturbing you in your. . .' he cast
a cold eye around the homely kitchen '. . .living room.
But I regret it is necessary to deal with this matter
immediately.'

He gestured to Sparrow, who pushed his captive
forward roughly. 'This, I believe, is one of your tenants.'

Antonia moved forward, seeing, with some concern
that the man had a bloody nose. 'Indeed, it is Josiah
Wilkins from the cottages at Brook End. Josiah, what
has happened to you? Has this person struck you?' She
turned angrily on the gamekeeper, recognising him as
the one who had so impudently manhandled her. 'You!

How dare you come on to my land and assault my tenants!'

'Sparrow was on my land, madam, and about his duties for which I pay him.' Lord Allington was grim.

Antonia turned a contemptuous shoulder on both master and man and spoke to her tenant calmly. 'Tell me what occurred, Josiah, and how you came by your injury.'

'Well, miss, it was like this,' he began readily enough, although with a wary eye on the keeper. 'I was shooting pigeons—got a brace, too, but they came down the wrong side of the brook. I didn't have my old dog with me, see, so I waded across to pick 'em up and this bullying varmint jumped on me.'

'You watch your language—I've got the measure of you, Josiah Wilkins,' Sparrow threatened. 'Who's to say where you shot those birds? I don't believe a word of it, my lord. All these Wilkinses are a parcel of idle rogues.'

'Hold your tongue, man!' Antonia snapped, remembering again with a shudder the keeper's insinuating touch on her arm. 'Speak when you are spoken to in my house!'

Sparrow threw her a darkling look and slouched back into the shadows.

'You may not welcome our intrusion, Miss Dane, but I am sure you will agree that I have every right to detain a poacher, and the man is condemned out of his own mouth.'

'I agree you have every right to apprehend a poacher, my lord: however, this man is not a poacher. He was shooting my game, on my land and with my permission. And forgive me, for I imagine my knowledge of the law is not as extensive as yours, but I know he was within

his rights to retrieve the birds from your land, providing
he did no damage.'

'What nonsense is this?' Marcus exploded.

'Kindly moderate your tone, my lord! All my tenants
have my permission to shoot, trap and fish over my land.
In the absence of crops in my fields, I harvest whatever
my land yields for the benefit of both myself and my
people. You were the one who told me to look to my
starving tenants, after all!'

Donna was talking in the doorway to Jem, who came
forward to help Wilkins out. 'See that he gets home
safely, please, Jem. And see if you can find his pigeons,
will you?' she added, with a vituperative glance at
Sparrow.

'Sparrow, leave us,' Marcus ordered between
clenched teeth.

As the man closed the kitchen door behind him,
Antonia remarked conversationally, 'I presume, my lord,
that you will be placing that man on a charge of common
assault for breaking Wilkins' nose?'

'Do not try my patience further, madam,' Marcus
ground out. 'This is madness! Are you so penurious that
you must give every ne'er-do-well in the county licence
to poach on your lands?'

'My hard-working and deserving tenants are merely
harvesting the land as I have explained. They are not
responsible for my father's recklessness, but they have
to suffer the consequences. I do what little I can to miti-
gate their poverty.'

'And your own,' he added quietly. 'I do not understand
your stubbornness, Miss Dane; I have made you a fair
proposal to buy, and I would offer you a fair price—for
the house as well, if you would accept it. It would allow

you to return to London and to live as a gentlewoman should. Not like this!' His scornful eye once more swept the bare flagged floor, the scrubbed deal table with the shabby chairs drawn up to it.

'Are you suggesting that this household is anything less than respectable, my lord?' Donna had re-entered the kitchen unobserved, her small figure bristling with indignation at the insult.

'Forgive me, Miss Donaldson,' he said with a satirical twist to his lips. 'I have no doubt that the moral tone of this establishment is as a nunnery. However, it strikes me that Miss Dane might have a better chance of catching herself a husband were she in London.'

Antonia had, for the most fleeting of moments, allowed herself to indulge in thoughts of the pleasures of living in Town: shopping in the Burlington Arcade, driving in the Park, congenial evenings at Almack's where she could dance the night away, her card full. But Marcus Allington's crude remarks about her lack of success in the Marriage Mart brought her swiftly to her senses.

'Catch myself a husband?' She pulled herself up to her full height, eyes sparking fire.

Donna, watching from the doorway, thought she had rarely seen her charge looking more magnificent, despite her old gown and simply dressed hair.

'Let me assure you, sir, that a husband is something I regret the lack of not one whit!' Her colour was up, flooding her naturally creamy skin with a warm glow, emphasising the fine strong bones of her features. Her figure was slender but, under the stress of strong emotion, her bosom rising and falling, she looked Junoesque.

Marcus, too, was stirred. 'Take it from a disinterested observer, ma'am, a husband to school and curb you would be a most desirable thing! Very well, then, you have made your hard bed—lie upon it. Perhaps after a country winter, you will apply a more reasoned judgement to my offer.' He paused to pull on his gloves. 'I can wait.'

'Then you will wait a long time, my lord. For I intend to lease this house and grounds forthwith to a most respectable tenant.'

'Indeed?' Marcus's dark brows drew together. 'And supposing you find a person deluded enough to take on this ramshackle estate, where do you intend to live?'

Antonia hesitated, at a loss. He had provoked her into a wild statement of defiance and now she had no answer to his very pertinent question.

'Why, in the Dower House, of course,' supplied Miss Donaldson calmly, from the shadows.

Chapter Four

Marcus's hard laugh rang round the kitchen. 'A neat device, ladies, I must congratulate you upon your optimism.'

'Optimism?' Antonia repeated with dangerous calm. 'Why describe a perfectly practical solution so dismissively, sir? Or do you wish me gone from here so much?' She realised, as soon as the words were out, that she wanted to know the answer to that latter question very badly indeed.

'Your whereabouts, Miss Dane, are of little concern to me, provided that you are not inciting your tenants to lawlessness as this episode would suggest.' Marcus smiled thinly as he pulled on his riding gauntlets. 'I shall watch with interest your attempts to gull some Cit into taking on this. . .liability of a house. I wish you good day, ladies.' He nodded curtly to them both and stalked out.

As the door closed behind him, Antonia clutched the edge of the table to support her shaking legs. The encounter had affected her composure more than she would have thought possible. Marcus Allington was having the most deleterious effect on her equilibrium: she wanted him to like her, to support her efforts to keep her family estates together despite overwhelming odds.

And yet he was so inexplicably hostile. She could only conclude that he disliked her—which, she was honest enough to realise, was a disappointment—but that he wanted her lands badly enough to maintain the connection.

'Well, that was a nasty show of temper,' remarked Miss Donaldson as she calmly tidied away the tea things. 'But I suppose we should be thankful for, after all, it provoked me into thinking of a solution. Do you truly think it is feasible for us to move to the Dower House?'

Antonia met Miss Donaldson's bird-like eyes, bright with excitement. 'But, Donna, I thought that was just something you said upon the spur of the moment to irk his lordship. Were you truly serious?'

'Yes, Antonia, I do believe we could live most comfortably there, for from what you told me it is just of a size for the two of us. However, it grieves me to admit it,' she added with a wry smile, 'but his lordship is quite correct about this house. How are we to lease it in its present state of repair? We have just agreed we do not have the resources to make it habitable.'

Antonia got to her feet and began to pace up and down the flagged floor, her underlip caught in her teeth. Where indeed were they to find the money? She passed her small income and the few pieces of jewellery she had inherited under review. Even with Donna's tiny pension it would not do. There was only one recourse. It came hard, for the example of her late father was ever before her, a man ruined by debt—but she had little choice.

Taking a deep breath, 'I shall borrow the money,' Antonia announced decisively. 'I can put the estate up for security and repay the loan from the rent.'

'Oh, dear—' Miss Donaldson creased her brow '—debt makes me so nervous! Only consider your late parent's predicament and what it has cost you to retrieve it.'

Antonia remembered only too well the awful moment when their man of law had explained how little remained of the previously substantial family fortune once Sir Humphrey's debts had been quit. But she had little alternative other than to borrow.

She leaned across the table and explained earnestly, 'But this is different, Donna. Father borrowed with no intention of repaying the money, unless by gaming! I do not intend to continue borrowing beyond this one contingency; look upon it as an investment, which should soon realise a return. Pass me *Pigot's Directory* and let us see which banks there are in Berkhamsted to whom I may apply.'

They scanned the commercial directory together. 'There is only one,' Miss Donaldson said, running her finger down the column. 'Perhaps it would be better if you went into Aylesbury.'

'But look—it says here that this bank is an agent for Praed and Company in London: nothing could be better, for they act for Great Aunt Honoria.'

'You do not intend to deal directly with the bank, I hope, it would be most unseemly,' Miss Donaldson admonished. They may have come to a pretty pass, but for a young lady of breeding to enter a place of business was unthinkable. 'You will be writing to your man of business, will you not?'

'No, for it will cause a delay we can ill afford. I shall go the day after tomorrow,' Antonia added decisively. 'I shall write now to the manager and make an appointment. Jem can take the letter.'

Miss Donaldson recognised when Antonia had made up her mind and knew all too well it would be fruitless to argue. 'Very well, my dear, if you insist, but I cannot like it. However, needs must: we shall attend to your wardrobe. If you go into town with your kid gloves in the state they are at present, our poverty will be only too evident to all!'

The kid gloves, after much sponging and brushing, were all a lady could desire. Antonia stood on the steps of the Aylesbury Branch Bank wishing her courage were as easily restored, for despite her brave words to Miss Donaldson she was feeling decidedly apprehensive. It was simply not done for ladies of quality to deal with matters of business, and she had neither knowledge nor experience of such proceedings.

Through the discreet veil which Donna had insisted on attaching to her bonnet, she stared at the burnished brass plate that gleamed brightly despite the dullness of the day: Agents for Praed's Bank—James Pethybridge, Manager. Antonia stepped down again and took a few agitated paces along the pavement, glad of its height above the roadway, which was muddy from the day's light drizzle. Even the dismal weather conspired against her courage today.

Perhaps she ought to walk along to the King's Arms and bespeak a cup of coffee in a private parlour. . . Even as she hesitated, the church tower clock chimed close by. Eleven o'clock, the hour set for her appointment in Mr Pethybridge's reply; Antonia swallowed hard and raised her hand to the knocker.

The clerk ushered her into the banker's inner sanctum with due deference but with a sideways glance that betrayed his surprise at finding her unaccompanied. As she shook hands and sat down, Antonia was gratified to see only a look of polite enquiry on the banker's face, for she had been fearing outright rejection, if not incredulity at the thought of a woman carrying out her own transactions.

Miss Donaldson's assiduous work on her walking dress and frogged jacket had obviously passed muster, and the addition of a new ostrich plume to her bonnet had transformed its appearance. She smoothed down the garnet red cloth of her skirts and smiled back at the banker with a confidence she was far from feeling.

Mr Pethybridge was an amiable-looking gentleman in his early fifties, rotund and greying. His avuncular manner encouraged Antonia as she began to explain her circumstances and the nature of her request, becoming more confident and persuasive as she spoke.

Twenty minutes later, with her optimism and spirits quite dashed, he ushered her out into the main office. 'I do hope you appreciate, Miss Dane, the force of my arguments,' he said fluently with the air of a man long practised in turning down ill-considered requests for advances. 'It would be most unwise for a young lady, circumstanced as you are, to enter into such an arrangement. Indeed, it would be most irresponsible of me to encourage you to take on such a debt at this time. . .'

He broke off as he became aware that another visitor was speaking to his clerk. 'I do beg your pardon, Miss Dane.' Mr Pethybridge was flushed with embarrassment at having been caught discussing business in the presence of others. 'Allow me to see you out.' He ushered her towards the door, bowing deferentially as he passed the newcomer. 'Good morning, my lord, I shall be with you directly.'

'Good morning, Pethybridge.' Antonia started at the familiar, lazily deep tones and struggled to compose her features as she passed Marcus Allington with a slight inclination of her head. She regretted not replacing her veil.

'Miss Dane, good day. I hope I find you well? May I be so bold as to enquire if your business has prospered?'

There was little doubt that his lordship's business prospered: there was no sign of the angry man in country riding clothes of the previous day. Marcus Allington had obviously driven into town; his multi-caped driving coat was carelessly thrown open over immaculately cut, long-tailed coat and breeches. His boots shone like ebony and had miraculously avoided contact with the mud that, despite her best efforts, had spattered Antonia's kid half-boots.

He had also permitted his valet to trim some of the unruliness from his dark blond hair where previously it had curled unfashionably long on his collar.

Antonia, realising she was staring, swallowed a bitter retort, brought up her chin defiantly, and replied, 'It has not prospered, as you will no doubt be unsurprised to hear, my lord.'

'Indeed? I am sorry to hear that.' Ignoring Antonia's disbelieving expression, Marcus continued, 'Perhaps I could offer some assistance? Doubtless with your man of business absent you found yourself at some disadvantage in explaining the circumstances to my friend Pethybridge here.'

Thus subtly reminded of the extent of his dealings

with his lordship, Mr Pethybridge hastened to usher them both back into his office. 'Allow me to send for some refreshment. Do sit down, Miss Dane, and permit me to explore the details further: his lordship is no doubt correct that in your understandable inexperience you have omitted to mention something germane to the case.' He was all unctousness now in his desire to please his lordship.

'Doubtless,' Antonia replied coolly, 'for I am sure his lordship is never wrong.'

To her intense embarrassment, the banker took this as permission to review the facts she had laid before him, thus exhibiting every detail of her financial circumstances to Marcus, who sat at his ease in a wing chair, seemingly unsurprised by what he heard.

Antonia scarcely attended to what the banker was saying, her mind in a whirl of speculation. What was Marcus Allington about, in so promoting her cause? Yesterday he had made it plain he thought her foolish in the extreme—and why should he do anything so prejudicial to his own interests in acquiring her land as to help her to a loan? That was not the way to snap up her property and expand his own. . .

Her speculation was curtailed by Mr Pethybridge announcing, 'In view of these facts, I see no reason not to advance you the sum you request immediately.'

Antonia was so astonished at this complete about-face that it was as much as she could do to manage the common civilities of thanks. What had Marcus said to sway the man? But she could hardly ask now, thus proving she had paid no attention to the proceedings—the men would think her a perfect fool!

The banker bowed them out with renewed

protestations of his desire to assist Miss Dane in any way he could.

Standing on the pavement, drawing on her gloves, she realised that Marcus was at her side. Startled into directness, she demanded, 'What game are you about, my lord?'

'What can you mean, Miss Dane?' he enquired urbanely, offering her his arm. 'Allow me to escort you to your carriage, the pavements are so slippery.'

'You may escort me to the King's Arms where Jem awaits me with the gig,' Antonia snapped. 'And you know what I mean! Pethybridge had no intention of granting me the loan until you intervened. Nothing, nothing, had changed and yet he reversed his decision, as you knew he would!' The effort of quarrelling in public with a man who retained his infuriating calm only fuelled her anger. 'Surely you do not expect me to believe you have no ulterior motive in securing me this loan, my lord?'

'Indeed I have, Miss Dane.' The more angry she became, the suaver his manner was.

Antonia was taken aback. 'Well, what is it? It seems to me to be an action quite against your own interests.'

'I have no intention of telling you that. And you must allow me to judge what my own interests are, Antonia.'

'Do not address me so, my lord—and you must tell me! I have no desire to be beholden to you.'

'Your desires are not the only ones at issue: and I have no intention of gratifying your curiosity.' Marcus glanced sideways at her, a small smile touching his lips. 'You were not paying a great deal of attention in Pethybridge's office, were you?'

She flushed at the veracity of his observation, but did not reply.

'That is understandable, for it must have been an ordeal for a lady, and I can understand you being distracted. But it is not sensible to undertake business with only half your mind on the matter.'

He guided her through the cobbled entry to the inn. 'Ah, your carriage awaits, complete with chickens in a coop and straw upon the boards, I see. Is it too much to hope that you will spend some of your loan on a conveyance more suited to your station in life?'

'Lord Allington, I have never in my life been tempted to strike another human being,' Antonia hissed in a low voice, aware of an interested audience of Jem and two lounging ostlers. 'But I am sorely tempted now! You are quite the most insufferable, patronising, arrogant individual it has ever been my misfortune to encounter. I must be grateful that you have helped me to obtain the funds I need, but do not think I do not harbour the deepest suspicions as to your motives.'

'Your imagination is too vivid, Miss Dane.' He steered her to one side as a farmer's gig swept through the yard. 'As I observed the other day, your addiction to Gothick novels has much to answer for. I bid you good day, Antonia.' Before she could upbraid him for using her Christian name again he had tipped his hat and had gone, striding through the archway into the High Street.

Jem prattled cheerfully as they drove home, very pleased with himself for the bargain he had struck over the coop full of chickens. Antonia made admiring noises, but her mind still dwelt on Marcus's extraordinary behaviour.

What had he meant by telling her she should have paid more attention in the banker's office? Had she missed some vital point? Antonia racked her brains, but in vain.

She opened her reticule and unfolded her copy of the paper she had signed: yes, she had mortgaged the house and land against the loan that she had taken out for a maximum term of one year.

She sat and stared heedlessly over the burgeoning hedges already white with May blossom, mentally editing a version of that morning's events for Miss Donaldson. Donna would only say 'I told you that you should send a man upon the business' in her most governessy tone, Antonia thought. But that was not what was so irksome about the matter; if her man of business had been easily available, she would have employed him.

No, it was because it was Marcus Allington. . . She had no desire to be beholden to him for his intervention with Pethybridge! But, more importantly, she did not want Donna to harp endlessly on about his possible motives—why, she would conclude that his lordship was attracted to Antonia. 'Too ridiculous for words!' she exclaimed aloud, then had to apologise to Jem, who had taken it as a comment on his commercial triumph and was most put out.

Donna was sitting by the open back door, engaged in turning a worn sheet edge to edge, her work basket at her feet, but she dropped the linen unregarded as she heard Antonia's step on the path. 'Well, my dear, back already! Did you have a nice drive?'

Antonia saw at once the anxiety which lay behind the bright words; Donna was steeling herself for disappointment, and was already braced to offer soothing words and encouragement. Antonia put her arms around her companion and hugged her fiercely. 'We have the money, Donna! Every guinea we need!'

'Hooray!' Donna threw her pincushion up in the air,

seized Antonia's hands and proceeded to jig around the kitchen, much to the consternation of the charwoman who emerged from the scullery, wiping her hands on her apron to see what all the noise was about.

Donna subsided into a chair in a billow of skirts, pink-cheeked and quite unperturbed by the amazement of Mrs Brown, who hastily took herself off to the kitchen garden shaking her head over the unaccountable ways of the gentry. 'Tell me all about it—every detail,' Donna demanded.

Antonia produced a highly edited version of her interview with Mr Pethybridge, carefully omitting any reference to Marcus Allington, then reached for the commercial directory in search of builders and carpenters.

'I cannot believe the thing was so easily accomplished,' Miss Donaldson persisted. 'I thought you would have the most enormous difficulty going unaccompanied.' She looked beadily at Antonia's betraying flush. 'Antonia, why are you looking so conscious? Have you been employing feminine wiles upon Mr Pethybridge?'

'Upon Mr Pethybridge?' Antonia's guilty indignation was fuelled by the knowledge that she had not told Donna the truth. 'Really, Donna, as if I would! Why, he is quite an elderly gentleman.'

'Hmm. . .' was the only reply from her perceptive companion who inwardly believed that even elderly gentlemen had an eye for a pretty young woman.

The next few weeks passed in a blur of activity as Antonia began to put her credit to good use. The house seemed full of workmen repairing the roof, reglazing windows, unblocking drains and repainting woodwork neglected for many years. Miss Donaldson thrived amid the chaos. She was in her element supervising the polishing of panelling and staircases and was all for redecorating the entire house from attics to cellars.

'Donna, the bank loan is not bottomless,' Antonia cautioned. 'And I intend spending some of it reroofing the tenants' cottages, for they are in a scandalous state. Besides, if all is sound and clean, the new tenant will be able to put his own stamp upon the decorations. I have had a most encouraging response from a Mr Blake, the agent for the gentleman who advertised in *The Times*— I shall suggest he comes down to see the house and, should he prove interested, we can discuss such details then.'

Lying in bed that night, kept awake both by the smell of fresh paint and the moonlight flooding in through the window, Antonia stretched luxuriously in the half-tester bed. The two ladies no longer had to share a room and Antonia now occupied one of the chambers at the side of the house overlooking the pleasure grounds. Restlessly, she rose and crossed to the window, admiring the greensward, newly scythed by Old Johnson after much grumbling.

The moonlight was almost as bright as day and even reflected off the river, a curve of which cut across the grounds. It was calm, still and almost unseasonably warm for April and Antonia felt no desire to go back to bed. Her days were very full, but at night, unless she managed to fall asleep at once, her mind kept turning to thoughts of Marcus.

She managed to curb unruly memories of being in his arms, of the touch of his lips on hers, but when she closed her eyes she saw his face as clearly as if he were

standing before her. It seemed more than just a few weeks
since she had last seen him.

Briskly she shook herself—this would not do! If she
could not sleep she should do something useful—or even
go for a walk. The light was good enough for a stroll
around the lawns, or even to venture as far as the river.

Something her brother Howard had told her years ago
when she was still living at Rye End Hall and he was
just a schoolboy came back to her; it was better to fish
at night, for then the fish rose more easily to the lure. It
was a mad idea, but why not try a cast tonight? It seemed
a very simple thing when she saw other people do it and
she knew where the rods and lines were. How surprised
Donna would be to find a nice fat perch on her plate for
breakfast!

Hastily dressing in a plain gown and pulling on a stout
pair of shoes, Antonia tiptoed downstairs before reason
could reassert itself and send her back to her bed.

The rods were in the store-room where she had last
seen them; there were several, all different, which was
confusing. Antonia tried a couple for weight, then selected the smallest before remembering she would need bait.
In the pantry, she cut rind from the bacon, lit a horn
lantern, then, feeling quite an old hand at the sport, crept
out and across the lawns.

The night was almost completely still; there was no
wind and, other than a faint rustling as a night creature
slipped through the grass, no sound. Antonia found a
patch of dry gravel to stand upon, set down her lantern
and attempted to bait the hook. This proved more difficult
than she expected: the hook was sharp and the bacon
slippery.

Eventually, she succeeded and, throwing her arm right

back, cast the line over the water. Nothing happened. Antonia peered at the rod in the lamplight and fiddled with the reel until it was running smoothly, then tried again. This time the bacon shot right across the river and snagged on the rushes on the opposite bank.

After several attempts, Antonia's arm was aching and she was realising that there was more to fishing than met the eye. 'One more try!' she muttered. To her great surprise, the line landed plumb in the middle of the river with a satisfying plop.

Despite this triumph, Antonia soon discovered that fishing was a less stimulating activity than she had been led to believe. The silence stretched on, broken only by an owl hooting as it drifted over the meadow. The line hung in the scarcely moving water and Antonia stifled a yawn.

She was just wondering idly what time it was and when the fish were going to start jumping when the rod in her hand gave a jerk and the line began to run out. She had caught a fish! Antonia grasped the handle of the rod firmly and began to reel in the line until the squirming silvery fish was clear of the water. She landed it clumsily on the grass, dropped the rod, then realised she had no idea how to proceed now.

She pounced on the fish, grabbing at it with both hands, alarmed to discover just how slippery and muscular a live fish was. She turned and twisted as the fish leapt in her hands then found herself thoroughly entangled in her own line as it wrapped around her ankles.

'Oh, keep still!' she pleaded with the fish, but it did not oblige, lashing its tail to soak the front of her dress. 'I should have known it would be you!' A voice half-weary, half-amused, sounded almost in her ear.

Antonia shrieked in alarm. As her hand jerked, it freed the hook from the perch, which leapt from her grip into the river. With her heart in her mouth, Antonia spun round to face Marcus Allington. He was quite at ease, leaning against the trunk of a willow that bent over the water.

'Is there no end to your talents, Miss Dane?' he enquired, his mouth twitching with suppressed laughter.

'Do not dare laugh at me,' she stormed. 'You scared me half to death and you made me drop my fish!'

'A very respectable perch by the look of it; a shame you let it slip through your fingers.' The angrier she became, the more amused Marcus appeared.

'*I* let it! If you had not crept up behind me like some thief in the night. . .' She took a hasty step forward and felt the fine line wrap itself more firmly round her ankles. 'Oh, bother this line, it has a life of its own!'

'Stand still and I will untrammel you.' Marcus sauntered over and dropped to one knee beside her.

Antonia stood looking down on his bent head, burning with embarrassment at the touch of his fingers at her ankles. She shifted uneasily, awkwardly unsure of what to do with her hands, and he admonished sharply, 'If you wriggle you will make it worse! Come,' he rallied her, 'this is no time for maidenly modesty, Miss Dane—do you want to be here till dawn?'

'Well, hurry up then,' she responded pettishly, glad that at least the moonlight would leach the colour from her flushed cheeks. 'Can you not cut it?'

'Cut a line?' He sat back on his heels and looked up at her, his eyes glinting in the subdued light. 'Really, Miss Dane, I can see you are no true angler. If you had not dropped the hook in the folds of your gown I could be quicker, but I have no intention of running its barbs into my thumb.'

'Well, do your best.' She subsided, quivering with a mixture of emotions ranging from indignation and embarrassment to a strange excitement and a terrible compulsion to let her hands run through the thick hair on the bowed head before her.

It seemed forever before he rose to his feet, the hook held securely between finger and thumb, the line trailing free on the grass. 'There you are—you can begin again now. Where is your bait?'

'Over there, but I think I have fished enough for one night.'

'Bacon?' He peered into the dish. 'What were you intending to catch with that, for goodness' sake?' The amusement was back in his voice again.

'Perch, of course. Bacon is excellent for perch—as you just witnessed.'

'A veritable Izaak Walton,' he teased. 'Here, take your hook and line.'

He held both out to her and the act of stepping forward to take them brought her disturbingly close to him. She held out a tentative hand for the hook, but he shook his head, 'No, on second thoughts, you are right, you have fished enough tonight.' He secured the hook onto the reel and dropped the rod.

Marcus stood regarding her, musing that, even in the plain, worn gown with her hair awry, the unruly curls falling about her cheekbones, Miss Antonia Dane was quite provokingly desirable, the more so because she was entirely without artifice. Even in the moonlight he could see the clear hazel eyes regarding him steadily, the lashes naturally sooty and curled. The light took the colour from the flawless skin, lending her the appearance of an alabaster statue.

'What are you looking at me like that for?' Antonia asked, her mouth suddenly dry. Encounters with this man in broad daylight were unsettling enough, but under the influence of the full moon she felt anything might happen.

There was amusement in the look he was giving her, but he was not laughing at her expense; rather the look was tender and appreciative and transformed his face, making him seem less harsh, more approachable. 'Oh, I was just thinking how charmingly you smell. . .of fish.'

'You. . .!' She raised a hand in fury, only for him to catch it lightly by the wrist.

'Please, do not slap my face—not covered as you are with fish scales and slime.' His voice was warm and insidious as he pulled her gently towards him as if she too were a fish on a line. Antonia found herself moving, unresisting, compliant.

'I really ought to wash my hands,' she faltered ridiculously, irrelevantly.

'No need, we can manage if you only keep them at your sides,' he remarked dispassionately before bending his head to kiss her.

His mouth was moving around the curve of her upper lip, gently nibbling. Antonia gasped with the intimate shock of the sensation, but made no attempt to break free. When he reached the full softness of her lower lip she capitulated utterly, tipping her face trustingly upwards. His hands still held hers captive at her sides, which made the embrace seem even more shocking and disturbing.

Marcus murmured into her hair, 'I must come night

fishing again; I would never imagine I would catch such a prize.'

'Marcus, I am not a fish!' she protested into his coat front, but it was only the mildest of reproofs. She had no desire to move out of the circle of his arms, away from his warmth and the strength that was evident even through the fine cloth of his coat. Did she feel like this because it was Marcus who was holding her, she wondered, or was it moon madness?

He sighed, his breath stirring the fine hair at her temple. 'Agreeable as I find this, we cannot stand out here all night, Antonia. What will the redoubtable Miss Donaldson think has become of you?'

'Nothing, I trust,' replied Antonia, trying not to feel disappointed as he turned from her to collect up her fishing tackle and lantern. 'She was asleep when I left, and I hope she still is.'

He took her arm, guiding her solicitously over the tussocky grass of the still-untamed pleasure grounds. 'Then you came fishing on a whim? What an extraordinary young woman you are.' The lantern was attracting small moths, which rose from the lawn at their feet so that they appeared to be walking in a small cloud.

'We cannot live on game alone; I thought fish would be a welcome variation.' She glanced at him sideways to see how he took this reference to her licensed 'poachers'.

'I am not going to rise to your bait, Antonia; it is late and I am tired. I am resolved not to mention your poachers again, unless we find any on my land—not that I am happy with the example you are setting. But why do you not set that lad of yours to fishing? He has no doubt been doing it in my rivers half his life.'

So, he had decided to let that quarrel lie, she mused.

Still, that did not explain why he had so unexpectedly come to her aid with the banker. 'It sounds dangerously as if you are resigned to my remaining at Rye End Hall, my lord.'

He stopped and looked at her, a glint that was not all amusement in his eye. 'Take care, Antonia. You may have a penchant for angling, but do not try to fish for my motives. I told you I would not discuss them, that day in Berkhamsted.'

Antonia was not so easily discouraged. 'Come, my lord, 'twas less than a week before that that you were violently opposed to our remaining here and wished to buy my lands. Are you no longer interested in acquiring them?'

Marcus tucked her hand under his arm once more and carried on towards the house. 'There is more than one way to skin a cat, Antonia,' he remarked casually, smiling faintly at her answering snort of exasperation. 'Now, which door did you come out by?'

'The side door—it is unlocked.'

Marcus looked at her in surprise. 'Really, Antonia, have you no care for burglars? You truly are the most extraordinary woman I have ever encountered.'

'If we are to talk of extraordinary behaviours, Marcus, why are you out at this hour? Why, it must be all of half past two.'

'A card party at Sir George Dover's. It was such a pleasant evening I walked over.' He named a near neighbour of hers whose wife had already made her call of courtesy. 'As you say, the hour is late. Goodnight, Antonia.' He lifted her hand, kissing the back of her wrist, well away from her fish-scaled fingers, and strode off along the footpath into the moonlight towards Brightshill.

A short while later, Antonia snuggled down in her bed and thought back on that extraordinary encounter. There was no doubting she had behaved most improperly, moonlight or not, but she could not regret allowing Marcus to kiss her.

Her fingers, now mercifully free of fish, strayed to her lips, tracing where his mouth had roamed. Surely he was not simply toying with her affections? There was no denying that her affections were engaged, and he was a gentleman, after all. Yet that casual remark about skinning cats, his refusal to discuss his motives for helping her with the loan—those nagged at the back of her mind. She had refused to sell him her lands—had he now some other ploy in mind?

Chapter Five

'Oh, Donna! Mr Blake writes to say they are most interested in my description of the property and my proposals!'

Antonia waved two sheets of hot-pressed notepaper at Miss Donaldson, who put down her needlework and asked placidly, 'Do you refer to your answer to the advertisement in *The Times*? Do stop jigging around the room, my dear, and let me see. . .'

Antonia, her eyes shining, whirled to a halt on the newly cleaned salon carpet and handed the letter to her companion. 'I am so relieved!' she exclaimed. 'After putting all this work in hand, I must admit to a severe apprehension that we would not find a tenant willing to take it.'

'I, too,' Miss Donaldson confessed, smoothing out the sheets to con them again. 'After all, it is almost four weeks since you wrote. So much money has been spent—although I must say it is most pleasant to be able to sit in here, instead of sharing the kitchen with Mrs Brown, especially now the weather is so clement.'

They both turned to look from the wide bay window

across the green swathe of lawn, finally responding to Old Johnson's frequent scything. The fine weather had allowed the workmen to complete almost all their work on the Hall; tomorrow, they would commence the smaller task of making the Dower House habitable again.

The river glinted in the sunlight, recalling her moonlight encounter with Marcus Allington. Antonia struggled to suppress the nagging feeling of disappointment that struck her every time she thought of that incident. She had honestly expected Marcus to call again, to start wooing her.

She had teased herself, wondering if he was interested in her for herself or her property, and then had felt most disheartened on learning that his lordship had left for London the following day. She told herself that it would teach her not to jump to conclusions, or indeed, flatter herself that a man like Marcus would have serious intentions towards someone with no fortune, no sophistication, no experience. . .

'Are you attending, my dear?' Miss Donaldson had obviously been speaking for some minutes. Antonia recalled herself and apologised. 'I was saying that this Mr Blake states here his intention of calling the day after tomorrow unless he hears to the contrary. I do believe we should send a positive response today, for we are quite ready to receive him.'

'You are correct; it would create a good impression and it is important that he convince his principal that this property is right for him.'

Antonia felt far from confident that she could negotiate the lease successfully. She had still not told Donna that it was only with Marcus's intervention that the bank loan had been granted. By herself, she had failed utterly with

Mr Pethybridge; Mr Jeremy Blake was probably cut from the same cloth. And this time she could hardly call on Lord Allington to negotiate on her behalf, even if he had been at Brightshill.

Two days later Miss Donaldson was flitting around with a duster polishing wood that already gleamed and driving Antonia to distraction. She was nervous enough about their visitor as it was. 'Please, Donna, come and sit down. Mr Blake is due at any moment and you are quite flushed. Oh, listen! Is that a chaise I hear now?'

Donna thrust the duster under the sofa cushions and patted her hair firmly under her cap. Antonia smoothed out the folds of her only respectable morning dress and cast a hasty glance in the overmantel mirror. She felt confident her appearance would impress an elderly lawyer: her unruly dark hair was caught back smoothly under a dark ribbon, her high-necked dress was trimmed chastely at collar and cuff with Brussels lace and her only ornaments were a good amber set inherited from her mother.

She turned as their newly appointed maidservant announced, 'Mr Blake, ma'am.'

A man scarcely older than herself stood on the threshold of the salon. Mr Blake was a pleasant-looking gentleman with a cheerful, plain face, neatly trimmed brown hair and immaculately fashionable, if sober, clothing. A far cry, indeed, from the dessicated lawyer they had been expecting. And if the ladies were surprised, so too was Mr Blake. He was not quite quick enough to conceal the look of, first, surprise and then pleasure as he took in the striking young lady stepping forward to greet him.

From the cool formality of the letter Miss Dane had
written him, Mr Blake had expected to find a formidable
spinster of indeterminate age. Instead, he was confronted
by an elegant young woman dressed with stylish severity.
She was not quite in the established mode, being too tall
and willowy, to say nothing of being a brunette when
the fashion was for blondes, but to him she appeared
entirely admirable.

He schooled his face and took her proffered hand as
she greeted him. 'Good day, Mr Blake, I trust you had
a pleasant journey from Town.'

'Thank you, ma'am. I spent the night in Berkhamsted
at the White Hart in tolerable comfort.'

'May I present my companion, Miss Donaldson.'

This lady was more in the style Jeremy had been
expecting. He exchanged polite bows with Donna and
accepted both the seat and the cup of tea that were
offered.

'I realise you have only had the most cursory of first
impressions of Rye End Hall,' Antonia said, attempting
to sound unconcerned, 'but may I ask if this is the sort
of property your principal is seeking?'

'Yes, indeed,' Mr Blake said warmly, then recollected
himself, adding more coolly, 'That is to say, the location
is precisely what Sir Josiah desires, and the house appears
charming.'

'Sir Josiah?'

'I think there is no harm in my revealing that I rep-
resent Sir Josiah Finch, who returned from the East Indies
some twelve months ago and is now desirous of settling
in this area from whence his family originated.'

'How very interesting; no doubt he will find the
countryside hereabouts a great contrast to the Indies!'

They continued to exchange pleasantries whilst the tea was drunk. Antonia talked on, not showing by a whit her instinct that Mr Blake was not only very favourably disposed towards the Hall, but also towards herself. It was very gratifying to feel one was admired, and she was enjoying the respectful admiration in Mr Blake's eyes.

'Another cup of tea, Mr Blake? No?' Antonia rose to her feet. 'Then may I conduct you on a tour of Rye End Hall?'

As they crossed the hall, Antonia paused to allow him time to observe its proportions before she asked, 'Are you well acquainted with Sir Josiah?'

'Indeed, I am, Miss Dane, we are related by marriage.'

'I asked, for I was wondering if he intended bringing his family; there is ample accommodation.'

'Sir Josiah is married—Lady Finch is my aunt—but alas, they are without surviving children; the Indies are a cruel place for those of tender years.'

Out of the corner of her eye, as she murmured words of regret, Antonia was aware of Donna slipping back into the salon, no doubt to peruse the pages of *Burke's Landed Gentry* for the records of the Finch family. Such a connection would explain Mr Blake's air of easy good breeding. And, Antonia mused, it should also make negotiations much simpler; no doubt he was fully in his uncle's confidence and would be able to make decisions without constant reference to his principal.

Mr Blake proved to be an undemanding visitor, although he made frequent notes in his notebook. He admired the number and proportions of the rooms, commented favourably upon the domestic arrangements and was fully in accord with their decision not to decorate extensively.

'Sir Josiah will be bringing a considerable collection of Oriental furnishings and art works,' he explained as they descended the staircase. 'And he will wish to hang some very fine Chinese wallpapers, if that is acceptable to you, Miss Dane?'

'Oh, certainly, I would have no objection. You sound as though you have already resolved to recommend Rye End Hall to Sir Josiah,' Antonia commented, attempting to conceal the eagerness in her voice.

'I think it would suit them admirably,' Mr Blake began, 'but the final decision is, of course, Sir Josiah's,' he added with a sudden return to lawyer-like caution.

'Would you care to take a little luncheon before seeing the pleasure grounds and Home Farm?' Antonia offered, determined to remain cool and businesslike, but quite unable to hide the pleasure and relief that flooded through her at his positive words.

Jeremy Blake blinked at the radiant smile which illuminated Antonia's face, transforming her from a cool and severe lady into a charming and vivacious girl. There and then he determined that not only was Sir Josiah going to lease Rye End Hall, but that he would make every effort to provoke Miss Dane into smiling at him like that again.

Miss Donaldson had left off from her scanning of *Burke's* long enough to order up a light collation to be served in the breakfast room. Antonia would have wished that the smell of beeswax polish was not quite so obvious, bespeaking as it did all the hard work and hope which had gone into preparing the house for this visit. Fortunately, Mr Blake seemed oblivious to such details of housekeeping.

'Most eligible. . .extremely well connected,' Donna

hissed excitedly in Antonia's ear as they entered the room. 'I have marked the page. . .'

'Donna. . .shh! Do take this seat, Mr Blake, it affords a fine view down to the river.'

'That puts me in mind of another question I must ask—thank you, ma'am, cold pigeon would be most acceptable—is the fishing good? And do you intend to retain the rights?'

To both his, and Miss Donaldson's, astonishment, Antonia blushed to the roots of her dark hair. Mr Blake frantically scanned his memory to find what he could have said to produce such a reaction while Antonia recollected herself hastily. 'I believe there are perch, but I really cannot say. I have no intention of keeping the fishing rights, none at all.'

Her vehemence was as puzzling as her confusion and she was very aware of Miss Donaldson's beady regard. She must pull herself together, stop falling into daydreams and reveries every time anyone mentioned the river. A sensible woman would conclude that, despite his dalliance on the river bank, Lord Allington's absence was a clear signal that the incident meant nothing to him. She became aware that Mr Blake was speaking again and remarked hastily, 'And no doubt pike are common.'

'In the stables?' Miss Donaldson interjected. 'Antonia dear, you have lost the thread of the conversation, we were speaking of accommodation for Sir Josiah's carriage horses.'

'I am so sorry. A syllabub, Mr Blake, or can I tempt you with a jelly?'

'Either, Miss Dane,' the lawyer responded warmly, causing Donna to cast up her eyes. The man appeared to be highly attracted to dear Antonia, which, considering his most eligible connections, was not to be discouraged. On the other hand, she had entertained hopes of Lord Allington, but that unfortunate disagreement over the poaching appeared to have driven him away. . .

An hour later, only the stables remained to be inspected. Mr Blake expressed his intention of setting forth immediately and set his groom to hitching up his pair while he looked around.

'I hope to regain London tonight and speak to Sir Josiah tomorrow morning,' he explained as they emerged from the carriage house into the sunlight once more.

'You will be very late, surely?' Antonia queried.

'I shall change horses at Stanmore and expect to make good time. Sir Josiah is impatient when it comes to matters of business—he will expect a prompt report.'

'May I enquire if you are still of a positive mind in recommending this house to Sir Josiah?' Antonia crossed her fingers in the folds of her skirts as she ventured the question.

'Let me just say that I shall ask the name and direction of your man of business before I leave,' Mr Blake replied, pencil poised over his notebook.

Antonia dictated the details and London address, making a mental note to write with all dispatch to Mr Cooke at Gray's Inn, who would otherwise be deeply confused to receive such an approach from Mr Blake.

She was slightly taken aback at the sight of Mr Blake's conveyance, a rakish sporting curricle pulled by a pair of handsome matched bays. She had expected a lawyer to be driven in a closed carriage, not to be tooling himself down the highway. But then, Mr Jeremy Blake was most unlawyerlike in many respects.

'Well, I must thank you for your hospitality, Miss Dane, Miss Donaldson,' Mr Blake began, taking Antonia's hand in his and looking into her hazel eyes warmly. 'And I hope to be able to give you an answer within a few days. . .'

He was in mid-sentence, Antonia's hand still clasped in his own, when, with a flurry of hooves on the gravel, Marcus Allington cantered into the stableyard astride a rakish chestnut. He reined in hard, but not before the carriage horses shied in alarm, the groom running to their heads.

Mr Blake immediately stepped between the ladies and the horses, glaring with unconcealed annoyance at the source of the intrusion.

Antonia's heart leapt in her chest as she stood there, a prey to mixed emotions. She was glad to see Marcus again after so many days, annoyed at herself for caring that he had not called, and acutely conscious of how they had last met. Her eyes flew to his face, searching for some glance, some acknowledgment of their encounter by the river.

Marcus had calmed the chestnut, but made no attempt to dismount, staring haughtily down at the stranger. Mr Blake squared his shoulders in his admirably cut coat, drew his brows together in an expression of some severity and remarked coldly, 'Sir, you have alarmed the ladies.'

It was as if he had not spoken. Marcus looked over his head, bowed slightly and greeted the ladies. 'Good day, Miss Dane. I trust I find you well, Miss Donaldson.'

Mr Blake, who had had more than his fair share of experience in dealing with arrogant aristocrats and who had a very good sense of his own breeding and worth, was not to be bested. This carelessly dressed man on the superb horse was obviously known to the ladies; none the less, that did not excuse his abominable bad manners.

He turned his shoulder on the rider, bowed slightly to Antonia and continued with his farewells as though Marcus Allington did not exist. 'Thank you again for your hospitality, Miss Dane; I hope to return to Rye End Hall very shortly. I will, of course, write at the earliest opportunity.'

Consoling himself with the thought that his carriage horses would pass muster with the most critical of horsemen, Jeremy Blake mounted his curricle, looped the reins neatly and set his pair in motion, sweeping past Lord Allington as if he were not there.

Antonia waved energetically at the departing carriage, noting with some pleasure the set expression on his lordship's face. She squeezed Donna's hand warningly, although it was unlikely that her companion would prattle of the lawyer's identity or purpose. It was too much to hope that this display of displeasure was jealousy because his lordship felt some partiality for her; on the other hand, it would do no harm to keep Marcus Allington guessing about her visitor.

Antonia stepped forward with a cool smile. 'Lord Allington, good day.' She might entertain warm—even romantic—feelings about him when he was absent, daydream about the pressure of his lips on hers, speculate about his intentions but, faced with the man himself, she found herself provoked by his arrogance. 'A very fine day, is it not? One really feels that summer is around the corner.'

Marcus dismounted, tossing the reins to a groom as he did so. 'Oh, a visit! How nice,' Antonia prattled brightly. 'I had assumed you were merely passing.

What a pity we have just finished luncheon.'

'I have eaten, ma'am, some time ago. I would not have intruded if I had realised you were entertaining company.' Marcus was chillingly polite.

'Of course you would not,' Antonia replied with what she hoped was maddening complacency. At that moment Miss Donaldson gave up all hope of Lord Allington as a suitor, made a hasty excuse and left. Antonia glanced sideways at Marcus's unsmiling face. 'You seem out of sorts, my lord.'

Marcus met her eyes steadily, then suddenly smiled, his brow clearing. Antonia had the distinct impression she had overplayed her hand. 'Not at all, Antonia. I merely called to see if you had experienced any more difficulty with the bank while I have been in Town.'

'Oh, have you been away? Now that I think of it, I do believe one of the servants mentioned that you were not at Brightshill. Have you been absent long? For ourselves, we have been so busy that time has just flown by. Thank you for enquiring, everything has proceeded most smoothly.'

They were strolling towards the house as they spoke. Antonia was very conscious of his nearness. From the very beginning, she had found him a dominating physical presence, but since experiencing his kisses she found herself acutely aware of his hands, of the breadth of his shoulders, of the very scent of him. It was most unsettling to find the sensations she had experienced under the moonlight recurring now in full daylight. There was no excuse for it, going as it did against all proper behaviour!

They had now arrived at the front door, which still stood open. 'Would you care to see the work we have had done?' Antonia asked, feeling that some conciliatory gesture was owing, considering that Marcus had been instrumental in obtaining the necessary funds for the work for her.

It became obvious as they walked through the house that he must take a personal interest in the practical details of his own estate. The questions he asked the plasterers and roofers who were putting the finishing touches to the attic rooms were informed, and Antonia was surprised by the easy demeanour he showed with the men.

It was partly explained when the plumber said, 'If you care to take a look at the roof, my lord, you will see we used the same way of fixing the leadwork as we did at Brightshill.'

Antonia stepped back into the shadows and watched Marcus talking to the men. They were deferential, she realised, not entirely because of his rank, but because in him they recognised someone who understood the needs of a big estate and of their place within it.

His face as he talked had lost all its severity and his whole frame was relaxed as he handled a damaged piece of leadwork handed to him by the plumber. Here was a far cry from the magistrate punishing a poacher, or the brusque landowner ordering his gamekeepers.

William Hunt the plumber was pointing at something out on the leads. To Antonia's astonishment, Marcus stripped off his jacket, rolled up his shirtsleeves and swung easily out of the cramped dormer window on to the flat section of the roof.

When the plumber and his mate had followed him out, she strolled across to the window and watched them. To her alarm, Marcus was leaning dangerously over the parapet, prodding at brickwork and throwing comments over his shoulder to Hunt. Incomprehensible remarks about flashing, downpipes and rain hoppers floated back to her.

Gradually her alarm abated. As Marcus got to his feet, Antonia found her eyes drawn to the play of strong muscles under the fine linen the breeze was flattening to his back. He stood, one foot on the parapet, looking out over the grounds; as he turned to toss a remark back to the plumber, the wind caught his hair, blowing unruly blond locks into his eyes.

'I agree, you had better talk to Miss Dane about those downspouts. A decision must be made one way or another,' he was saying prosaically as he pushed back the hair and met her eyes.

Across the space their gazes met and locked, his eyes holding a question she could not decipher. As she searched his face, Antonia realised with a jolt that she was falling in love with Marcus Allington and that if he made any answering sign of partiality she would run to his side, however many workmen were present, however inappropriate the setting.

The moment seemed endless, but only a few seconds could have passed for Hunt was saying to her, 'It's like this, ma'am; the weight of rainwater coming down off this roof is too great for the size of hopper, it's difficult to explain without you seeing it. . .' He scratched his head, at a loss for the words that could better explain the situation to a lady who could not hope to understand technical matters of this sort.

Marcus strode across to where she stood at the window and extended his hand. 'Come, Miss Dane, you will be safe in my care. It is quite flat for the most part.'

Willingly, Antonia let Marcus take her hand. His grasp

was warm, firm and sure and she experienced no fear as she stepped up on to a box, then stooped to climb over the window ledge.

'Thank you, Hunt,' Marcus said to the plumber. 'I am sure you want to be getting on inside: I will show Miss Dane the problem.'

'Oh, look, you can see for miles,' Antonia exclaimed, gazing out over the greening Hertfordshire countryside and the great beech woods rolling over the scarp edge of the Chilterns towards the Vale beneath.

She leaned on the brick parapet, her eyes fixed on the distant horizon, happily unaware of the height until she made the mistake of looking downwards. The paved terrace four storeys below seemed to swim up to meet her as she recoiled with a gasp of terror.

Marcus took her in his arms and spun her round so that his body shielded her from the drop and she was held hard against him.

Antonia's eyes were tight shut; she had never been at such a height before with so little between her and the ground. Her heart was beating sickeningly, her breath tight in her chest.

'You are not going to faint,' he informed her firmly. Antonia felt rather than heard the command as her ear was pressed against his shirt front. The breeze had cooled the linen, but through it she could feel the heat of his body. He smelled faintly of cologne, leather and something which was indefinably Marcus.

'Are you certain?' Antonia quavered. She had never fainted before, but the mixture of sensations she was now experiencing made her feel she might do so at any moment.

'Quite certain,' Marcus assured her. He set her firmly

at his side, his body between her and the drop, his arm still protectively about her shoulders. 'You see, you cannot possibly fall. Come, over here and sit down away from the edge. You cannot go in until I have explained the deficiencies of your rainwater system or Hunt will be quite unable to proceed.'

Antonia glanced up, wondering at his mood, and caught the glint of amusement in his dark eyes. 'Do you truly understand these matters?' she asked as he handed her to a low brick wall safely away from the edge.

'But of course, and so should you. I trust you also understand about the correct dimensions to ensure a chimney draws properly and the desirable fall of drains away from the house. . .'

'I find nothing desirable about drains under any circumstances,' Antonia stated firmly, trying not to wish he would put his arm around her again.

As though answering the thought, Marcus sat down beside her and almost casually tucked her arm through his. The thought of protesting at the familiarity flickered through her mind, only to be dismissed. It was certainly most improper, but then, who was there to see it? And it was broad daylight; he had kissed her in the moonlight yet had taken no further liberty. This was safe enough for propriety, Antonia told herself, although it was wreaking havoc with her sensibilities.

'Those are fine chimneys on the Dower House,' Marcus remarked, pointing them out through the trees. 'Have you decided what you will do with it?'

'The men have begun work on it this week, although there is little amiss with the structure. Donna and I will be quite comfortable there.'

'Then you will be selling this?' He half-turned to face

her, evidently surprised. 'You have changed your mind since I made you an offer for it?'

'Indeed, no, I have no intention of selling Rye End Hall, it is my family home. I am to lease it. Do you not recall? You were most slighting about the suggestion. I am grateful that, thanks to your intervention, I have the capital with which to do the work here: I assumed you knew why I wanted the money. I was quite clear about it, I believe.'

'I had thought those just hot words thrown at my head.' Marcus smiled at her. 'We were, after all, somewhat intemperate in our discussion of the matter, and I must admit I did not take your scheme seriously.'

Antonia turned a puzzled countenance to him. 'But what did you believe I wanted the money for, if not to renovate the house in order to lease it?'

'Why, to live in moderate comfort as is befitting of your station.'

'So you influenced the banker solely out of concern for my comfort? You must have wondered how I intended to repay the loan,' she exclaimed in a rallying tone. But underneath she felt a sudden surge of hope that he may have acted to keep her in the neighbourhood because he had a partiality for her.

'I would hope that I always act for the comfort of others,' Marcus replied drily. 'But there is an overriding consideration. . .'

Antonia could scarcely breathe waiting for him to finish the sentence.

'. . .it is of great concern to me, and our neighbours, that a fine estate such as Rye End Hall should not fall into rack and ruin. It leads to poverty, which in its turn brings about lawlessness and want.'

'If your motives are so altruistic, sir, I am amazed you felt unable to air them the other day when I asked you directly why you had secured the money for me!' Really! Just when she found she was liking the man—she could not bring herself to even think the word love—he said something insufferable. 'You will be pleased to hear that I am in hopes of securing a most respectable tenant for the house and the Home Farm,' she added stiffly, spots of colour touching her cheekbones.

'Ah, I thought I smelt a clerk this morning!' Marcus seemed quite unaware of her discomfiture. Antonia sensed only his satisfaction at placing Mr Jeremy Blake.

'No clerk, sir! Mr Blake is a lawyer with the highest connections. I am most hopeful his principal—and uncle—will take the Hall.'

'You are warm in your defence of—what is his name, Black?'

'Blake. I found him a most amiable and intelligent person to do business with. And, of course,' she added slyly, recovering her equilibrium, 'such a gentleman. It would be a considerable asset to our social circle locally if he were to accompany his uncle here.'

'I shall look forward to making his acquaintance,' Marcus said politely. 'But we stray from the point—you intend taking up residence at the Dower House?'

'Certainly. Both Miss Donaldson and I expect to be most comfortable there. It is entirely the right size for two unattached ladies, the gardens can be made charming. . .'

'So you intend to dwindle into respectable spinster-hood there, do you? No doubt you will be able to devote many fascinating hours to constructing a shell grotto in the grounds or perfecting your tatting.'

Antonia was taken aback by his sarcasm, then

recollected that he must be disappointed that she had not chosen to sell the property to him. 'Dwindle! Indeed not! We have every intention of entering fully into the social life of the district as soon as we are established at the Dower House. I have retained control of the lands other than those attached to the Home Farm, so I shall have tenants to oversee. . .indeed, I have every expectation of being rushed off my feet.'

'I am reassured to hear it.' His brow quirked with what Antonia had come to recognise as hidden amusement. 'May I hope you will visit Brightshill? I have a houseparty assembling soon—we may even muster enough couples to get up a dancing party on occasion.'

'I should like that very much,' Antonia responded formally, although the thought of finding something in her wardrobe to match the London gowns of his guests was somewhat daunting. The light breeze suddenly strengthened and Antonia shivered in her light gown. 'We should go in, Donna will be wondering what has become of me.'

Marcus took her hand to help her across the roof, but at the window ducked through it, before turning and holding up his arms.

'I can climb down by myself, thank you,' she said, blushing at the thought of so close a contact.

'Antonia, there are two ways of doing this; either I turn my back while you scramble down, doubtless tearing your gown in the process, or I lift you down—in the most respectful way, of course!' Laughter danced in his eyes. She knew he was laughing at her, but suddenly she did not care. She would be in his arms, however briefly, would feel his strength keeping her safe.

Wordlessly she reached down to him and found herself swung effortlessly over the sill and into the attic. Marcus held her for a fraction longer than was needful, before setting her down on the dusty floor. 'Tell me,' he began, looking down at her.

'Yes?' Antonia faltered, lifting her eyes to his, noticing a smudge of whitewash on his cheekbone, a cobweb caught in his unruly dark blond hair and ruthlessly suppressing the urge to brush it away.

'Have you retained the fishing rights?' He smiled, teeth white in the gloom.

So, standing here so close to each other evoked the same memories in him, too. 'No, I am convinced I would never make a good fisherwoman, no matter what,' she said with a shaky laugh.

'Practice is what you need, Antonia,' he murmured, his eyes warm on hers. 'You must come to Brightshill and let me teach you.' He put up one hand as if to touch her face, but dropped it as heavy boots sounded on the floorboards outside. By the time William Hunt joined them, there was a clear five-foot space between them and Marcus was commenting on the state of the plasterwork.

Marcus took his leave soon after and Antonia drifted back to the small salon, half-excited, half-irritated with herself. She had been out for several Seasons, had engaged in elegant flirtations with eligible men at balls and dinners: why did Marcus Allington have this effect on her? Her heart told her she was in danger of falling deeply in love with him, yet her head told her it was impossible.

She had been thrown into his company in the most extraordinary circumstances, hauled up before him as a common criminal. And their meetings since then had been characterised by an intimacy which was most unseemly. Antonia told herself firmly that it was this

improper proximity that was fascinating her. And as for
Lord Allington, he no doubt flirted with any lady willing
to indulge him, and her circumstances were perhaps
unusual enough to have piqued his interest.

By the time she rejoined her companion she had the
satisfaction of having her unruly emotions firmly under
control, or so she believed. Miss Donaldson, however,
missed very little.

'His lordship has gone?' she enquired, putting aside
her needlework.

'Some minutes ago,' Antonia replied indifferently. 'He
and Hunt appear to have settled a most difficult question
to do with the downspouts.'

'Indeed. And that necessitated you romping all over
the leads?'

'Hardly romping.' Antonia laughed lightly, flicking
through the day's post. 'The height is most disconcerting,
although the view is wonderful.'

'So you spent the entire time up there discussing drain-
age and the view?'

'Oh. . .we spoke of our plans for the Dower House.
And his lordship was kind enough to extend an invitation
to Brightshill shortly—he is assembling a houseparty.'

'Then I am not entirely without hope,' observed Miss
Donaldson archly.

'Hope?' Antonia turned to regard her companion.
'Of what?'

'Of your moving in Society, of course, as is fitting.'
Miss Donaldson kept her countenance schooled, but
Antonia had the distinct impression that that was not her
meaning.

Chapter Six

'My dear Antonia!' Miss Donaldson exclaimed. 'If you cannot find any rational occupation within the house, then please go out and take the air—for I declare you are quite fraying at my nerves with this incessant fidgeting!'

The uncharacteristic sharpness of her companion's tone startled Antonia. 'Am I fidgeting? I am so sorry, I was not aware of it.'

'You have done little else the past two days,' Donna replied more kindly. 'You have embroidered two flowers on that scarf, only to pull both out again; the pages of that new volume of Shelley's poetry are still uncut; there are two letters awaiting reply from your cousin Augusta. . .'

Antonia put up her hands to stem the flow. She knew Donna was right, but she felt she could not settle to anything now the workmen had left and the big house stood ready for its new tenant. Outside the windows, the trees were heavy with fresh greenery, the newly planted pleasure grounds were breaking with new growth and the very air was heavy with the promise of summer just around the corner.

'If only we knew what was happening—whether Sir Josiah has decided to take Rye End Hall! It is a week now since Mr Blake's visit—I had expected to hear from him several days ago.' She paced restlessly across the drugget protecting the newly laid carpet, then burst out, 'Oh, Donna, what if Mr Blake has failed to persuade his uncle! What shall we do then with all this money laid out and no way of repaying it?'

Miss Donaldson came to put her arm around her young companion. Knowing Antonia as she did after nearly a decade together, she recognised the strain she was under. A surge of real anger shook her normally well-schooled emotions. This was all the fault of Sir Humphrey Dane and his son! How could Antonia's father and brother have been so feckless, so selfishly uncaring as to leave her the sole inheritor of debt and disarray!

'It is only a week, dear,' she began soothingly when the sound of hooves crunching on gravel caught their attention. 'Ah! No doubt that is Lord Allington come to call. Now that I think of it, it must be a week since we last saw him. The diversion of a visitor will turn our minds from these worries.' Miss Donaldson spoke brightly but was precisely aware of how long it had been since his lordship had been at the Hall, and had been feeling quite cast down at his lack of attention to Antonia. She had entertained such hopes of the pair of them. . .

'Mr Blake, ma'am.' Anna the housemaid was bobbing a curtsy in the open doorway.

'Why, Mr Blake! We had not looked to see you in person—what an unexpected pleasure.' All the relief Antonia felt—for surely he would not have come in person to give her an answer in the negative—was in Antonia's radiant smile as she offered him her hand.

Jeremy Blake shook the proffered hand and bowed to Miss Donaldson, whilst reflecting that his arrival on business was not normally greeted with such warmth. His eyes lingered on Miss Antonia Dane: her slender figure was enhanced by the simplicity of the muslin gown she was wearing. He could scarcely believe, for he was a modest young man, that it was his appearance that had prompted the sparkle in her dark eyes or the warm colour heightening her creamy complexion, but he was susceptible enough to appreciate it none the less.

'Do, please, take a seat, Mr Blake. May we offer you some refreshment after your journey? Anna, bring the decanters.' Antonia sank down gracefully on the sofa, prey to a sudden fear that he had bad news and was kind enough to bring it in person. 'Have you ridden over from Berkhamsted this morning?'

'No, ma'am. I have taken rooms at the Green Man in Tring. It is rather more conveniently situated for riding here daily, which I hope you will permit me to do, for there are many practical details to be settled. . .'

'Then Sir Josiah is minded to take Rye End Hall?' Antonia could hardly contain her excitement and relief in order to speak calmly.

'Indeed yes, Miss Dane. He was most happy with my account; both he and my aunt feel this will be the ideal country establishment for them.'

'You must feel very gratified that Sir Josiah and Lady Finch place so much trust in your judgement as to take the house unseen,' Antonia responded warmly. 'And I must thank you for your persuasions on our behalf. It is such a relief to know that Rye End Hall will be let to such a notable person as Sir Josiah and will regain its place amongst the estates of the area.'

Mr Blake flushed slightly at the compliment. 'I thank you, ma'am, but I assure you that once presented to him, the merits of the estate were such that Sir Josiah needed little persuasion by me. And it is you and Miss Donaldson who should be congratulated on the taste and propriety of the renovations.'

Setting his glass on one side, Mr Blake removed some folded papers from his breast pocket and handed one, closed with a seal, to Antonia. 'I act as messenger from your man of business whose letter you have there. Between us, we have drawn up a contract which I trust you will find acceptable: may I hope you could give me an answer upon it if I return tomorrow?'

'But surely we can close on this today!' Antonia exclaimed. 'If you will allow me an hour to peruse it before luncheon, then, unless I have any questions, I can sign it and the deed is done. You will stay for luncheon, Mr Blake?'

'That would be most acceptable, ma'am, thank you.' Mr Blake got to his feet. 'With your permission, I will use the time until luncheon to ride around the estate: there are some notes Sir Josiah has charged me to make, and it is a most beautiful day.' He bowed to the ladies and left.

Antonia seized Donna's hands and danced her round the room in a jig of joy and relief. 'We've done it, we've done it, we've done it!'

'Antonia, dear! What if Mr Blake should see us!'

'He has gone—and what if he does see us? I do not care!'

'Antonia, please, I am quite breathless. And this is most indecorous!' But Donna was smiling.

When Mr Blake rejoined them for luncheon Antonia

greeted him with the words, 'I am most happy to sign this contract. My man of business recommends it to me, and I am more than happy to vacate the Hall by the date specified.'

A look of anxiety crossed Mr Blake's pleasant features. 'I had feared that a date only two weeks hence might be too precipitate for you. Are you quite certain it is convenient?'

'Let us discuss it over luncheon.' Antonia led the way through to the breakfast-room, which served them as a small dining-room. 'Please sit here, Mr Blake: will you carve the ham? I tell you truly, Miss Donaldson and I would be ready to move to the Dower House within the week. All the building work there is done: it only remains to hang the curtains, make up the beds and remove our personal possessions.'

'I am most relieved to hear you say so, Miss Dane,' he rejoined, passing a platter of carved ham to Donna as he spoke. 'If I may, this afternoon I had hoped to ride over and see your tenant at the Home Farm. I will need to spend one or two days with him this week, and then there are numerous measurements Lady Finch has charged me to make in the house, if that will not be inconvenient to you.'

'Not at all,' Antonia assured him warmly. 'I will give you a note of introduction to Thomas Christmas at the farm, and as to the measurements, you are to make yourself quite at home and not stand on ceremony. Come and go as you please.'

The rest of the meal passed most pleasantly for the ladies as Mr Blake proved to be an unexpected source of anecdotes about London Society. It was obvious he mixed freely with the Quality and Antonia could well imagine him gracing the floor at Almack's. She felt he perhaps viewed life a little too seriously—a product of his profession, no doubt—but he was most agreeable company.

'Are you frequently away from home upon Sir Josiah's business?' Miss Donaldson enquired. 'I only ask because, for a young man such as yourself, absences must put a strain upon domestic harmony.'

Antonia flinched at what was, to her ears, an obvious attempt to discover whether he were married or not. Mr Blake, however, showed no sign of discomfiture at the probing.

'Fortunately, ma'am, I have my own apartments within Sir Josiah's London residence and come and go as I please with no inconvenience.'

An expression, which Antonia recognised as the nearest Donna ever came to smugness, crossed her birdlike features. So, Mr Blake was not married and was even now being added to Donna's mental list of suitable suitors for Antonia.

Jeremy Blake, mercifully unaware of his hostesses' thoughts, soon took his leave, taking the signed contract and a note for Thomas Christmas from Miss Dane urging the farmer's complete co-operation with his new landlord.

Antonia stood on the sunwarmed steps watching as he cantered off towards the Home Farm. Halfway down the driveway, he encountered another rider. Both gentlemen doffed their hats as they passed one another and Antonia recognised Marcus's blond locks in the sunlight.

He dismounted at the front door, tossing his reins to the groom who was riding at his heels. 'Ten minutes, Saye,' he ordered. 'Keep them walking, this breeze is

fresh. Good afternoon, Miss Dane.' He bowed slightly
to Antonia. 'I trust I find you well?'

'Very well indeed, my lord. You find me on my way
to the flower garden. Would you care to accompany me
and protect me from Old Johnson, who refuses to believe
any of his blooms are for cutting?'

Marcus strolled alongside her, wondering what had
occurred to put her in such high spirits. For, though
Antonia's manner was controlled, her eyes were sparkling and her whole figure seemed animated with
suppressed excitement.

'Did I recognise that London clerk visiting again?'

Antonia hid a smile at his apparently casual probing.
It seemed Mr Blake piqued his lordship's interest, which
could only be flattering to herself. 'Indeed, it was Mr
Blake. I see no reason why I cannot tell you now that
his principal, Sir Josiah Finch, has decided to take Rye
End Hall. I expect Sir Josiah and Lady Finch—she is
Mr Blake's aunt, by the by—will be in residence here
within the fortnight.'

'I congratulate you!' Marcus pushed open the wicket
gate into the garden and held it for Antonia to pass
through. 'You appear to have scored a veritable triumph
with your tenant: a very notable nabob, indeed.'

Antonia scanned his face, looking for signs of sarcasm,
but saw only genuine admiration for her business acuity.
'You know Sir Josiah?'

'No, but I have heard of him. I believe he has been
returned to this country from the Indies for almost a year,
and the *on dit* is that he has amassed a great fortune in
his years in the East. He and Lady Finch do not go much
into Society, although she, of course, is widely connected

with some of the best families. He, I believe, is a self-made man. . .'

'And none the worse for that,' Antonia exclaimed hotly.

'I had intended no slur on your nabob. I am sure he is a most excellent man and will adorn our local society.'

Antonia was surprised. She had expected Sir Josiah's origins in trade—however exalted—would be despised by an aristocrat such as Lord Allington, as they would certainly have been by her own father.

'You do me an injustice,' Marcus continued evenly, 'if you believe I would condemn the man for such a reason. If he proves a bad landlord, I may revise my opinion.'

Antonia suspected there was a veiled hint about her 'poachers' in that last remark but, warmed as she was with her success and the admiration of Mr Blake, she chose to ignore it, not wishing to provoke an argument.

Old Johnson greeted them with a look of deep suspicion and a grunt. When Antonia asked him for a basket he produced one with bad grace. 'And some scissors, please, Johnson,' she requested firmly, knowing how the old man hated her to pick 'his' flowers.

'Ain't got none,' he muttered, but was foiled by Marcus producing a pocket knife.

Marcus held the basket while Antonia snipped her selected blooms, wandering up and down the paths under the old man's hostile eye. 'He appears to have taken a great dislike to me, as well as to your flower picking,' Marcus observed.

'Small wonder,' Antonia responded crisply, 'as you are the cause of his son's present condition.'

'I? And what condition might that be?' He looked

down into her indignant eyes, noticing for the first time
that in their hazel depths there were flecks of green.

'He is languishing in Hertford gaol, sent there by you
for poaching, and meanwhile his old father must support
his family.!'

'I remember him now—and I doubt his father is supporting his family, which consists of numerous by-blows
scattered from here to Berkhamsted. The son is a ne'er-
do-well who has never done an honest day's work in his
life and who crowned a career of poaching, thievery and
wenching by clubbing a keeper so savagely the man lost
the sight of one eye. No, ma'am, save your sympathy
for those who better deserve it.'

Antonia shivered at the chill in his voice and in his
eyes. 'I am sorry,' she stammered. 'I should not have
spoken without knowing the full facts. Was the injured
man one of your keepers?'

'Yes,' Marcus replied shortly, then seeing her stricken
face, relented and explained. 'He is the younger brother
of Sparrow, my head keeper. He works in the stables
now, for his sight is quite poor at night.'

Antonia remembered Sparrow's rough grasp. 'No
wonder Sparrow is so hard on poachers.'

'Indeed, Miss Dane. It is as well to remember that not
every picture is painted in black and white.'

She stooped to snip off some greenery, averting her
face from his. 'I accept your reproof, my lord. I acknowl-
edge that I become so passionately engaged sometimes
that I fail to see the shades of grey.'

Marcus put one hand under her elbow to help her
upright. Even through her gown and the leather of his
glove she could feel the warmth of him. 'I would not

wish to see you any less passionate about anything, Antonia,' he murmured.

She could not meet his eye, glancing away in confusion, to encounter instead the rheumy regard of the old gardener. This was no place to engage in. . .whatever was occurring between her and Marcus. Was he flirting with her, or merely teasing her? She could hardly tell, and her growing partiality for him was clouding her own judgement.

'I have filled my basket as full as I dare,' Antonia said lightly, nodding to Johnson as she led the way out of the garden. 'Donna will be wondering what has become of me, for she wanted to fill the vases in the hall.'

Marcus took the basket from her and they strolled back towards the house in companionable silence. At the front door he handed her the flowers and remarked, 'I had almost forgot the purpose of my call. I am assembling a houseparty at Brightshill next week—I believe I mentioned it before—and I hope Miss Donaldson and yourself will do me the honour of joining us for dinner on Tuesday evening.'

'I would be delighted, my lord, as, I am sure, will be Miss Donaldson.' Antonia spoke calmly but inside her heart had leapt at the thought of mixing with society again after so many months. And to see Marcus in his own setting, to see Brightshill in all its glory, filled with people. . .

But those people, she suddenly realised, would be of the height of London Society, fashionably dressed, *au fait* with the latest gossip and news. She had neither the gowns nor the gossip to mix comfortably with such a set; what would Marcus think when he saw her in such a company? He might find her amusingly unconventional now, but what appeared refreshing as a country diversion would seem gauche and soon lose its charm set against Town polish.

'Antonia? Is anything wrong?' Marcus appeared preternaturally alert to her mood today.

'Oh, no. . .I was merely woolgathering.'

'Forgive me, you must have much to be doing and thinking about. I shall leave you to your housekeeping and look forward to your company next Tuesday.'

Antonia held out her hand to shake his and was startled to find him bending over it to brush the back of her knuckles with his lips. 'Adieu, Antonia.'

She watched him, unconscious of bringing her hand up to her cheek as she did so. Saye came up with the horses and the two men were trotting off down the driveway before she recalled herself.

'Donna, Donna!' she called, running up the steps.

'There you are with the flowers.' Miss Donaldson emerged from the salon, a vase in each hand. 'What an age you have been, Antonia, I could not imagine what was detaining you.'

Antonia recognised the teasing note in her voice. 'You know full well Lord Allington called! Oh, Donna, he has invited us to dinner at Brightshill next Tuesday. His house party will be assembled—what are we to wear?'

'I shall wear my garnet silk, of course,' Donna replied composedly. 'It is perfectly suitable, and my attire will not in any case signify. No, my dear, the real question is, what are you to wear?'

Antonia dumped the flowerbasket unceremoniously on the side table and wailed, 'I have not a notion! I do not even know what is the latest mode—although you may be certain that not a garment that I own will be in it!'

'Then we must set to work immediately. Anna can arrange these flowers; we must review our wardrobes and see what will pass muster. Now,' she began, ticking items off on her fingers as she ascended the stairs. 'Gowns, those must be new, then there are your stockings, gloves, slippers. . . Anna! Where is that girl? We must see if there are any of your old gowns that will cut up. . .'

Antonia hurried after her companion, bemused that for once Miss Donaldson was not taking the opportunity for remarks on the folly of fashion and the impropriety of a mind set upon adornment.

An afternoon spent in turning out both their wardrobes swiftly passed. At length, they sank down gratefully with a cup of tea and reviewed their findings.

'It is as I feared,' Antonia said gloomily. 'We each have one pair of respectable evening gloves, there is enough ribbon to furbish up your gown and your slippers are presentable. But our stockings are woeful, my evening slippers unwearable and not a single gown of mine is in such a condition that I could either wear it or cut it up to make another with any pretensions to style.'

'None of this is insurmountable,' Miss Donaldson said firmly, setting down her cup and raising her voice. 'Anna!' The girl hurried in, only to be dispatched to find Jem and order his presence with the gig the next morning. 'We can try what Berkhamsted has to offer and go further afield if necessary.'

'But, Donna,' Antonia protested, 'we cannot afford to shop for any of this!' She was utterly bewildered by Miss Donaldson's enthusiasm.

'Nonsense! You have money left from the loan; look upon this as an investment.'

'You cannot be suggesting that I use that money for husband-hunting!'

'I did not say anything of the kind. But you cannot go into Society attired like a milkmaid. And if you are not to go into Society, pray tell me why we have been wasting so much time and money to establish ourselves in the Dower House?'

'Oh, very well,' Antonia conceded, knowing there was no gainsaying her companion in this mood. 'But we only have a week in which to prepare.'

'It will suffice. If luck is with us, we shall be able to obtain copies of the *Ladies' Intelligencer* in Berkhamsted, which will give us an inkling of the current mode. I have already found an excellent shop for haberdashery—I told you of it when I bought the linens last month—and there are several drapers. One, at least, must have some acceptable silks.'

'But we do not know which dressmakers to trust,' Antonia protested.

'Dressmakers? No time, my dear—we will sew the garment ourselves. With my skill—for I believe I do not flatter myself—in pattern cutting, and your fine stitchery, we may save several pounds and no one be any the wiser. Now, let us have some supper and retire early: we have a busy day before us tomorrow.'

'Now this will become you very well,' Donna said with satisfaction, holding up the dull gold silk against Antonia's creamy skin. 'That subtle counter-stripe in the weave quite picks up the brown of your hair.'

'Indeed yes, ma'am,' Mrs Mumford the linen draper

hastened to add her voice. 'If you intend to make this gown here—' she gestured to a striking fashion plate open on the counter '—I can think of nothing that will cut and drape better.'

'It is very expensive,' Antonia demurred, wistfully fingering the soft sheen.

'Quality will out, madam, if I may make so bold an observation.'

'Quite right,' Miss Donaldson declared. 'We will take a dress length of this, and the lining we had already agreed upon. Now, trimmings. . .'

Another delightful half-hour was passed deciding between the rival merits of mother-of-pearl buttons or covered silk ones, floss edgings or corded ribbon and whether to add a sprig of artificial flowers at the neckline or an edging of fine lace.

'And will you be bringing in your slippers for dyeing, ma'am?' Mrs Mumford enquired as the girl made up the parcels. 'I can recommend Thomas Hurst in the High Street for kid slippers, but his dyeing isn't all it ought to be.'

After negotiating with the shoemaker to send the new slippers to Mrs Mumford, they retired to a private parlour overlooking the inn yard at the King's Arms and sent for coffee and biscuits. Antonia made herself comfortable in the window seat and surveyed the bustle below. 'Oh, Donna, do look at Jem. He is sitting up in the gig with his arms folded, aping the groom in that curricle over there.'

'He is a good lad,' Donna remarked with a smile. 'I am glad we are able to give him employment. The yard is very busy, is it not? Here comes another post chaise— and I do declare, is that not Lord Allington coming out of the inn?'

It was, indeed. Antonia, from her vantage point, could look down on Marcus as he strolled out into the sunlight and stood waiting for the post boys to let down the steps of the chaise. Although he was wearing riding dress as usual, Antonia noticed he was more carefully attired than normal. As he lifted his tall hat, she saw he had submitted his tawny locks to the attentions of his valet, for the nape of his neck, newly shorn, showed paler against skin tanned by outdoor pursuits.

The door of the chaise swung open as soon as the vehicle came to a halt and, without waiting for the steps to be let down, a boy of about nine years tumbled out. For a moment Antonia thought he was about to throw his arms around Marcus, then he checked himself, pulled himself to his full height and with great dignity thrust out a small hand. Lord Allington solemnly shook it, then bent and scooped the boy into his arms.

The lad's face broke into a huge grin which persisted as Marcus set him on his feet again just as a small blonde whirlwind threw herself at his lordship's knees. Marcus rocked slightly, then stooped again to pick up the child who snuggled her face into his neck and clung firmly.

Antonia drew back slightly against the drapes, feeling excluded from the affectionate reunion.

Still holding the child, Marcus stepped up to the carriage door and held out his hand to assist the young matron who had one foot on the steps. She was laughing up into his face as he bent and allowed his cheek to be kissed and Antonia realised, seeing the two dark blond heads together, that they must be brother and sister.

'What an elegant ensemble,' Donna remarked approvingly, her eye on the lady. 'That moss-green pelisse and bonnet set against the paler green of her skirts—so tasteful and understated!'

'And so flattering to her colouring,' Antonia commented. 'I had no idea Lord Allington had a sister—as indeed she must be, for they are so alike—and certainly not that he was an uncle.'

His sister was saying something to Marcus that caused him to set his little niece down and step once more to the post chaise. Another lady was hesitating prettily on the top step, almost as if the unaided descent was too much for her fragile frame.

'Well! That is most certainly not a sister, and possibly not even a lady!' Donna remarked tartly, disliking the woman on sight.

'She is very pretty,' Antonia said, seeking to be fair in the face of Donna's hostility.

'Artifice, pure artifice. She owes a great deal to the arts of her modiste and coiffeuse, and no doubt to the rouge pot!'

'Donna! We are too far away for you to know that. How uncharitable you are this morning!'

They both fell silent as the lady allowed Marcus to hand her down, swaying towards him with one hand to her brow and a brave smile trembling on her lips. 'Huh! Showing him what a dreadful headache she is suffering, but how brave she is being despite all,' snorted Donna.

The apparition was swathed in madder rose silk with a velvet pelisse, cut with fluttering edges, each trimmed with a gold tassel. She was poised carefully on the cobbles, as if reluctant to place her dainty kid boots on the horse-trampled ground.

'She is tiny,' Antonia observed, and indeed, as she stood, one hand firmly on Marcus's arm, the stranger stood no higher than his shoulder. 'No doubt another member of the houseparty, yet if I am not mistaken, Marcus is surprised to see her.'

'Do you think so? Well, you know him better than I, my dear.'

It might not be apparent to Donna, but to Antonia, whose mind's eye was so often full of every nuance of Marcus's tall figure, a certain rigidity in his shoulders and an expression of bland politeness showed a change of mood.

The party was returning to the carriage, the post boys in their big boots swinging up on to the horses' backs, and Saye was leading out Marcus's mount. In a flurry of hooves the carriage and the two riders turned and were out of the yard, leaving it strangely empty to Antonia's watching eyes.

Donna got to her feet and summoned the parlourmaid, giving her instructions to carry their parcels down to Jem. 'Tell him we will be at least another hour,' she ordered, 'and send him out some bread and cheese and ale.'

'Donna? Why are we not returning home?' Antonia demanded as she found herself being hustled down the stairs and into the High Street once again.

'We are going back to Mrs Mumford's shop,' her companion announced firmly. 'We are going to buy several ells of ribbon to furbish up your russet walking dress, some velvet for a new pelisse, a new bonnet and,' her gaze fixed on Antonia's sensible walking shoes, 'some kid boots.'

'That is dreadfully extravagant!' Antonia protested as they passed St Peter's church.

'No more than you deserve,' Donna riposted.

'This is not a competition,' Antonia said drily,

recognising the source of her companion's sudden burst of extravagance.

'Is it not?' Miss Donaldson's lips compressed with finality.

Mrs Mumford was almost overcome to receive further patronage from the ladies of Rye End Hall. She was commenting effusively on the elegance of taste shown by their selections while the assistant tied the parcels, when the shop bell jangled and in walked Mr Jeremy Blake.

'Ladies!' He doffed his hat and bowed politely, an expression of pleasure on his amiable features. 'I trust I find you well?' Although, looking at Miss Dane's glowing complexion and sparkling eyes, he could not doubt it. 'May I be of assistance to you with your parcels? I have only a small commission—some cravats, if they can be furnished—and then I am at your disposal.'

The ladies accepted gratefully—Donna, because she could never reconcile herself to her charge going out without a footman to carry her parcels, Antonia simply because she found Mr Blake's company so congenial.

The cravats were soon added to the pile of purchases and the party made its way back along the High Street towards the King's Arms.

'I was intending to call upon you tomorrow,' Jeremy observed as they crossed the street. 'But as we have happily encountered one another, I wonder if I might raise the matter now.'

'Please do so Mr, Blake. Have you heard from Sir Josiah?'

'Indeed I have, ma'am. I would find it most helpful to know when I may order the paperhangers to begin.

But,' he added hastily, 'I would not want to inconvenience you in the slightest.'

'Thank you for your consideration. It must be an object with us to oblige Sir Josiah and Lady Finch in any way that we can.' Antonia turned to Miss Donaldson. 'I believe we can undertake to have vacated Rye End Hall by today week, could we not, Donna?'

'The Dower House is already cleaned and aired. All we need to do is remove our personal possessions, and that is but the work of a day. I am sure we can oblige Lady Finch.'

'I am most grateful. Is there any assistance I can lend you in your removal?'

The ladies assured him that they had matters well in hand and thus they parted, Mr Blake on some further errand in the town, the ladies to rejoin Jem and drive home.

'Well, my dear,' Donna said briskly as the gig bowled past the castle ruins, 'we shall be busy indeed! What with establishing ourselves in the Dower House and undertaking all that dressmaking, we shall scarce have a minute to spare. But we will prevail!'

'You are enjoying the prospect, are you not, Donna?' Antonia enquired drily.

'I am, indeed. We have the prospect of a change of scene, of congenial company in Sir Josiah and Lady Finch and the house party at Brightshill, and some hard but rewarding work ahead. How far we have come from our first dismay at seeing Rye End Hall in March!'

'How far, indeed,' Antonia agreed, musing that her life had indeed changed greatly since that first, singular, encounter with Marcus.

Chapter Seven

Lord Allington leaned negligently against the frame of the parlour door at the Dower House and crossed his booted feet at the ankles. Having found the front door standing open and no servant to announce him, he had strolled through, tossing his hat and riding crop on to the hall chest, before hearing the sound of a chair being scraped across wooden boards in the front parlour.

Antonia was standing upon the chair before the window, stretching up to catch a length of muslin on hooks. She was so absorbed in her endeavours to achieve a pleasing drape she was quite unconscious of being observed from the doorway.

His lordship was in no hurry to attract her attention. He was used by now to finding pleasure in the sight of Miss Dane, but she was looking more than usually striking that morning. Her luxuriant hair was caught back simply by a black velvet ribbon, she was clad in a plain gown which showed off her figure to advantage, and her movements had a natural grace as she reached up to the window.

She stretched further, then the muslin slipped from her

124

fingers and dropped to the floor, remaining suspended only by the far corner. 'Oh, bother!'

'Allow me.' Marcus stepped forward.

Antonia spun round on the wooden seat, which tipped precariously, precipitating her into his lordship's arms, which were very ready to receive her. 'Oh! My lord. . . you quite startled me.'

'My fault entirely, Miss Dane.' He smiled down at her, causing Antonia's heart to flutter uncomfortably. 'We are being very formal this morning, are we not? However, I feel I must mention that something appears to be stabbing me in the right shoulder.'

Antonia hastily dropped her hands, which had been clasping his lordship's coat. 'It is my pincushion—see, I have it tied to my wrist.'

She held up her hand to show him, and blushed when Marcus caught her wrist between his fingers and bent his head over the velvet pad.

'Marcus, you are tickling me!'

'I am sorry, I have never appreciated the complexity of needleworking devices.'

'Now you are laughing at me.'

'Not at all, but I must wonder why the mistress of the house is scrambling about on chairs when she has servants to do this sort of thing.' He released her hand and strolled across the parlour, surveying it as he did so. 'You have made a great difference here in a short time— I should never have believed this place could look so elegant.'

'Hardly that, although I flatter myself we have made it tolerably comfortable and homely. I have no fear of headless ghouls now.' Antonia cast him an arch look from under her lashes, but failed to provoke any response other than a slightly raised eyebrow. 'And as for the servants, they are assisting Donna with our trunks.'

'In that case, allow me to assist you.' He stopped to right the fallen chair and set it to one side. 'I believe I can reach the hooks if you will direct me how you desire the fabric to hang.'

Antonia, surprised that his lordship would stoop to such trifles, hesitated briefly before gathering up the muslin and handing it to him. 'I am trying to achieve a soft curve across the top of the window. . .a little more. . .a little more fullness on the left—perfect! If you can just secure it there. . .'

They stepped back together to admire the finished effect. 'Now, what is the next task?' Marcus asked agreeably.

'My lord. . .I am certain you did not come here to hang curtains! I really cannot trespass on your time, especially when you have a house party assembled at Brightshill to claim your attention.'

Marcus appeared not to have taken in a word she had said, for he was gazing at her in an abstracted manner, a slight smile on his lips.

'My lord?' she prompted.

'I do beg your pardon, Antonia, I was quite some distance away. I was in fact in contemplation. . .'

'That much was plain, my lord,' Antonia responded somewhat acidly. 'Might I enquire what it was you were contemplating?'

'Mm? Yes, of course you may. Matrimony.'

'Matrimony!' Antonia's eyes flew to his face. 'What can you mean?'

'I mean that I am intending to make an offer of marriage, Antonia.'

Her heart sank towards her kid slippers as the image of a fragile blonde figure emerging from the post chaise filled her mind. With a great effort of will, she forced a small smile to her lips. 'I am flattered that you regard me as a friend to be confided in on such a delicate matter.'

He took her hand in both of his and looked straight into her troubled eyes. 'I do not make myself plain, Antonia, and perhaps I should not have approached you thus; although, in the absence of either father or brother...in short, Antonia, will you do me the honour of becoming my wife?'

Antonia felt as though all the breath had been sucked from her lungs by the shock of his declaration. She knew he found her attractive—his kisses had left her in no doubt of that—but she had never allowed herself to hope that anything more would come of it than a light-hearted flirtation.

She wanted to say 'yes, with all my heart', but her common sense held the words back. After all, he had made her no declaration of love, but in the past he had made a declaration of another strong motive for an alliance—his desire for her lands. A young lady of her class would be expected by Society to marry for position, yet she had seen at first hand the destructive sadness of a marriage where the love of one partner—her mother—had not been returned by the other.

His hands were warm and strong holding hers, she felt his eyes on her face but could not raise hers to meet them, for if she did she knew she would lose all level-headedness. She swayed towards him, wanting to bury her face in his coat front, drink in the scent of him, give herself up to him.

Instead Antonia took a deep breath, gently freed her

hands and sat down in the chair. 'I am very sensible of the honour you do me, my lord,' she began, surprised to find her voice so steady when her pulse was leaping.

'But—you are going to refuse me, are you not?' Marcus's voice was equally steady.

'Oh, no!' She did look up then, searching his face for emotion and finding none. 'I must. . .my lord, I must ask for time to consider my answer.'

'I see. You would advise me not to give up all hope, then?' he enquired drily. 'How long would you require to make your decision?'

Chilled by his lack of ardour, Antonia's reply was equally cool. 'A few days. . .a week at most.' He could at least have seemed disappointed!

'Then we are agreed: I will raise the matter again a week from today, and until then, we will not refer to it. I trust you will still feel able to dine at Brightshill tomorrow. My sister is much looking forward to meeting you.'

'Your sister?' Antonia was grateful for the change of subject. 'Is she married? Is she accompanied by her family?'

'Yes, Anne is the wife of Charles, Lord Meredith. He will join us later today, but my nephew and niece accompanied their mother.'

'It must be pleasant to have children about the house.' They must have been the charming children she saw arriving at the inn, greeting their uncle with so much affection.

'Indeed: young Henry has already dug holes in the lawn for his cricket stumps and his little sister Frances appears to regard me as an endless source of sugar plums.'

Antonia laughed, remembering the little girl clinging tightly to Marcus's neck in the yard. 'You pretend to be severe, my lord, but I can tell you are a fond uncle!' They both seemed relieved that the tension between them had passed. 'And do you have many other guests?'

'My sister was accompanied by a friend of hers, Lady Reed. She comes alone; her husband is at Brighton, commanding a regiment of foot.'

A friend of his sister's, indeed! Antonia remembered the sharp little feline face smiling up into his with a great deal of warmth and felt a deep stirring of unease.

'Two friends of mine are also with us already, and my sister is chaperoning a Miss Fitch. Her mother and mine have some matrimonial enterprise in hand, but who the lucky man is to be, I have no idea as yet.'

'You, perhaps?' Antonia asked lightly.

Marcus laughed. 'Good lord, no! I have it on good authority that she considers me to be almost in my dotage.'

Antonia looked at the tall rangy figure, the thick blond hair, the firm set of his jaw and wondered if Miss Fitch was in need of an oculist. No, Marcus Allington was in his prime. . . Swiftly burying these thoughts she cried, 'Unkind, indeed! Why, you cannot be more than five and thirty, my lord.'

'I am thirty, Miss Dane. However I am flattered you consider me so mature.' His tone was severe, but his eyes were twinkling with amusement at her teasing.

'Antonia dear, this hem. . . Oh! My lord, forgive me, I had not realised you were here.' Miss Donaldson had her arms full of dull gold silk which she was trying to conceal without crushing it fatally.

'I was just leaving, Miss Donaldson, I would not dream

of intruding further as you are so much engaged with
domestic affairs. Good day, ladies.' He paused in the
doorway. 'I look forward to your company tomorrow
evening. I shall send the carriage at seven, if that is
convenient.'

As soon as he was gone, Donna spread the dress out
over a chairback, tutting over the creases.

'Donna, what are you about with my new gown?'

'I came down for your advice on the length of the
hem. But I was so put about by finding his lordship here,
I fear I have creased it,' her companion twittered. 'Do
you think he will recognise the dress when he sees it
tomorrow?'

'What if he does?'

'I would not have him know you are reduced to making
your own gowns.' She smoothed it down anxiously.
'There, after all, it is not too badly crushed, it will
steam out.'

'I doubt whether Lord Allington, in common with most
of his sex, would remember such a thing from one day
to the next.' Antonia was sorely tempted to tell her companion of Marcus's declaration, but swiftly thought better
of it. Miss Donaldson would see no obstacle to acceptance—indeed, would regard it as the height of her
ambitions for Antonia, and would never enter into a
rational discussion of Antonia's misgivings on the matter.
'Now, let me see what remains to be done with this
gown, and while we work I will tell you what Marcus
told me of his guests.'

'It seems strange to be setting out in evening dress when
it is so light,' Antonia remarked as they settled themselves against the luxuriously upholstered squabs of

the carriage Marcus had sent as he had promised.

'Not so strange when you consider it is but a few weeks from the longest day,' Miss Donaldson observed prosaically. 'But for me the strangeness lies in going out into company at all—it must be quite nine months since we last put on long gloves!' She looked down complacently at her own, and adjusted a pearl button.

Antonia smiled back, thinking how like a neat little bird her companion was in her elegant dark garnet-shot silk with its modest infill of lace at the bosom. Miss Donaldson had never been a beautiful woman, even in the first flush of youth, but now, in her mid-forties, she had character and style and a surprising taste for fine fabrics and Brussels lace.

'How pleasant it is to travel in such comfort,' Antonia observed, running an appreciative hand over the seat beside her. 'One would hardly credit that this is the same track over which we are wont to jolt with Jem in the dog cart.'

The observation started a train of thought in Miss Donaldson's mind. 'It would be such a relief to me to see you settled into a mode of life suited to your breeding,' she sighed.

'Mmm?' Antonia pretended not to hear. 'Oh, do look at the setting sun on the west face of Brightshill, turning the grey stone pink! How very pretty.'

Marcus came out onto the steps as the carriage pulled up, sending Miss Donaldson into a flutter by handing her down with a bow. Antonia, waiting until Donna was safely out, had the leisure to observe his lordship. She reflected that his rangy figure and long well-muscled legs could bear the fashion for tight trousers better than most. His coat of dark blue superfine set superbly across his broad shoulders and his shirt front gleamed white in the now-lengthening evening shadows.

His glance as he handed her down was openly appreciative and his fingers found, as if by chance, the gap between the pearl buttons at her wrist, lingering caressingly on the smooth flesh there. Antonia shivered and met his eyes. There was banked fire behind the bland politeness of his expression, a danger she had only glimpsed before when he was angry. But he was not angry now. Antonia, recognising raw desire for the first time in her twenty-four years, dropped her gaze and swallowed hard.

It was only a few minutes later when, still shaken, she was following Lady Meredith's maid to a bedchamber to divest herself of her cloak, that she wondered why he had not shown those feelings when making his declaration. How could she have resisted him then?

Donna, observing Antonia biting her lip, came over and pinched her cheeks, saying, 'Indeed, yes, you do need a little colour, you have gone quite pale, my dear.'

The butler was waiting at the foot of the stairs. Not by a flicker of his well-schooled features did he show that he had ever set eyes on Miss Antonia Dane before, although it had been a scant three months since she had been manhandled through this very hall by two burly gamekeepers.

'Miss Dane. Miss Donaldson,' he announced, throwing open the salon doors with a flourish.

Antonia, summoning up all the poise necessary to confront the patronesses of Almack's in critical mood, straightened her spine, took a deep breath and sailed into the room.

The men sprang to their feet, but Antonia was

conscious only of Marcus's eyes upon her.

Lord Allington was accustomed to considering Miss Dane an exceptionally handsome young woman, but he had never seen her in anything other than plain, workaday gowns with her hair dressed simply. Tonight she was resplendent in dull gold silk, her bare shoulders rising creamily above the seductive slopes of her bosom revealed by the cross-cut of the bodice.

Diamond eardrops trembled against the bare column of her throat and her hair had been caught up severely and allowed to tumble from the crown *à la* Dido.

Marcus stepped forward, ruthlessly suppressing the desire to sweep her into his arms and kiss her insensible. 'Miss Dane, welcome to Brightshill.'

'Thank you, my lord.' Antonia dropped a curtsy, thrilling to the knowledge that this man desired her. 'It is not, of course, the first time I have visited here.' She had the satisfaction of seeing his eyes narrow warily, before adding, 'I have a vague memory of coming here with my grandfather, many years ago.'

He turned to greet Miss Donaldson, but not before Antonia caught the hint of a sensual smile of recollection on his lips. It heightened her recollection of that audacious kiss in his study and her colour was becomingly warm when he turned to her again.

'May I make you known to my sister, Lady Meredith and to her friend, Lady Reed.' The two ladies rose and exchanged curtsies with the new arrivals, Anne Meredith with a warm smile, Lady Reed with a speculative glance that was not lost on Antonia. 'Miss Fitch. . .' The young lady, only just out of the schoolroom, blushed charmingly at being the centre of attention and retreated hastily to her place beside Lady Meredith.

'May I also present Lord Meredith. . . Mr Leigh. . : Sir John Ollard.' The gentlemen bowed in their turn.

Antonia found herself seated next to her hostess, who was making polite enquiries about the move to the Dower House. Within minutes she felt herself quite at her ease with Marcus's sister, who appeared to have none of her younger brother's hauteur.

As Antonia had observed in the inn yard, Anne Meredith shared Marcus's colouring and bone structure, making her a handsome rather than a pretty woman. She made the best of her looks by dressing *à la* Turque in dramatic jewel-coloured silks and a turban-like head-dress. The regard of her husband was amply demonstrated by the very fine suite of emeralds at her neck and ears and Antonia admired the manner in which she carried off the entire ensemble.

They were comfortably moving on from the perils of house removal to the best way of approaching the layout of a small pleasure garden when Antonia became aware that someone was watching her intently.

Lady Reed was quite openly assessing Antonia, her chilly blue eyes moving from the diamond eardrops to the little kid slippers, so newly dyed bronze to match the stripe in the silk. Antonia felt uncomfortably as though she was being priced on a market stall—and being found wanting.

Nettled, Antonia turned with a chilly smile, determined to outface the older woman. But it was too late; Lady Reed got to her feet and strolled, with maximum effect on the onlookers, to talk to Mr Leigh.

Donna had been making small talk with Miss Fitch, an uphill battle with so shy a child. 'Is not Mr Leigh the younger son of the Earl of Whitstable?' she enquired.

'Yes, he is the Honourable Richard,' Sophia confided, blushing rosily.

Ah ha, Donna thought, so that's the way the land lies, amused to see Miss Fitch casting a dark look at Lady Reed.

The young man in question appeared less than comfortable at being the target for her ladyship's attention. She was resting one small white hand confidingly on his sleeve, her little face upturned to his, her eyes big and appealing as she hung on his every word.

Antonia caught Donna's eye and almost collapsed into giggles as Miss Donaldson cast her gaze ceilingwards. Still amused, she glanced round and saw Marcus watching the tableau stony-faced.

She was speculating upon his thoughts when the butler announced that dinner was served. Lord Meredith offered her his arm and the entire party made its way through to the dining room.

Antonia blinked in the dazzle of light from the two magnificent chandeliers suspended over the table. Despite having had three of its leaves removed to accommodate a party of only nine, the table still dominated the room with its burden of crystal, fine china and decorative pieces.

With five women and four men the seating plan at the table was, of necessity, unbalanced. Lady Meredith, as hostess, had sought to overcome this as best she could: she and Marcus faced one another down the length of the board. He had Lady Reed to his right and Antonia on his left. Lord Meredith on Antonia's left faced Miss Fitch and Miss Donaldson and Lady Meredith was flanked by Sir John and Mr Leigh.

Conversation was at first general as servants poured

the wine. Antonia chatted lightly to Marcus of the original-
ity of the display of flowers down the centre of
the table.

'Yes, the hothouses are producing particularly well
this year,' Marcus replied. 'You must allow me to
conduct you round them one day soon, Miss Dane. I
would value your opinion on any improvements we
might make.'

Antonia's heart leapt at the use of the word 'we'. But
no, she was reading too much into the word; doubtless
he meant his gardening staff and not the two of them as
man and wife.

The ambiguity had not been lost upon Claudia Reed
either. Across the table, she glanced sharply from
Antonia's flushed cheeks to Marcus's inscrutable
expression and immediately began to talk to him of
mutual acquaintances in London. 'I do declare, Marcus,'
she drawled, touching his sleeve, 'your hothouses are
now far superior even to Lord Melchitt's. I remember so
clearly the advice you gave to him when we were in
Bath last spring.'

She looked at Antonia as she spoke, her blue eyes
signalling quite clearly the message that she and
Marcus had a history, shared not only friends, but
experiences, too.

Antonia smiled sweetly back, refusing to be drawn,
and began to converse with Lord Meredith, who was
offering her the dish of poached turbot. Marcus's chef
had excelled himself: the fish dishes were followed by
elaborate entrées of truffled roast chicken, glazed ham
and roast larks in pastry cases.

Antonia caught Donna's eye across the table and
smiled at her companion's carefully schooled expression.

After months of frugal housekeeping and good, plain fare culled from the land or their garden, this sumptuous menu with its rich sauces was almost overwhelming.

Lord Meredith proved to be genial and entertaining. Antonia guessed that he was less intellectual than his wife, and more concerned with his estates than with the arts or politics. He cast fond glances at his spouse, who appeared to be discussing the state of the Whigs with Sir John.

'Intelligent woman, my wife,' he confided in Antonia with immense pride. 'Don't understand why she finds politics so interesting—rather go hunting, myself—but I like to see her enjoying herself.'

Antonia followed his gaze and thought how magnificent her hostess looked, her strong features animated by intelligence as she rallied Mr Leigh on his views on the government.

She was guiltily aware she had been talking far too long to Lord Meredith and should be devoting some of her time to Marcus. It was an effort to turn back into Claudia Reed's glittering sights, but she did so.

'Might I trouble you for the powdered sugar?' Marcus enquired, taking it and passing it to her ladyship who began to dip early strawberries into it before pressing them to her lips with little cries of pleasure.

Antonia regarded the spectacle with carefully veiled distaste, wondering exactly what was, or had been, the relationship between these two. Could she have been his mistress? Such things were not uncommon in polite society, she knew; after all, Marcus was no stripling. She could not, however, admire his taste.

And, if Claudia Reed were his mistress, what was she doing here when he was courting Antonia? Was he

motivated simply by his desire for her lands and a degree
of attraction to her? Antonia acknowledged that her
breeding, if not her present circumstances, made her an
acceptable match. But she was never going to be able to
employ the wiles and artifice of such a highly finished
piece of nature as Lady Reed.

'Marcus tells me that you and Miss. . .er. . . Dickinson
have set up housekeeping in some quaint Tudor ruin,'
Lady Reed smiled sweetly with her lips, but her eyes
remained cold. 'How quixotic of you!'

'Miss Donaldson,' Antonia corrected evenly. 'And,
indeed, it would be most quixotic if the Dower House
were a ruin, but in fact it is a most charming place,
requiring only a little care and attention to make it a
comfortable home once again.'

'And that despite the headless ghoul,' Marcus added
with a shared smile towards Antonia.

'Will you never stop teasing me about my foolishness—' she began to replied but was interrupted by a
squeak from Claudia.

'A ghost! Oh, Marcus, I am so relieved to be staying
here at dear Brightshill! I know from past experience,'
she added to Antonia, 'that there are no spectres here and,
even if there were, I know Marcus would protect me.'

Only the memory of her own folly in flinging herself
into Marcus's arms saved Antonia from making an acid
rejoinder. Claudia's intention was quite plain: she had
established that she had been a guest at Brightshill
before—and perhaps more than just a guest. She spared
a passing thought for Sir George Reed, drilling his troops
at Brighton. What was the man about to leave his wife
to her own devices? Surely he must know her for what
she was?

'Ladies? Shall we?' Lady Meredith was on her feet, gathering the attention of the female guests. 'I suppose we must leave these wretches to their port, and what they always assure us is not gossip but a serious discussion of affairs!'

In the drawing-room, Anne Meredith linked arms with Antonia and began to stroll up and down the length of the room. 'What a charming gown, my dear. May I ask who your modiste is—surely not a provincial dressmaker?'

Antonia was just deciding whether to be frank or to turn the question when she was saved by the intervention of Lady Reed. 'Yes, charming simplicity—almost naïve, is it not? And that gold is such a difficult colour unless one is somewhat swarthy! For myself with my porcelain skin, I have to choose only the purest colours.'

Antonia suppressed the desire to grind her teeth in the face of such comprehensive spite and replied, 'How trying for you.' Really, she fumed inwardly, men could be such fools. What did Marcus see in her? Then she looked at the perfect figure, the pert bosom displayed by expensive dressmaking, the pouting red lips and told herself not to be such an innocent. And with Sir George so safely out of the way in Brighton it would not be ghosts wandering the corridors of Brightshill at midnight. . .

Antonia's first instinct was to have no more to do with Marcus. If he thought she was so complacent—or such a fool—as to tolerate his mistress, then he had sadly misjudged her character. Then the doors opened and the gentlemen rejoined the party and she looked across the room and saw him.

Marcus was standing in the doorway, regarding her without expression. Haughtily Antonia raised her brows;

in reply, his lips curved into a smile so intense, so full of promise that her resolution melted and her heart lurched with love for him. She smiled back into his eyes, seeing only him, conscious only of him, the sounds in the room fading into nothingness.

She was still arm-in-arm with her hostess and was jolted back to the moment by Anne exclaiming, 'Ah, good! The gentlemen! What say you we make up a table or two of cards? Mead, set up the tables over here.'

As the butler directed the footmen, Miss Fitch protested softly that she had no head for cards. 'I am very foolish, I am afraid,' she confessed.

'Never say so!' Richard Leigh protested. 'Will you not play for us, instead? I would be delighted to turn the music for you.' He waved aside her blushing protests, lifting the lid of the pianoforte and adjusting the stool for her. 'What piece shall we start with?' he asked her, coaxing her out of her shyness.

After a moment, under cover of the first bars of a Mozart air, Lady Meredith remarked, 'How charming! The child really does play beautifully.'

'If one has a liking for the insipid,' Lady Reed commented. 'It is as well she has some talent to attract, I suppose, for she is otherwise unremarkable. So gauche!'

'No more so than any debutante of her age,' Antonia retorted. 'I find her refreshing. But then I have always preferred the natural to the contrived, and it would appear that I am not alone in my opinion.' She nodded towards Mr Leigh, who was assiduously turning the pages, his dark head bent close to Sophia's soft brown curls.

Lady Meredith skilfully turned the conversation, but not before Antonia had caught a gleam of approbation in her eyes. It seemed to Antonia that her hostess had no more liking for Claudia than she, which made it even more obvious that the woman was there not at her invitation but at Marcus's.

'Now, let us set to partners,' Lord Meredith exclaimed, tearing open the seal on the first pack of cards. 'Miss Donaldson, do you care to play?'

'Well, my lord, I must confess a distinct partiality for whist,' Donna admitted.

Antonia laughed. 'I warn you, my lord, she is a demon player!'

'In that case,' Lady Meredith declared, 'I shall claim her for my partner.'

'Then I will partner you, Meredith,' Sir John offered, 'unless either of you ladies, or you, Allington, wish to take my place. No? Very well then, Meredith, I am with you and we must hope the ladies will be gentle with us!'

Antonia moved to a sofa where she could listen to the music and watch the card players. Lady Reed, sighing heavily, drifted off to the other end of the room where she posed decoratively against a table and began to turn over the pages of an album of engravings.

Marcus was turning towards Antonia when his sister called to him. 'Marcus, I need you! This hand is beyond everything—if I do not have your assistance, I must throw it in immediately.'

To cries of 'Unfair!' from the men, Marcus pulled up a chair and sat at his sister's side.

Antonia sat, the intricate melody on the edges of her consciousness, her eyes on Marcus as he teased his sister, dropping his head into his hands as she played a disastrous card. He was totally natural and at ease, his good humour and his affection for his sister evident.

Antonia had known for some time that she was in love

with him, but seeing him like this, all his coldness and arrogance gone, she realised she liked him very much as well. And she could not deny that she could imagine herself mistress of Brightshill. . . .

She sat there, warmed by her thoughts, dreaming a little, unheeding of time when she was brought back to the present by laughter at the card table.

Lord Meredith was totalling points and saying teasingly to his wife, 'My dear, you and I will play the next rubber together and permit Miss Donaldson a partner more worthy of her skills!'

The table broke up and resettled itself amid Miss Donaldson's laughing protests and Marcus got to his feet, strolling over to the sofa where Antonia sat.

'Antonia, I feel in need of some fresh air. Will you join me on the terrace? It is quite warm.'

'Yes, I would like that.' She looked up into his face, her dark eyes meeting his frankly. She saw his face change, soften, as he extended his hand to her and led her towards the long windows, which were open on to the balmy night. He handed her across the low threshold, then, when they were both standing on the flagstones, tucked her hand under his elbow and strolled towards the balustrade.

Antonia watched their shadows precede them across the terrace, lengthening as the light diminished behind them. Her heart beat strong but steady and her certainty grew that Marcus would take her in his arms as soon as they were out of view.

He led her round the corner of the terrace, into the moonlight that bathed the garden. Moths fluttered around and the perfume of night-scented stock hung heavy on the warm air. Neither of them spoke. Antonia rested her hands on the cool roughness of the stone balustrade, quite content to wait for what would come.

The fine cloth of Marcus's sleeve brushed against her arm, and so aware was she of him that it felt like his touch. After a long moment, he put his hands on her shoulders and gently turned her to face him. Antonia tipped up her face trustingly, inviting his lips. When the kiss came she returned it with ardour, melting into his embrace.

She was very conscious of his body hard against hers, of his breathing, of his desire for her. Finally he freed her mouth and looked down at her. His face was shadowed, but she could still read the question in his eyes.

'Yes, Marcus,' she said simply.

'Yes?'

'I will be your wife.'

He raised her hand to his lips, kissing her fingertips. 'You have made me a happy man.' It seemed as if he were about to claim her lips again, but he checked himself, glancing over her shoulder towards the house. 'Come, let us rejoin the others, I would not have our absence remarked upon.'

Despite her happiness, Antonia felt a tiny chill at his correctness, his formality. She wanted him to sweep her up, cover her face with kisses, say how much he loved her. . .

As they rounded the corner of the terrace, Antonia glimpsed a figure slip back through the far windows and recognised Claudia's flounced skirts.

Perhaps that was why he was being so restrained——he

wanted to protect her from Lady Reed's acid tongue. There was time enough to talk of love when they could be sure they were alone.

Chapter Eight

Antonia felt she was floating across the threshold, hardly needing Marcus's guiding hand on her arm. She was so suffused with happiness that she felt everyone in the room must be aware of it the moment they looked at them. It seemed they had been gone for hours, yet the card game was still in progress, Miss Fitch was still playing her pretty airs on the pianoforte and the clock on the mantel was just chiming eleven.

'Shall we tell them now?' Marcus whispered in her ear.

'Oh, yes, I want everyone to share in our happiness,' she whispered back, glowing.

Marcus pressed her hand, gazing deep into the luminescent hazel eyes that promised him so much. He looked round the room at his friends, who were now becoming aware of their re-entrance, opened his mouth to speak, then was forestalled by a quavering cry.

'Ohhh. . .' On the chaise-longue, Lady Reed raised a trembling hand to her brow, moaned again, and slid gracefully from the low silk seat to the carpet where she lay motionless.

At once Marcus and Antonia were forgotten in the

rush to the swooning woman's side. Lady Meredith was there first, kneeling on the carpet, her hand under Claudia Reed's head. Donna knelt beside her, chafing one small hand between her own capable ones.

'My dear,' Lady Meredith commanded over her shoulder to her husband who was standing somewhat helplessly behind her, 'pray, ring for Mead. I fear we may need to call for the doctor, and we must certainly have her woman here.'

'I shall do it, ma'am,' Sir John rejoined, striding to the fireplace and tugging hard at the bell pull.

Miss Fitch had started up from the piano stool in alarm and now stood clutching her throat, almost as pale as Lady Reed. Antonia, seeing her distress, crossed swiftly to Mr Leigh and whispered, 'See to Miss Fitch, or we will have another patient on our hands. Why not take her out on to the terrace—the fresh air will revive her.'

'Willingly, Miss Dane, but do you think it entirely proper that I should do so in the absence of her chaperon?'

'Indeed, yes!' Antonia was losing patience with such a backward lover. 'I can see perfectly well from here if you just step outside the window.' She gave him a gentle push, and with a grateful look he put one arm protectively around Sophia and ushered her out of the window.

Marcus had stepped across to speak to the butler, who turned and hurried from the room to summon his minion. Antonia cast a tolerant glance at the young people on the terrace before strolling across to the chaise-longue.

She felt no great concern for Lady Reed, convinced she was merely playacting, but, standing next to Lord Meredith and looking down at the prone figure, she began to have doubts for the first time.

Claudia was as pale as marble, the blue veins visible on her eyelids, her lips pinched and chalky. She was lying in what must have been an exquisitely uncomfortable position without a sign of movement and appeared unresponsive to Lady Meredith's ministrations. 'Oh, she is very convincing,' Antonia muttered to herself, not quite under her breath.

'I beg your pardon, ma'am? Did you speak?' She had forgotten Lord Meredith at her side.

'I said, "I fear she is sinking",' Antonia extemporised hastily. 'Where can her maid be?'

At that moment the woman hurried into the salon, vinaigrette in hand, and bent over her mistress to administer the smelling salts. Despite the strength of the salts, the only effect was a low moan and a brief fluttering of eyelids before they closed again. All Antonia's concern vanished as she caught the swift assessing glance around the tableau of helpers that Claudia made in that moment.

She was looking to see where Marcus was, the devious baggage! All this was a device to divert his attention from Antonia. Well, we will see about that, Antonia thought grimly. 'Oh, dear,' she declared out loud in a voice of deep concern, 'I fear such a long lasting swoon must surely be injurious to her health. We must revive her!'

As she spoke, she picked up a glass of water from the table that had been placed beside Lady Meredith as she sat at cards. With one swift movement, she dashed it into the face of Claudia Reed.

With a shriek Lady Reed came to, sitting up so swiftly she almost overturned the women kneeling beside her. Her mouth was opening and closing with shocked outrage while the water trickled down her face, turning her blonde curls into rats' tails and sending the cunningly applied lamp black on her lashes running down her cheeks.

'You. . .you. . .' she began to splutter, turning venomous blue eyes on Antonia.

'No, do not thank me, I am only relieved that my actions have restored your senses!' Antonia hastened to assure her.

The men had tactfully turned away and Anne Meredith and Donna, assisted by the maid, helped Claudia to the chaise. Donna glanced up, catching Antonia's eye, her expression a mixture of amusement and censure.

The maid began mopping her mistress's cheeks. When Lady Reed saw the black staining the cloth, she gave another shriek and demanded to be taken to her chamber. 'Give me your arm, you stupid girl!' she railed at the unfortunate maid. She stumbled from the room, Lady Meredith in attendance, leaving a stunned silence behind her.

'Poor gel!' Sir John Ollard commiserated clumsily after a moment. 'Quite understandable, though, that she should swoon. It is a devilish close night. Very quick thinking on your part, Miss Dane, I have to confess I was becoming anxious myself.'

Antonia, who by this time was feeling thoroughly ashamed of herself, merely coloured and glanced uneasily at Marcus. His face was impassive as he tugged on the bell pull again, but Antonia thought she could detect a hint of a smile at the edges of his lips.

Mead appeared with his usual quiet calm. 'My lord?'

'Please ascertain from Lady Meredith whether she requires you to send for Dr Rush.'

'I have already done so, my lord, and James has taken the gig to collect him.'

Antonia's conscience was still pricking her. 'Does Lady Meredith require any assistance, do you know, Mead?'

The butler turned to her with his usual gravitas. 'I believe not, Miss Dane. However, I will enquire.'

Another short silence ensued, broken this time by Miss Donaldson. 'When it is convenient, my lord, I do believe it is time Miss Dane and I returned to the Dower House. Pray bid goodnight to Lady Meredith for us.'

At that moment Miss Fitch, becomingly flushed, was helped across the threshold from the terrace by Mr Leigh. Donna gave the young woman a somewhat beady look and said in a tone she had often used to Antonia, 'My dear Miss Fitch, perhaps it would be better if you too retire now.' Blushing, Sophia complied, whispering her goodnights and hurrying from the room.

Marcus turned from holding the door for her. 'I believe I can hear the wheels of the carriage on the drive. Let me accompany you to the front door, Miss Dane, Miss Donaldson.'

He took advantage of the slight flurry whilst Miss Donaldson settled herself in the corner of the carriage to say, low-voiced, 'I will call on you tomorrow morning, my dear.'

Antonia pressed his hand responsively and let him hand her into the carriage. It took all her social training and self-control not to lean out of the window for a last glimpse of him as they turned the bend in the drive.

Donna was uncharacteristically silent. Antonia, braced for an inquisition, found it hard to tolerate and finally broke into speech herself. 'I wonder what can have been the matter with Lady Reed,' she mused disingenuously.

'Admittedly, the evening is warm, but she could hardly be said to be overdressed.'

It was difficult to descry Donna's expression in the gloom of the carriage, but when she spoke her voice was dry. 'I doubt it was anything to do with the heat.' She paused, then added, seemingly changing the subject, 'You were out alone on the terrace with his lordship for a long time, my dear.'

Antonia knew her companion too well not to catch her drift. The temptation to tell Miss Donaldson of her acceptance of Marcus's suit almost overcame her, but then she thought better of it. Donna would be full of questions, none of which she could answer. No, better wait until Marcus had visited her tomorrow and then she could give her the glad news and a date for the marriage.

'The air was very pleasant, quite refreshing,' she said lightly. 'Did you not observe how completely it revived Miss Fitch?'

'Hmm!' Donna snorted. 'What revived that young lady was having Mr Leigh hold her hand for twenty minutes! I am sure Lady Meredith would not approve—I was in two minds whether to go out there myself.'

'Why did you not?' Antonia encouraged, happy that the conversation had turned from her own sojourn on the terrace.

'Because I was more concerned with what you were about!' Donna was tart as she leaned forward to look into Antonia's shadowed face. 'To dash water into Lady Reed's face in that way was quite outrageous!'

'It did revive her most effectively.'

'Do not seek to be so disingenuous with me, Antonia—I can read you like a book. No, it is not Lady

Reed's health that causes you concern, and well I know it.'

'Do you think she was Marcus's mistress?' Antonia enquired daringly.

The improper question had the desired effect of completely distracting Miss Donaldson from the scene in the salon. 'Antonia! What an unseemly question! You should know nothing of such things. . .I am sure his lordship would not. . .'

'His lordship is thirty years old,' Antonia retorted tartly. 'He has hardly lived as a monk, and Lady Reed is an attractive woman—even if she does black her lashes—with a complaisant husband hundreds of miles away.'

'Antonia, stop it—you should not have such thoughts! Well, at least, if you do, you should not voice them aloud. A well-bred young woman pretends not to know how men go on.'

'Oh, stop this pretence, Donna, we both know what goes on!' Her voice dropped and trembled slightly. 'Do all men have mistresses, Donna, even after they are married?'

'Some do,' Donna admitted, then rallied with a happy thought. 'But those who have married for affection and who retain their feelings for their wives do not—why, look at Lord Meredith, can you imagine him keeping a mistress?'

Antonia leaned back against the squabs with a sigh, looking out at the silent countryside now bathed in moonlight. She was suddenly very tired, all the excitement of the evening, of Marcus's declaration, ebbing away to leave her feeling somewhat low.

Entering the Dower House, she was glad of Donna's

silence and bade her goodnight on the landing with only a few words.

She had been certain she would fall asleep as soon as her head touched the pillow, but in the darkness the foolishness of her behaviour came back to haunt her. How could she have thrown that water at Lady Reed? And in doing so, had she not behaved just as badly as the other woman?

Miserably, Antonia could not but fear that Marcus would think less well of her because of it, for she knew he had not been gulled by her expressions of concern for Claudia. She loved him, wanted to appear wholly admirable in his eyes. In the darkness she tossed and turned, scourging herself with reproaches. A lady would have behaved with dignity: after all, she was the one whom he had asked to marry. Why then descend to such jealous behaviour?

The night seemed endless, sultry and oppressive. When Antonia finally slipped into sleep it was only to dream vividly of Marcus—his lips hot on her throat, his arms binding her tightly to his body. When she woke it was to find the sheets tangled round her, her hair damp and tousled on the pillows.

Consequently, it was a wan-faced and subdued Antonia who faced Donna across the breakfast table the next morning.

'My dear, you look quite pulled down,' her companion said anxiously, scanning her face. 'I am sure this weather is unhealthy. Shall I send for Dr Rush after breakfast? You must go and lie down with a nice cup of tea. . .'

'No, please do not concern yourself, Donna. It was so close last night, I felt I was stifling. When I did sleep, it was very fitful and has done me no good.' Antonia listlessly spread some butter on her bread, looked at the conserves and found the decision between honey and jam quite beyond her.

Donna was still worrying on. 'I think you should return to bed. I will make you a tisane—'

She broke off as Anna the maidservant bustled in with a tray and fresh tea. 'Anna, please go directly and make up your mistress's bed and open the windows wide. It is fresher this morning, my dear, I am sure there will be a breeze and you will sleep more easily in the cool.'

'Thank you, Donna, but I am expecting Lord Allington to be calling on me this morning. Perhaps I will lie down when he is gone.' What he would think when he saw her wan face and the dark shadows under her eyes she could not imagine. The comparison with the exquisite Claudia Reed could only be unfavourable.

Antonia sighed heavily. She wanted to see Marcus again so badly, to be in his arms, hear him at last tell her he loved her. Yet she felt so drained, so guilty that she had behaved badly the night before. She was ashamed of being jealous, ashamed of thinking ill of Marcus. And in some far less worthy part of her mind, she acknowledged that she had shown her hand to the other woman. If Claudia Reed had been in any doubt about Antonia's feelings for Marcus, the incident last night would have made them crystal clear.

By her own actions, she had given that unscrupulous female the upper hand—and Claudia was living under the same roof as Marcus. She was a married woman, entirely unconstrained by the strict social rules that governed Antonia in her dealings with Marcus.

'You do not seem very pleased that Lord Allington is

calling this morning,' Donna observed. 'Is something amiss? He appeared most attentive last night as he saw us to the carriage.'

Her eyes were beady with pleasurable curiosity. Surely he could only be calling in order to make dear Antonia a declaration! The foolish child had been tossing and turning all night in anticipation. No wonder she was feeling so enervated.

'If we are expecting a visitor, it would certainly not do for you to retire to your bedchamber,' she continued briskly, biting back the torrent of questions which filled her mind. What had Lord Allington said to her dear Antonia last night? She had had to overcome all her instincts as a chaperon to allow them so much time alone together on the terrace, but it appeared to have paid dividends.

Antonia found herself being steered firmly out of the breakfast parlour and up the stairs to her bedchamber. 'If we brush out your hair—really, tying it back so tightly makes you appear quite schoolmarmish!—and I think we can conceal those dark shadows with just a touch of rice powder. . .and your new jonquil muslin is most becoming. . .'

Donna bustled round the room as she spoke and Antonia passively allowed herself to primped and preened. But she had to admit, looking in the mirror afterwards, that sitting in the cool room had refreshed her, and Donna's ministrations had transformed her into some semblance of her usual self.

Her skin was still pale, without its normal glow of health, but it was flawless. Her abundant brown hair clustered in a tumble of curls on the shoulder of the pale jonquil gown and her eyes were clear, although the heavy lids still spoke of her sleepless night.

'There!' announced Donna with satisfaction. 'You look quite yourself again. I am sure his lordship will notice no difference.'

Antonia smiled back at her companion, her spirits rising. How strange that one sleepless night could put things so out of kilter, disturb the balance of her emotions so! It was she Marcus wished to marry, and today when he came to her he would tell her that he loved her. Now he was betrothed, some former associations would inevitably cease.

Hoofbeats sounded on the gravel drive. Both women hurried to the low open casement and looked out, but the rider below was not Marcus.

'It is Saye, his lordship's groom,' Antonia observed as the man reined in his black cob and leaned down to hand a folded paper to Anna, who had run out at the sound of his arrival.

The girl slipped the note in her apron pocket, but made no move to go back into the house. She was looking up at the sturdy young man with coy admiration, her cheeks pink. Antonia could not catch what the groom was saying, but the two appeared to know each other well, for he was laughing and chatting easily to the girl.

He gathered up the reins to leave, but bent down at the last moment and snatched a quick kiss from the maid before cantering off down the drive. Anna stood looking after him, her fingers straying to her cheek.

'Anna!' Donna's voice came sharp on the morning air. 'Stop standing there like a moonstruck calf and bring that note in at once!'

The girl started and stared upwards in alarm. 'Yes, ma'am, sorry ma'am.'

She was still very pink as she handed over the missive to Antonia. 'And just what are that young man's intentions?' Antonia demanded. 'I am not aware you have asked Miss Donaldson's permission for a follower to call.'

'Intentions? I don't know what you mean, miss,' the girl stammered. 'I've known Josh Saye all my life— friend of my brother's, he is, miss.'

'Indeed,' Miss Donaldson observed coolly, but not unkindly. 'I am sure if he is one of his lordship's men he is respectable, but even so, if he is to call on you, then I must know and you can both sit in the kitchen in a proper manner. And,' she added, 'no dallying on the front doorstep!'

'Yes, ma'am, thank you, ma'am.' The girl scuttled from the room, relieved to have got off so lightly.

'Oh!' Antonia said blankly, scanning the letter.

'Why, what is wrong, my dear?'

'His lordship writes that he is unable to call this morning after all. It seems the parish constables have brought a most complicated case before him and he must sit— perhaps all day—to hear the evidence against them before committing the men to the County gaol.'

She could have handed the letter to Miss Donaldson without a qualm, for the businesslike lines in his firm black hand contained nothing beyond the simple message, his formal regrets and his intention to call later that evening.

Antonia was conning the household accounts after luncheon when Jem was admitted to the small parlour.

'I've brought the post, miss.' He held out the papers in one slightly grubby hand and hesitated, looking hopefully at Miss Donaldson, who was ensconced in the window-seat stitching a pillowcase.

'Have you eaten, Jem?' she asked, just as he had hoped.

'Not since a bite of bacon at breakfast, ma'am. Long time ago, that was,' he added, managing to sound half-starved.

'Then go to the kitchen and tell Anna I said you were to have a bowl of soup and some bread. And when you have finished, go to the kitchen garden and see if there is any weeding you can do for Johnson.' The lad grinned and dashed off.

Antonia spread the handful of letters on the table. 'There is a note from Great-Aunt Granger—that is a hopeful sign, her handwriting seems much firmer. And a bill from the corn chandler for the chicken feed. Oh, I think this is from Mr Blake.' She broke the seal and spread out the crackling sheets. 'Yes. . .he writes that Sir Josiah and Lady Finch will be arriving at Rye End Hall the day after tomorrow.'

'How interesting.' Donna put down her sewing and gave Antonia her full attention. 'How soon do you think we should call? We must not be backward in paying our respects to our new neighbours; yet, they will no doubt be fatigued after their removal and one would not wish to intrude.'

'Then let us leave our cards in four days' time.' Antonia finished scanning her great aunt's letter and handed both it and Mr Blake's note to Donna. 'Great-Aunt does indeed seem more like her old self, I am glad to say.' She pushed the ledger away and stood up. 'These figures are giving me a headache. I think I will go for a walk. Will you accompany me?'

'No, thank you, my dear, I think I will remain here

and finish this linen. Keep to the shade and do not forget your hat,' she called after Antonia.

Antonia strolled along the river bank, idly swinging her broad-brimmed straw hat by its ribbons and taking deep lungsful of the warm air. Above her, skylarks sang in the clear sky without a hint of cloud. The river glinted in the sunshine as it hurried along, its surface disturbed as fish rose to take flies from the surface.

She paused to pick dog roses as she went, sucking her finger as she pricked it on the thorns. Her spirits were rising as she walked and she began to sing under her breath. The trees closed in over the river in a green tunnel and she strolled beneath them, grateful for the shade and uncaring how far she had walked.

It seemed to her that she had her heart's desire: she was in love with a man who wished to make her his wife, whose every action showed his desire for her. She had secured her family home from ruin and by her actions in the neighbourhood had made the name of Dane respected once more. To have found a husband so close to home was an added joy, for she had grown to love the rolling beauty of the countryside, to value the good relations she felt she had forged with her tenants.

With a start she realised how far she had ventured. Although she had never walked so far along this path before, she guessed she was on Brightshill land. In fact, she calculated, if she walked on around that bend, she might be able to glimpse of the roof of the house where Marcus was. The evening, when he would come to her, seemed a long way away. . .

The turn of the river revealed a summerhouse built as a small classical temple on shorn grass. The lawns swept up towards the house, almost hidden by the rise of the land. All seemed deserted, shimmering in the heat of the afternoon. Antonia gazed towards the house for a long moment, hardly believing that she would be mistress of it, perhaps before the year was out.

The classical portico of the temple was casting tempting shade; Antonia realised just how far she had to walk back and decided that a few moments' rest would be welcome, for if anything the day was getting hotter. She sank gratefully on to a wrought-iron bench and fanned herself with her hat. Through gaps in the trees she could see the sky was no longer cloudless and great thunderheads were building, threatening a storm later.

Antonia got to her feet and decided to set out again before she was caught in the rain.

'What are you doing here?' Marcus's voice enquired from behind her.

She whirled round, her heart beating with delight at the sound of his voice, then found she could not see him. Puzzled, she descended the short flight of marble steps and rounded the far corner of the summerhouse.

Trees had been planted to surround a grassy glade where the wild flowers had been allowed to grow unchecked in the natural style. A semi-clad goddess in marble gazed out to the river with unseeing eyes, a docile fawn recumbent at her feet.

For a moment Antonia stood, enchanted by the tranquility of the spot, then she saw Marcus. A hammock had been slung between two trees, providing a shady resting place, and he was lying, coat discarded, shirt open, a book and pitcher on the ground beside him.

Whoever Marcus had spoken to, it was not Antonia. His gaze was fixed on someone within the grove of trees, someone who at that moment emerged.

For a dizzy moment Antonia believed the statue had come to life and descended from its plinth, then she realised it was Claudia. Her hair was caught up in classical ringlets, her form molded by the diaphanous muslin of a white gown. The garment, confined only by a crisscross of ribbons at the bosom, was to Antonia's horrified eye, quite outrageous.

Claudia skirted the foot of the hammock to stand at Marcus's side, her back to Antonia. As the sunlight caught the gown, the wearer's limbs were clearly defined beneath skirts that must have been dampened.

They were talking, low-voiced. Antonia, frozen to the spot, was unable to hear what passed between them, but she could clearly see Claudia reach out to brush the hair from Marcus's forehead before leaning down and fastening her lips on his.

Surely he would rebuff her, push her away! Then, before Antonia's startled eyes, his arms encircled Claudia, pulling her into his embrace. The hammock swayed wildly, the slender trees supporting it bent inwards and Claudia, ever graceful, subsided on to Marcus's broad chest.

Seconds later the hammock tipped, tumbling them both onto the grass sward, where they lay in a tangle of limbs, lips still joined.

With a sob Antonia whirled round and ran blindly back along the river bank, stumbling over roots, briars catching at her skirts.

Behind the summerhouse, Marcus freed his lips from the voracious, experienced mouth above him and pushed Lady Reed from his chest with more force than gallantry.

He raised himself on his elbows, panting slightly, and

glowered at Claudia, who still sprawled enticingly at his side.

'Damn it, woman! Have I not told you to behave with more circumspection? Anyone could have seen you.'

Claudia pouted prettily. 'Why so hot for respectability, my love, when you used to be so hot for me?'

He snorted, pushing himself into a sitting position. 'When was I ever your love, Claudia? Admit it, you love only yourself.'

'And you, Marcus? I suppose you are going to tell me now that you love that. . .female. What is it that attracts you, my dear? It surely cannot be her clothes, her lack of style and connections? She is all ungainly legs and country complexion.' Her drawling tone did not quite disguise the malice behind the words.

Marcus got to his feet in one easy movement. 'Enough.' He stooped to take Claudia's hand and help her up. 'I intend to marry Miss Dane. It is an entirely suitable match.'

'In terms of land, I suppose it is wise,' Claudia conceded. 'For I can see the advantages of connecting the two estates, they march together so well. I am quite fatigued, my dear, and bored with talking of your little country mouse.' She slipped her hand through his arm, 'Let us go back to the house and take tea.'

As they began to stroll up the long sloping lawns, Antonia had reached the last stretch of river before the Dower House. She had sobbed as she ran, and now, breathless and dishevelled, sank to the bank edge.

She could not go into the house like this, unless she was prepared to tell all to Donna. Antonia bent, scooping up cold water to splash on her hot eyes, and eventually felt calm enough to return home.

In the parlour Donna was sipping tea, the mended linen in a basket at her feet. 'My dear!' She started up at the sight of Antonia's flushed face and heavy eyes. 'Come and sit down. You have walked too far, undone all the good work of this morning. I do hope you are not sickening for something.'

'I think it is the weather.' Antonia was surprised at the matter-of-factness she could achieve, although her heart felt as though it were breaking. 'See, the clouds are banking up, we will have a storm soon.' Despite the heat, she felt as though something had frozen inside her. It was as though she had known all along that he did not love her, that he had offered only for her land, not for her love.

You fool, she told herself, as she mechanically drank the tea Donna passed her. You have been living in a fool's paradise: after all, he had never spoken of love. She could not fault him in that. It was all her own foolishness, her own romantic daydreaming. Her own inexperience had ensnared her, leading her to believe that a man's passions were all allied to love. But men, she was learning, could desire a woman with their affections entirely unengaged. And, it seemed, could feel that desire for more than one woman at a time.

And several hundred acres of land were, no doubt, a powerful inducement to desire.

She was still more despising of herself than angry with Marcus when, an early supper eaten, she sat waiting for him in the garden. Donna, in obvious expectation of a proposal, had tactfully made herself scarce.

The air was heavy with a threatening chrome yellow tinge to the banked clouds. Lightning flickered over the

Vale and thunderflies swarmed above the flowerbeds. Antonia, despite the light summer gown, felt as if she were wearing furs, so oppressive was the heat.

She was fighting to keep calm, rehearsing the dignified, frigid speech with which she intended to withdraw her acceptance of his offer. She had no intention of bringing Claudia Reed's name into it. No, she would say in measured tones that she had thought better of it, that they would not suit. After all, she could never admit she had seen them that afternoon.

The old longcase clock from the hallway struck seven, the sound echoing faintly across the garden from the open casements, set wide to catch what little breeze there was.

Where was he? The longer she waited, the harder it became to maintain her fragile composure. Then she heard the hoofbeats and started to her feet, her heart beating painfully.

Marcus, trotting up the driveway, saw the tall, slim figure in the pale yellow gown against a rose bush and turned his horse's head. Tossing the reins over a branch he strode across the lawn towards her, a smile warm on his lips.

Antonia knew her face was set—try as she might, she could not arrange her features into any semblance of welcome. As he neared her and saw her expression his changed, too, into a look of questioning concern.

'Antonia, what is wrong?' He took her hand in his, raising it to his lips.

Antonia pulled her hand away, her legs suddenly weak with longing for him, for his touch. She could not allow herself to falter, weaken, or she would be lost, loving him as she did.

'My lord,' she began formally, her lips stiff. He began

to speak, but she held up her hand to forestall him. 'My lord, I have to tell you that, flattering as your offer to me yesterday was, I feel my acceptance of it was mistaken. Upon mature reflection. . .' her voice wavered slightly as a frown gathered between his brows, but she pressed on bravely '. . .upon reflection, I must decline your proposal, sensible though I am of the honour you do me. My lord, we should not suit,' she finished baldly.

This was as far as she had gone with her prepared speech. Her imagination had not allowed her to envisage Marcus's reaction.

'Should not suit!' His voice was incredulous. 'Antonia, what can you mean?' She was having an attack of maidenly vapours, no doubt, although he had not thought it of her.

Antonia drew herself up and took a steadying breath. 'I mean what I say, my lord. We should not suit. I am only grateful circumstances were such that we made no announcement last night.'

He let out a short bark of laughter. 'We may have made no announcement, but our friends know what to expect.'

'I have done nothing to lead them to draw conclusions,' she said stiffly. 'What you have done, my lord, is your affair.'

'Damn it, woman, will you stop calling me "my lord"!'

'How dare you use such language to me!' The thunder cracked and rolled overhead, causing Antonia to start nervously.

Marcus did not hesitate. He seized her in his arms, fastened his mouth on hers, feeling its hard resistance soften and yield beneath his lips. Antonia felt close to swooning, the pounding of her heart finding echo in the skies above. His hands were roaming tantalisingly, finally settling on her shoulders, hot on the bare skin exposed there.

She wanted him so much, and when his tongue invaded her mouth she opened to him, welcoming the intimacy. Her hands tangled in his hair, and as they did so a picture of Claudia flickered against her closed lids.

Antonia stiffened in his arms. It was as though she could taste the scent of the other woman on his lips and it repelled her. With a gasp, she wrenched herself free of him.

'My God, Antonia,' he exclaimed, running his hand through his disordered hair. 'How can you claim we do not suit? I have never known a woman respond so, with such passion. . .'

'And you have known so many, my lord,' she riposted, her colour high, her bosom heaving.

So that was what it was all about! Damn Claudia. This was what he feared would happen when she had turned up uninvited and against his wishes. He had implored her to be discreet, not flaunt their relationship. But he should have known that the slightest hint of competition would drive Claudia to a display of ownership as provocative as it was indiscreet.

'If this is about Claudia—' he began, with fatal misjudgment.

'About Claudia! You have the effrontery to invite your strumpet to your home at the very time you make me a proposal and you wonder that I reject you? I had a better opinion of your understanding than that, my lord!'

Heavy rain drops began to fall, plopping weightily on the dusty earth. Neither heeded the wetness, so caught up were they in their battle.

'Strumpet! That is fine language for a lady to use! And Claudia Reed is not my mistress, if we must speak plainly of such things.' His eyes were narrowed in the failing light, but she could still see the angry glitter through the rain that now lashed down.

'Do not lie to me!'

'How dare you!' His voice was like the thunder above.

'I dare because I speak the truth! I cannot deny the evidence of my own eyes!' As soon as she uttered the words Antonia realised how she had betrayed herself.

'What evidence? What are you speaking of?' The water was running down the hard planes of his face, his hair was as sleek and dark as an otter's.

'I saw you this afternoon,' she cried out. 'I saw you behind the summerhouse with your wh—' She almost used the shocking word, but some vestige of restraint held her back.

'Those who creep about spying should expect to see unpalatable sights, madam.' Marcus's cheeks were flushed, although whether from anger or shame she could not tell.

'You do not deny it, then?' she accused hotly.

'I am not going to justify myself to you, Antonia. If you are not prepared to take my word, then you are correct: we would not suit.' He bowed stiffly, clapped his hat back on his sodden head and strode to where his horse sheltered miserably under the tree.

She stood, unheeding of the torrent, until she could no longer discern the sound of hoofbeats, then, her gown winding wetly about her limbs, she stumbled back towards the house.

Chapter Nine

The heavy rainstorm of the night before had ruined all but the most sheltered roses in the Dower House gardens. Antonia lifted up the water-weighted branches to try and find some buds fit for cutting, grimacing in distaste as the pulpy petals clung to her hands.

The storm had cleared the air: the morning had dawned bright and fresh and a slight breeze was fast drying the gravel paths. Antonia was resolved to keep herself occupied, but her mind felt numb. Her thoughts flickered to the events of the day before, then flinched away as though she had touched a burn. She could not bear to think of Marcus and of what she had lost by spurning him. . .

Hoofbeats sounded in the lane beyond the high quickthorn hedge and she dropped the basket, her hand flying to her throat. 'Marcus!' she said out loud as the hoofbeats slowed and the rider turned into the carriageway of the Dower House.

It was Marcus. . .her eyes strained against the bright sunlight, then the silhouetted rider became clearer. The man was shorter than Lord Allington, his hair a neatly barbered brown and the horse he was riding obviously a hired hack.

Antonia bent to hide the dismay on her face, righting the basket and dropping the scissors in beside the roses. By the time she was ready to face Mr Jeremy Blake, she had composed herself. He had dismounted and was waiting politely for her to notice him, the reins looped over his arm.

'Mr Blake, what a pleasure to see you again. I must thank you for your letter; we are looking forward greatly to meeting Sir Josiah and Lady Finch. May I offer you refreshment?'

Antonia called to the maidservant, as the girl, warned by their voices, threw open the front door. 'Anna, please show Mr Blake where he can leave his horse and then bring some refreshment to the drawing-room.'

She entered the house, placing the basket of roses on the hall table before examining her reflection in the glass. How was it possible to feel so unhappy and yet for it not to show on her face? True, there were smudges of purple under her lashes and she was paler than usual, but she looked quite composed in her fresh sprigged muslin, her hair tied back in a simple ribbon.

Hearing noises, she went in search of Donna and found her, as she had expected, sewing in the small parlour. 'Mr Blake is come. I have told Anna we shall receive him in the drawing-room.'

Donna laid aside her work, and her worries about his lordship's failure to call yesterday as expected, and hastily patted her already immaculate hair into place. She approved of Mr Blake: a most well-mannered and well-bred young man, although not, of course, such a catch as Lord Allington would be. . .

Consequently she beamed upon the young man as he was shown into the drawing-room by Anna a few minutes later. It would do no harm, she reflected, to encourage Mr Blake in his association with them. His lordship was showing alarming signs of taking her dear Antonia for granted—a rival to pique his jealousy was all to the good.

Jeremy Blake found himself greeted, therefore, with a distinguishing degree of warmth by both his hostesses. Miss Dane, smiling though she was, seemed to him to be almost wistful behind her welcome. What could have put her out of countenance? He could not conjecture, but resolved to defend her against whatever had caused that slight crease between her pretty brows, the shadows beneath those soft hazel eyes.

He sat in the proffered chair, flicking up the tails of his new riding coat, pleased he had decided to wear it that morning. Crossing one leg over the other, he was conscious that, although his valet might not use champagne in the blacking, he still achieved a most creditable appearance to his master's boots.

Fortified by the fact that he was appearing at his best, and by the sip of Canary from the glass at his side, he turned his mind to the matter in hand. 'I am charged with messages from my principal and his good lady. Sir Josiah wishes me to say how obliged he is at the expedition with which you have instructed your man of business to proceed and Lady Finch asked me to present her compliments and to hope that you both will call upon her at Rye End Hall at your earliest convenience.'

Donna beamed upon him, feeling that these formal attentions were entirely in keeping with how her dear Miss Dane should be treated. It was a scandal that she had had to endure poverty and social obscurity because of her father's outrageous behaviour. Now at last, received at the two great houses of the neighbourhood, she was moving in circles appropriate to her breeding.

She recalled herself from dreams of social advancement for her protégée to find that Mr Blake had moved on to less formal matters. 'And in the carriage house, right at the back, I found a whisky. Just a one-horse carriage, of course, but in very good condition and eminently suitable for a lady to drive in the country. The terms of the lease do not include any vehicles other than the farm carts, so, of course, I had intended sending it round to you. I thought perhaps you had overlooked it. . .'

'How delightful,' Antonia cried. 'As you say, it is just the thing.' Then her face fell. 'But no, it would not be practical, for we have no horses, and to purchase one simply for this purpose would be profligate indeed.'

The room fell silent for a moment, then Mr Blake brightened visibly. 'I believe I may have a solution, ma'am, if you would not object to performing a favour for me. I shall be bringing up my riding and carriage horses from London, and Sir Josiah is most willing to stable them for me as I shall be here so much in future.'

The ladies nodded in comprehension, Antonia concealing a small glow of pleasure at the thought of furthering their acquaintance with such a congenial gentleman. 'However, I have one carriage horse for which I no longer have a use as I only drive a team these days. I am reluctant to sell it, for I have had it for many years, yet I do not feel I can pension it out on Sir Josiah's land. It is most suitable for a ladies' carriage. If you could give it pasturage, I would be delighted for you to have the full use of it.'

Mr Blake leaned back in his chair, pleased with his

tactful solution. He wondered if Miss Dane could drive. Pleasant fantasies of long summer afternoons teaching her to handle the reins flitted through his mind.

'How very generous and thoughtful,' Antonia began, then commonsense reasserted itself. 'But we have no groom.'

Donna hastened to interject. 'My dear, we were only speaking of this yesterday. Did we not agree that we needed a man to assist with the heavier work about the place? Jem is too young and Old Johnson too infirm. There must be a suitable and honest youth in the village looking for employment.'

'If you will permit me, ladies, I will speak to the estate manager and ask him to recommend a reliable man and send him over for your approval.'

The matter thus satisfactorily concluded and his messages delivered, Mr Blake rose to go. Antonia waited for him at the front steps while he rode round from the yard. He reined in, doffing his hat and leaning down as he realised she wished to speak to him.

'Mr Blake.' She held out her hand and he took it, holding it as he looked down at her. 'I must thank you again for your kindness. We would be happy if you would call again—please do not stand on ceremony.' She smiled up at him, her hand feeling safe in his. He seemed so uncomplicated and honest and his admiration warmed her chilled heart.

At that moment, another rider passed the gate, slowing almost to a standstill. Jeremy's mount tossed its head at the presence of another horse and they turned to see who it could be. Lord Allington, sitting tall and erect on his rakish hunter, regarded them coldly for a moment, then clapped his spurs to his horse's flanks and cantered off.

'His lordship appears out of humour again,' Mr Blake remarked more laconically than he felt.

'Indeed, yes,' Antonia agreed with a small sigh.

So that was how the land lay, Jeremy mused as he trotted down the drive and turned towards Rye End Hall with a last wave of his hand. Lord Allington was the cause of Miss Dane's unhappiness, was he? He had seen more than enough in London of eligible aristocrats playing fast and loose with the affections of young ladies without the protection of watchful male relations. He would have a quiet word with his aunt, Lady Finch. Without daughters of her own, she would be charmed to take Miss Dane under her wing.

Antonia drifted back into the house, her pulses still racing from the unexpected sight of Marcus. Had he been intending to call and been deterred by the presence of the other man? Unconscious that her thoughts were chiming with those of Jeremy Blake, she told herself that she may be Miss Dane of Rye End Hall, Hertfordshire, but she was still dowerless and unprotected.

Antonia felt she had been naïve: Marcus had proposed for her lands, expecting her to be a complaisant Society bride, willing to overlook his mistress—and no doubt his gambling and sporting entertainments—in return for a title and an establishment. Like any foolish village girl, she had expected love and courtship and fidelity.

Well, foolish she might be, but she was not willing to settle for less. How much better to have discovered this now than to have married Marcus and faced humiliation and disillusion when she had no escape!

Borne up by a new sense of resolution, Antonia went to find Donna. The latter was arranging the battered roses in a pewter jug in the small parlour, a frown on her face.

'Was that Lord Allington I saw just now riding past?' her companion enquired bluntly.

'It was.' Antonia fiddled with a discarded stem, rolling it between her fingers, unwilling to meet Donna's eye.

'Antonia, what is afoot? I thought the man was coming to propose to you.' Donna regarded her beadily. 'Is he playing fast and loose with you, because if he is. . .?'

Antonia knew she had to stop Donna's speculation before she confronted Marcus and demanded to know what his intentions were. 'He proposed to me and I have refused him,' she announced flatly, subsiding wearily onto a bench.

There was a moment's shocked silence, then Miss Donaldson repeated slowly, 'You have refused him!' She, too, subsided into a chair, too amazed to stay on her feet. The scissors dropped unheeded to the floor. 'But why, Antonia? He is the most eligible man, and I was certain you were in love with him. When you came in from the terrace the other night, your happiness was almost palpable. . .'

Antonia swallowed down the lump in her throat at the thought of that happiness, of how much she still loved Marcus. 'I have discovered that his moral character is not such as I could tolerate in a husband. I must be able to respect the man I marry.'

As she had expected, this completely persuaded Donna. Moral instability was one thing she would never tolerate—and one subject on which she would never feel able to question Antonia further.

Donna got to her feet and began to pace the room, her small frame a-quiver with indignation as she spoke. 'Well, my dear, it is indeed fortunate that you discovered how deceived we were in his lordship. We will cut him, of course—he will not be welcome in this house again, that is for sure! It is a lesson, is it not, how one may be taken in by a handsome face and an air of breeding!'

Despite everything, Antonia could not help but be amused at the thought of the redoubtable Miss Donaldson making her displeasure clear to Marcus at their next meeting.

Donna was employing her happy knack of finding a silver lining in even the blackest cloud. 'And the arrival of Sir Josiah and Lady Finch could not be more providential, for we shall not lack congenial company. And if Mr Blake is to be residing here—' she glanced at Antonia under her lashes '—no doubt parties of younger people will frequently be present.'

Any further speculation was interrupted by the unceremonious arrival of Jem into the room. 'Begging your pardon, miss, but come quick, Old Johnson's having a seizure in the rhubarb patch!'

The ladies hastened after the small figure as Jem scuttled out through the kitchen and into the back yard. The old gardener was indeed visible, slumped on a log, his face ashen, his gnarled hands wringing the hem of his smock.

'Johnson! Are you ill?' Antonia turned to Donna. 'Could you fetch him some of the port wine?'

The old man struggled with his emotions and finally found his voice to utter a string of curses which caused Antonia to clap her hands over her ears. Seeing her reaction, he controlled himself with difficulty and growled, 'Begging your pardon, ma'am, but it's more than flesh and blood can stand, that it be!'

Donna hastened up with a tumbler of wine which the old man swigged back in one, wiping the back of his

hand across his mouth. 'God bless you, ma'am! Real
gentry, you are, not like that bastard up at Brightshill.'

'*Johnson!* Mind your language!'

Jem, seeing the look of bewilderment on Antonia's
face as Donna continued to remonstrate with the
gardener, hastened to explain. 'He's had a shock, see.
It's his other three sons, ma'am. They've been sent to
Quarter Sessions by his lordship for fighting with his
keepers. And they'll be transported, sure as sure, to
Botany Bay—and that's miles away, Essex at least!'
Jem's eyes were huge with the wonderful horror of it all.

'And our Sim withering away in Hertford gaol these
last three months,' the old man moaned, 'and all due to
his lordship's terrible hardness. Now he's took all my
boys. Starve, I will, and their wives and little ones
along'a me!'

'No one is going to starve,' Antonia declared robustly,
her mind trying to place the Johnson families amongst
her tenants. 'Are there many children?'

'Fifteen at the last count, ma'am,' Johnson said
gloomily, 'and young Bethan in the family way, I'll
be bound.'

'That's one of his granddaughters,' Jem supplied helpfully. 'I expect the father'll be Watkins up at Brightshill.'

'Well, he will just have to marry her,' Antonia said
firmly.

'His wife'll have something to say about that—he's
married already with six children,' Jem replied helpfully.

Antonia's brain reeled. There were ways and means
of keeping the families from starvation, but they needed
their menfolk home as soon as possible. Really, she could
not comprehend how Marcus could be so harsh, all for
the sake of a few pheasants! Obviously the men were in

the wrong to have gone on to his land, but she knew only too well how ready his keepers were to attack. Look at the way she had been manhandled!

'Those brutes of keepers!' she exclaimed. 'I am sure your sons were only defending themselves. I shall speak to his lordship directly. Jem, help Johnson home and go by the kitchens with Miss Donaldson on your way, I am sure there is some food you can take for the children.'

Antonia swept inside on a tide of high dudgeon, calling her maid. No doubt the Johnson clan were among the more feckless of her tenants—there had to be a few in every village—but if they were kept in poverty, they were bound to be tempted into crime!

An hour later, attired in her best walking costume, parasol tilted against the sun, she ascended the steps to the front door at Brightshill and pulled the bell handle.

'Miss Dane.' Mead the butler bowed respectfully as he held the door for her. 'How may I be of assistance? I believe her ladyship is at home. A warm day, is it not? Most clement.' Miss Dane appeared more than a little heated, her hair was coming loose under the brim of her bonnet and the colour was high on her cheekbones. Not that her spirited looks were in any way marred, he thought appreciatively.

'I wish to see his lordship.' Antonia was in no mood for polite chit-chat about the weather with his lordship's upper servants.

'I will ascertain whether his lordship is at home, ma'am. Would you care to step into the white salon while you wait? I will send refreshment in.' He ushered her into a cool, high-ceilinged chamber and bowed himself out.

Antonia was not inclined to admire the charm of the

room, a feminine confection of white picked out in gold
with ormolu enhancing the delicate French furniture.
During the hot walk up to Brightshill, she had decided
angrily that not only could she do without the responsibility for three wives, fifteen children and an old man—
not to speak of the unfortunate Bethan's predicament—
but that Lord Allington was entirely responsible for the
entire sorry coil.

By the time his lordship joined her, she had quite
forgotten all her embarrassment at meeting him again.
He closed the door behind him, and walked slowly
towards her, a look of quizzical tenderness softening his
face. 'Antonia. . .' he began to say, then must have seen
the stormy expression on her face, for he stopped, his
brows drawing together into their familiar hard line.

'Don't you Antonia me,' she snapped. 'I have come
to demand that you release my men immediately.'

'Your men?'

'Job, Boaz and Ezekiel Johnson, the men you have
had dragged off to prison, leaving their families to
starve!' Marcus was regarding her with astonishment.
Antonia stamped her foot in exasperation. 'Come, sir, it
was only yesterday! Do you sentence so many men that
you have forgotten them already?'

'Please sit down, Miss Dane.' Antonia sank gratefully
onto a sofa, her legs suddenly weak with reaction. He
appeared about to speak again as he pulled up a chair
opposite her, but he was forestalled by the entrance of a
footman with lemonade and orgeat.

By the time the servant had left, Antonia was calmer,
but as she sipped the cooling drink her hand was shaking
and her bosom rose and fell with emotion.

'Now, Miss Dane, perhaps you can explain to me why

it is a matter of concern to you that three violent rogues
are about to receive their just desserts?'

Antonia met the hard eyes, remembering with a shiver
the day she had been dragged before him as a poacher.
'Just because they had a set-to with your keepers—who
are all too ready to use violence themselves—does not
make them violent criminals! These men have families
to support: why can you not relax your implacable opposition to a little local poaching? You do not need all those
birds, and this is a time of such agricultural hardship.'

'The law is the law, ma'am, and should be observed.
You do no good with your meddling. I am sworn to
uphold His Majesty's peace—what would you have me
do when it is broken?'

'Meddling! Can you show no mercy? You may uphold
the letter of the law, but there are moral laws as well—
I hold you entirely responsible for Bethan Johnson's predicament.'

'And what might that be?' he enquired, only the white-
ness around his mouth betraying the mounting anger
within him.

'She is with child.'

'I assure you, ma'am, I am not the father. I have no
recollection of the wench, and whatever your opinion of
me, I can assure you I always ask their name first before
seducing village virgins.'

Antonia leapt to her feet, her cheeks burning. 'How
dare you speak of such things to me!'

Without answering, Marcus strode across to the fireplace and tugged the bellpull sharply. Antonia turned
away from him to hide her flushed cheeks and stared out
stormily across the tranquil park. Behind her she heard
him order, 'My curricle, at once, with no delay!'

A furious silence hung in the room until they heard the crunch of gravel beneath hooves. Marcus took her by the elbow in no gentle grip and marched her out of the door and down the steps to the curricle.

'Where are we going?' Antonia demanded when she found herself seated on the high-perch seat. She had not struggled with him in front of the servants, but she had every intention of demanding he let her down the moment they were out of sight of the house. 'How dare you manhandle me so! Stop and let me down at once!'

'No, there is something you should, and will, see.' All she could see of Marcus's face was his grim profile.

'If you do not let me down, I will jump,' Antonia threatened, gathering her skirts in readiness.

In response, he transferred all the reins and the whip to his right hand, throwing his left arm across her to pinion her to her seat. The horses, unsettled by the sudden shift of balance, plunged in the shafts and broke into a canter. Antonia felt herself thrown back against the seat, his arm like an iron bar across her. 'Do not be such a damn fool,' he snarled, controlling the horses one-handed. Even in her distressed state, Antonia could not help but admire his mastery.

It was only a few minutes before he drew up in front of a neat lodge at one of the side gates into the park. Another vehicle, a modest gig, was standing outside; as Marcus handed her down, Antonia recognised the local doctor emerging from the back door of the lodge.

'My lord, Miss Dane, good day to you. A bad business this, but he is young and strong and will come to no harm in the end. I will call again tomorrow.'

'Thank you, Dr Rush. Whatever he needs, he must have. You will send your account to me.'

The doctor mounted into his gig and drove away with a polite tip of his whip. 'Why have you brought me here?' Antonia asked, a strange feeling of apprehension gripping her.

'To see the handiwork of your innocent and starving tenants,' he replied tautly, pushing open the door without knocking and ushering her through.

Antonia found herself in a small but neat kitchen. A little girl was rocking a cradle by the hearth. She turned a tear-stained face towards them and Marcus patted her gently on the head. 'Are you being a good girl and helping your mother, Jenny?' The child, no more than four, nodded mutely. 'We will just go and see your father; the doctor says he will soon be well, so don't you cry now.'

In the back room, a woman was spooning water between the lips of the man laying on the bed. When she saw Marcus, she put down the spoon and laid the man gently back against the bolster. 'Oh, my lord. . .'

'Do not get up, Mrs Carling. How is he?'

Antonia saw with horror the white face of Nat Carling the underkeeper. His head was swathed in bandages, his eyes black and blue and his nose askew. He seemed barely conscious, except for a faint groan which escaped his lips every time he breathed.

'In a deal of pain, my lord. The doctor says his ribs are broke, but his skull's not cracked, thank the lord.'

'What has happened to him?' Antonia gasped in horror, although with a sinking heart she could guess.

''Twas them Johnsons, the whole pack of them, miss. Set upon him last night as he came home from the ale-house. Three against one, it was,' the woman added bitterly. 'And them with cudgels. If Vicar hadn't have been coming back from Berkhamsted and disturbed them, my Nat'd be dead now.'

'But why?' Antonia asked, appalled, staring down at the bruised face on the pillow, the stubble stark on the deathly face.

'He'd reported them to his lordship for poaching again, ma'am. Setting snares all through his lordship's Home Wood, they were, 'tother night, bold as brass. Ran off when Nat and his old dog disturbed them, but he could see 'em by the moon.'

'But to beat him so. . .'

'And kick him, too,' Marcus said grimly. 'Let me have a look at those ribs, Nat lad.' He eased back the coarse sheet with infinite care and Antonia gasped at the sight of the man's ribs, covered in bruises with the clear marks of hobnails on the flesh.

Antonia turned away, her hands pressed to her mouth, nausea rising. She heard Marcus behind her, talking low-voiced to the woman, assuring her the doctor's bills would be met and promising that the housekeeper would send down food and cordials from the house daily. 'One of the stable lads will come down and sleep in your shed, Mrs Carling. He can do the heavy work and help you with Nat. Now do not fret, he will mend soon.'

Outside Antonia gripped the side of the curricle, taking great gulps of the warm dusty air. Marcus took her arm and began to walk back into the park, leaving the horses standing. 'You are not going to faint,' he stated coldly.

Antonia looked up at him, startled by his frigid tone. 'What has happened to that man is terrible!'

'Indeed it is, and much to your discredit.'

'Mine! What have I to do with it?'

'You have coddled and encouraged not only the

deserving and unfortunate amongst your tenants, but the rogues also. They laugh at you for being so gullible! What did you think you were about?' His voice grew harsher as she turned hurt and bewildered eyes to his face.

'But they were starving. I only sought to feed them.'

Marcus took her by the shoulders and shook her. 'You fool, all you did was to teach them to steal. You have undermined the right of the law. Why did you not employ your own keepers? You could have instructed them to take the birds and distribute them to the deserving and those in genuine need and you would have given the keepers respectable employment besides.'

'Why did you not tell me sooner?' Antonia stammered. 'I never thought to employ my own keepers. I thought I was doing good, helping my tenants. . .'

'I did not know myself the lengths to which you had gone. Sparrow only told me today what has been the talk of the alehouses for weeks. I was coming to tell you of it this morning, but you were otherwise engaged.'

'Why did not Sparrow speak to you sooner? I so wish he had. . .I have misjudged the man.'

There was an uncomfortable pause before Marcus replied, 'He felt there was a degree of attachment between us that would make it impossible for him to speak critically of you without offending me.'

'How foolish of him,' Antonia replied between stiff lips.

'Indeed,' Marcus replied, dropping his hands from her shoulders.

She shivered, feeling bereft without his touch. 'Can you recommend a suitable man to act as keeper for me? And is there any other foolishness of mine which you should draw to my attention before I do any further damage?' she added, bitterness in her voice.

'I will find someone for you, if that is what you wish. As to your...foolishness, perhaps you will remember that I recommended you to return to London. It would have been as well for all of us if you had taken that advice.'

Antonia turned her head away so he could not see the tears starting in her eyes. He could not have put it more plainly: he wished rid of her, and his instincts from the beginning had been correct. Marcus, having failed to secure her lands, now wanted her out of his sight.

'I must thank you for an instructive afternoon, my lord,' she said, her head still averted. 'I trust you will let me know if there is anything I can do to assist Mrs Carling and her family. Good day.'

'Let me drive you home, Antonia.' Marcus put a hand on her arm, but she shook it off angrily. 'We should not part like this. I spoke harshly in my anger, but we can deal better together than this.'

'Sir, I am grateful for your concern, but we are neighbours, nothing more.'

'We have been more than that, and could be again.' He put his fingers under her chin, turning her face to his. Before she could protest he bent his head and kissed her lightly on the lips, then turned and walked away.

Chapter Ten

'I can hear a carriage,' Donna remarked, leaving a pile of linen unfolded as she hurried to peep discreetly from the bedroom casement. 'I wonder who that can be? I do not recognise the barouche.'

Antonia joined her, attempting to descry the crest on the carriage doors. 'I do believe it is Lady Finch. How very gracious of her to return our call so promptly!'

The ladies abandoned their work and hastened downstairs to greet the visitor. They had called at Rye End Hall two days previously to leave their cards and had been gratified to be received by Lady Finch herself. Sir Josiah, she had explained, was not with her because he had been detained in London on business, but was expected daily for he was most eager to establish himself in his new home.

Since their visit to their old home, Donna and Antonia had found much to talk of. Lady Finch had proved welcoming and open, delighted to make their acquaintance and full of praise for Rye End Hall and their preparations. She was obviously very well bred, but years abroad had lent a refreshing informality to her manner that captivated Donna particularly.

Antonia had noticed the ready affection that Lady Finch evinced for her nephew: a pastel sketch of him was one of the few pictures that had already been hung. 'I do hope dear Jeremy has been able to accommodate all your wishes in the arrangements,' Lady Finch had said. 'He is generally such a thoughtful individual, but you must appraise me immediately if anything has been overlooked.' The warmth and pride that tinged her voice when she spoke of Mr Blake indicated that she regarded him more as a son than a nephew.

'Lady Finch,' Anna announced, showing the older woman into the drawing-room.

There was a flurry of greetings and curtsies before the three were seated, tea poured and macaroon biscuits offered. 'What a charming old house,' Lady Finch enthused. 'After so many years in the Indies, it is such a pleasure to see a fine example of the antique English style. Are you comfortable here? It has a welcoming and homely atmosphere.'

Both Donna and Antonia found it easy to talk to Susan Finch and the half-hour visit quite flew by. At length, their guest stood up, drawing on her gloves, and looking out over the garden as she did so.

'What magnificent roses, Miss Dane. I hope you will allow Sir Josiah to visit your garden, for he has lately developed a keen interest in gardening. It is such a struggle to maintain a truly English style in a hot climate: there must be constant irrigation and all one's favourites just wither and die. I confess that, after a few false starts, we simply gave up.'

'I would be delighted, for gardening is one of my joys

also—' Antonia began to say when they were interrupted by the sound of carriage wheels on gravel.

'I must bid you farewell, for you have other visitors,' Lady Finch was saying when the newcomers came into view, trotting up the drive in a neat curricle. 'Why, it is my husband and Mr Blake!'

The two men were ushered in by Anna, flushed with importance at receiving so many guests in one morning.

'Sir Josiah!' his lady cried. 'I had not looked for you until tomorrow.' She held out her hands to her husband and Antonia was touched by the unfashionable warmth with which Sir Josiah kissed his wife.

'Miss Dane, I must make my husband known to you.' Antonia curtsied, liking Sir Josiah on sight. Where his wife was thin, her complexion made sallow by years of heat, he was rotund and still tanned on the top of his bald head. His shrewd eyes twinkled cheerfully in his open face and Antonia knew instinctively that she was meeting an honest man.

The enlarged party settled again, Sir Josiah accepting a dish of Bohea while he explained that his London business had been accomplished with more expedition than he had expected. He had hastened down, eager to view his new demesne, to be greeted by Mr Blake with the news that his wife was visiting Miss Dane.

'Naturally, I could not hesitate to make your acquaintance, ladies. My nephew has told me of your gracious assistance in rendering the Hall all that we would wish it to be.' The shrewd eyes slid sideways over the top of his tea cup to catch the slight flush on Mr Blake's cheeks.

Sir Josiah, tragically deprived of heirs of his own, was of a strongly dynastic turn of mind and was deeply fond of his nephew by marriage whom he intended making heir to his considerable fortune. Mr Blake had been admirably discreet on the subject of Miss Dane, but Sir Josiah knew enough of his nephew to recognise a man with a marked partiality.

Miss Dane was chatting easily to his wife and Mr Blake, allowing Sir Josiah to observe her whilst exchanging pleasantries with Miss Donaldson. A very handsome and prettily behaved young woman, he concluded. Somewhat tall, perhaps, and not dressed in the first stare of fashion, but unmistakably well bred.

Accustomed to assessing fabrics with the eye of a merchant, he approved of the jonquil muslin gown, but could not help but imagine Miss Dane gowned in one of the more striking shot silks his warehouse had recently imported. He must mention it to Susan; perhaps the opportunity for a small gift might arise. . .

His wife rose, catching his wandering attention. 'My dear, we must not impose on Miss Dane and Miss Donaldson's time further this morning. However, I have secured a promise from Miss Dane that she will show you her roses before much longer.'

'Capital! A fellow gardener—I could not have wished for better. Lady Finch, tell me, what is the state of our kitchens? When can we hope to entertain, for I would wish to hold a dinner party for our good neighbours as soon as may be?'

'Thanks to the perfect order in which all was left, I believe we could name this Saturday—that is, if you are free, ladies?'

Miss Donaldson coloured with pleasure at the compliment to her housekeeping and hastened to accept the invitation. The Finches departed, Sir Josiah begging the honour of sending his carriage over to collect the

Dower House party on the appointed evening.

Donna was obviously burning to discuss their visitors but Mr Blake, by remaining when his aunt and uncle had gone, forced her to silence.

'I wished to ask if the groom the estate manager sent down met with your approval,' he enquired. 'If so, I will arrange to have my carriage horse sent over immediately with the whisky.'

'Indeed, Fletcher appears a most respectable and willing man,' Antonia approved warmly. 'He has righted a stall in the old barn, so we can house both horse and carriage suitably.'

'Then would you wish me to drive the whisky over tomorrow?' he asked, his eyes smiling into hers. 'And perhaps it would be wise, with a horse that is unfamiliar to you, if I were to accompany you on your first drive.'

'But Antonia, dear,' Donna intervened hastily, 'have you not told Mr Blake that you never learned to drive?' Antonia knew all too well that Donna, having consigned Lord Allington to the ranks of Unsuitable Suitors, was already looking to Jeremy Blake to replace him.

'But you must allow me to teach you,' he cried enthusiastically. 'It would be my pleasure, for I am sure you will prove an apt pupil.' Antonia accepted, but in restrained tones. She liked Mr Blake—he was congenial and pleasant and good company—and she wanted to learn to drive, but Donna's unsubtle encouragement of the young man was unwelcome.

The parting from Marcus was still bitter. She loved the man, still dreamt of him at night, still longed to see his eyes smiling into hers with that unspoken promise. Donna could switch allegiance for her at the turn of a card, not knowing how strongly her affections were engaged, but her own heart was not so fickle, nor did she wish to give Jeremy Blake false encouragement and perhaps to hurt him.

Jeremy Blake was as good as his word: a groom delivered a note the next morning proposing a drive later that day and containing an invitation from Lady Finch to Miss Donaldson to take tea.

'She says here that, unless she hears to the contrary, she will send the carriage at three for me.' Donna's sallow cheeks were flushed with pleasure at the invitation. 'How kind her ladyship is, to consider my entertainment while you are engaged.'

'I am sure she is most considerate,' Antonia responded, 'but I am certain she also wishes to become better acquainted with you. After all, you have much in common. Was your father not stationed in several of the places in India she spoke of yesterday?'

'Indeed, he was. What a pleasure it will be to hear her descriptions of those scenes! I wonder if she has any sketch books?'

Mr Blake arrived at the appointed time, but Donna was not downstairs to admire the whisky and the neat bay horse he was lending them. She was still in her chamber, dithering over the choice between her three decent day gowns, a most uncharacteristic way for her to carry on.

Although thinking Miss Donaldson a pleasant woman, Jeremy Blake felt no chagrin at her absence—it allowed him free rein to admire the picture Miss Dane presented. She was sensibly dressed for driving in a pale fawn muslin gown with jonquil braid about the hem and a neat bonnet shading her eyes. He stood in the hallway admiring her elegant figure as she pulled on a pair of tan gloves and called up the stairs, 'I am leaving now, Donna! I will see you later, please give Lady Finch my regards.'

'Where would you like to go, Miss Dane?' Jeremy enquired as he handed her up into the little carriage and gathered up the reins. 'It is a very warm day, and the flies are so bad in the park, I wondered if you would care to drive out onto the Downs. There will be a breeze, and a fine view and I found a trackway the other day where you can take the reins without fear of other traffic.'

'That would be delightful,' Antonia agreed. 'I think I know where you mean, and I had intended to go there myself, but the weather has turned far too hot for such a long walk.'

'You would not consider such a long distance on foot, surely?' Jeremy's eyebrows shot up as he turned left into the lane. 'It is all of three miles in each direction: you are a most energetic walker, Miss Dane, if you considered such an expedition.'

'Why so surprised, Mr Blake? Did you think me a drawing-room miss who would never deign to do more than stroll around a pleasure garden? I must confess to enjoying vigorous exercise. Why, if I thought Donna would permit it, I would even dig the garden!'

Jeremy Blake looked at her sideways and said warmly, 'I never thought you a conventional young lady, Miss Dane. Making your acquaintance over the past few weeks has convinced me that you are quite out of the ordinary. Ah, here is the start of the track. Would you care to take the reins now?'

'Yes, please. I have been observing how you handle

the reins and I believe I can manage, if he only walks
to start with. . .'

Jeremy pulled up and transferred the reins into
Antonia's gloved hands. 'It is not so very different to
riding when you are driving only one horse: there, you
have got it just right.' There was a fleeting pressure
of reassurance from his fingers through the fine kid of
her gloves.

Antonia clicked her tongue and shook the reins and
the obedient bay walked docilely forward, little puffs of
chalky dust rising as his hooves struck the hard ground.

The hot air was full of the vanilla scent of gorse
blossom. Overhead larks sang and spiralled out of sight
in the cloudless blue sky and chalk blue butterflies and
fritillaries danced away from the horse's progress.

The track rose gradually as they climbed to the top of
the Downs. Antonia's spirits rose with their progress; the
feeling of freedom was so intoxicating. As they came
out onto the short cropped grass and saw the view of the
whole Vale stretched out before them, still and shimmering in the heat, she reined in instinctively.

'That is very good,' Jeremy encouraged. 'You have a
very light hand on his mouth—see how well he goes for
you. I do believe you are ready to trot.'

'Oh, let us just stay here a moment!' Antonia begged.
'It is so lovely here—so wide and open and the breeze
is fresh. When I am here, I do not miss London one jot!'

'You must have many friends and acquaintances in
Town who miss you, however,' he said gallantly.

'We had a wide circle of acquaintances when I lived
with my great-aunt,' Antonia acknowledged. 'But it was
quite remarkable how quickly they fell away when we
had to move to less fashionable lodgings.' She turned

luminous hazel eyes on Jeremy and spoke with emotion.
'I will not attempt to hide the truth from someone who
knows our circumstances as well as you: after the death
of my father, we were in most straitened circumstances.'

There was a small silence as they both gazed across
the tranquil vista beneath them, then Jeremy spoke carefully. 'I will be equally frank and say I much admire
the courageous way in which you have retrieved your
fortunes. Now, shall we try trotting?'

As the bay responded to Antonia's tentative signals
with a neat trot, the young lawyer reflected how easily
he could find himself in love with Antonia Dane. And
that was no part of his plan: he had his way to make in
the world, and he could not yet afford the financial—or
emotional—burdens of domesticity. One day he would
inherit Sir Josiah's fortune, but he was too proud a man
to wile away his days as his uncle's pensioner.

Jeremy indulged himself by putting a restraining hand
on Antonia's slender wrist as the bay's stride lengthened.
A small sigh escaped his lips. A sensible plan and laud-
able ambitions and hard work were all very well, but
Miss Dane was a delight to be with and to look at.

He wished he could ask her about Marcus Allington,
but that, of course, was out of the question.

There was a fine stand of perhaps a dozen beeches
ahead, casting a broad swathe of shade over the turf.
'The track goes around that copse,' he directed. 'Try
taking the bend at a steady trot—you are doing so well
on the straight, it should give you no trouble.'

As they rounded the curve, they found themselves
almost on top of a picnic party assembled under the
shade. There was a welcoming cry of 'Miss Dane!
Please stop and join us!' and Antonia recognised Anne

Meredith waving from a rug spread on the grass.

'Why, it is the houseparty from Brightshill! Do you have any objection to our stopping a while, Mr Blake?'

'Not at all, although you must introduce me, for I know only Lord Allington in the party.'

The picnickers had apparently arrived in two open carriages, which were drawn up some little distance away; as Antonia turned the bay's head towards the group, a groom hurried down to take its head.

Jeremy Blake helped her down from the whisky with rather more care than the modest height of the little vehicle demanded. He despised himself for permitting his hackles to rise whenever he came across the arrogant Marcus Allington, but he could not curb the desire to stand between Miss Dane and the man he was sure was playing fast and loose with her affections.

The picnic party had thrown all formality to the wind in the heat of the day. The gentlemen had cast aside their jackets and loosened their cravats and the ladies were reclining languidly against heaps of cushions on the ground. Only the children were unaffected and were playing hide and seek in the bushes, sun hats bouncing on the ends of their ribbons despite pleas from their mother to cover their heads.

Marcus, who had been lying stretched out at his sister's feet, a book open in one hand, his chin propped on the other, dropped the volume and got to his feet with an easy grace that belied his height.

Antonia swallowed hard and fought for composure as he strolled towards them. They had last met, and parted, in anger, but her feelings for him still burned as strong as ever. Marcus's eyes were fixed on her face and she lowered her chin so that the brim of her hat shadowed her expression.

The glimpse of bare skin where his shirt fell open, the play of muscles as he walked, the sun glancing off that tawny head, all conspired to rob her of her breath, of her senses. She remembered that last puzzling kiss and yearned for the feel of his lips again.

This was madness! She had made her decision, rejected him. Where was her pride that she could long for him so, knowing what his relationship was with Claudia Reed? Antonia made no effort to free herself from Jeremy's light grasp on her elbow; let Marcus think what he might!

Her chin came up and she faced him out, her colour high, but her eyes wide and sparkling. 'Lord Allington! Good afternoon. What a very pleasant spot for a picnic. You know Mr Blake, of course? He is teaching me to drive. Is that not kind of him?'

Antonia did not wait for a reply but sailed past Marcus, leading Jeremy to where Lady Meredith was sitting up and straightening her hat. 'Lady Meredith, may I make Mr Blake known to you? Mr Blake is the nephew of Lady Finch, our new neighbour.'

'Miss Dane, what a pleasure to see you again. Good afternoon, Mr Blake—do please excuse our informality. Will you not sit down and have some lemonade? I will introduce you.'

Mr Leigh helpfully piled up some cushions for the newcomers while Miss Fitch poured lemonade and the rest of the party was made known to Mr Blake. Antonia saw his eyes widen as Claudia languidly raised herself from a nest of pillows, revealing a scandalously flimsy and low-cut gown and an outrageously large straw hat.

'Mr Blake, how do you do?' she purred, her eyes

narrowing as she took in the lawyer's well-cut clothes and handsome figure. He bowed formally, but to Antonia's delight made no move to approach Lady Reed, seating himself beside Antonia and Lady Meredith.

Marcus sat down again, not beside Antonia, but next to Jeremy, whom he began to engage in conversation.

'Neat little bay, that, not too long in the back,' he observed pleasantly.

'A little long in the tooth now, my lord, but it is a nicely bred animal and ideal for a lady learning to drive.' Jeremy was polite but guarded.

'Ah, so it is yours, then? I wondered if Miss Dane had made a fortunate purchase.'

'Yes, it is mine, but Miss Dane is kindly stabling it for me.' Jeremy began to relate the tale of discovering the whisky and engaging Fletcher the groom for the ladies and the men began to fall to a general discussion of horseflesh, the others rousing themselves to participate. Lord Meredith, Mr Leigh and Sir John all had tales of difficult beasts and astute purchases to exchange and the ladies were soon quite forgotten.

Lady Meredith leaned over and touched Antonia lightly on the arm. 'Well, we have lost their attention for a while! Once men start talking of horses, I declare it would take an earthquake—or their dinner—to divert them.'

Anne Meredith glanced around. The men were oblivious, Miss Fitch had taken up Marcus's book and was engrossed and Claudia Reed appeared to have fallen into a light doze against an abundance of cushions. Although how she managed to sleep with her mouth set in such a pretty pout was beyond her hostess's comprehension.

Marcus's sister had liked Antonia on sight and had

entertained strong hopes that her exasperating brother had finally met his match in all senses of the term. Miss Antonia Dane was no vapid debutante, but refreshingly different, and Anne had had high expectations of an announcement.

But something had gone wrong, something had passed between Antonia and Marcus. Marcus had been like a bear with a sore head, even though he managed to hide it from everybody else. But she knew her elder brother—and she could guess the cause of the trouble. She glanced at Claudia and, in doing so, caught Antonia's eye.

'It is remarkable how that woman manages to cast her lures at every man she meets,' Anne whispered.

'And sometimes makes a catch,' Antonia murmured in return.

Ah ha! This remark was not lost on Lady Meredith. So that was how the ground lay! Anne knew there had been a discreet affaire some months ago—her brother, after all, was no monk—but she had believed it at an end. She had been surprised when Claudia had inveigled her way into the houseparty at Brightshill, discovering too late that Marcus thought she, Anne, had invited her, when she had believed Claudia was there at Marcus's behest.

Somehow Claudia had managed to poison the relationship between this delightful young woman and her beloved brother, but what could Anne do about it? Anne brooded thoughtfully. She could hardly eject the woman from Brightshill—it would cause a scandal. No, there had to be some other way to clip her wings. She would write that evening to Colonel Reed, inviting him to join the party, providing the regiment could spare him. Marcus would not like it, but he could not refuse to honour her invitation—and she could manage her brother!

Antonia wondered what had promoted the small smile of triumph that suddenly curved her hostess's lips, but her thoughts were interrupted by the children tumbling onto the rug beside them, hot and thirsty.

Mr Blake, obviously unused to boisterous children, shied away and broke off from a discussion of Tattersall's prices to suggest to Miss Dane that it was time they returned to Rye End Hall.

Antonia responded very promptly to Mr Blake's urgings with a pretty, biddable air that caused his lordship to raise an eyebrow, but he did nothing more than get to his feet politely as they left.

Mr Blake was assiduous in his daily lessons and by the end of the week Antonia was confidently taking gateways at the trot and even able to back the whisky for a short distance. Their drives had to be taken earlier and earlier during the day as June moved into July and the heat became oppressive by noon.

Antonia slept fitfully, her dreams full of Marcus, but by day she managed to push him to the back of her mind, enjoying Jeremy's undemanding company. She was certain now that he had no romantic intentions, although it was obvious that he admired her still and enjoyed her company in turn.

She would have felt less complacent if she had been aware of the conversations his aunt and Donna were having about them, for the ladies found one another's company so congenial they met almost daily and were soon on terms of the utmost confidentiality.

'What a match it would be, my dear Miss Donaldson!'

Lady Finch opined, pouring more tea for her guest. 'He has such a good nature, nothing ruffles him—so like my dear sister. And he is certain to achieve great things in his profession—I declare he would be most eligible, even if he were not our heir.'

'He is everything I had hoped for my dear Antonia,' Miss Donaldson confided. 'A steady, good, high-principled man. Not some flighty aristocrat who thinks his position allows him to toy with a young woman's affections.' This was said with a darkling look in the general direction of Brightshill, which Lady Finch had no trouble in interpreting.

The ladies were comfortably ensconced in the deep shade of a magnificent old cedar of Lebanon where they had spent the entire afternoon in pleasurable gossip. They were interrupted by the arrival of Sir Josiah who, broad straw hat on head, had been touring his gardens, a reluctant Old Johnson at his heels.

'Ladies! A fine day, is it not?'

Donna, fanning herself against the intense heat, moaned faintly. 'I fear it is just a little warm for me, Sir Josiah.'

'Reminds me of our days in the Indies!' He sank down, fanning himself with his hat and gratefully accepted a cup of tea from his wife. 'And what are you ladies plotting?' he enquired archly.

'Sir Josiah!' his lady protested. 'What a suggestion! Miss Donaldson and I were just discussing...er...'

In the face of the scepticism on her husband's face, she faltered. 'Well, if you must know, we were speaking of dear Jeremy and Miss Dane.'

'Ah ha! So that is how the land lies!' The nabob contemplated his cup for a few moments. 'I cannot pretend I am anything but delighted.'

Miss Donaldson, flustered by this frank speaking, hastened to set the story straight. 'Sir Josiah, please, I believe you run a little ahead of us! Nothing has been said between the young people.' She broke off, looking pensive. 'At least, I believe not—Lady Finch and I were merely speculating upon the desirability of the match.'

'Well, well.' Sir Josiah was unperturbed. 'We shall see. But I have every hope. . .two handsome young people thrown together. . . Nature has a way of dictating events. . .' He tipped his hat over his nose and dozed off, leaving Miss Donaldson tutting in horror at the unseemly notion of Nature, and Lady Finch hiding her smiles behind her fan.

The two handsome young people in question had spent the morning bowling along the dusty country roads in perfect harmony, happy in each other's company, but without a romantic notion in their heads.

Mr Blake, no fool, had drawn his own conclusions about Miss Dane's feelings for Lord Allington. However unsatisfactory he considered her choice to be, he was far too pragmatic a man to waste time pining for what could never be his.

Miss Dane, too honest to mistake liking for love, was content to enjoy Jeremy's company. The attraction to her that she had sensed in him on their first meeting had tempered to liking and mutual respect and if she could not—would not—have Marcus, then she would settle her mind to being an old maid. . .but one with many good friends.

*   *   *

By one o'clock the next morning, with the moonlight flooding across the bedchamber floor as bright as day, Antonia's resolution to be a happy old maid had quite deserted her.

Marcus had filled her dreams and now, fully awake, she could not shake his image from her mind. She was also very hot, the low-ceilinged room seemed oppressive and suddenly she had to be out in the fresh air.

Antonia pulled on a light muslin gown and kid slippers and slipped quietly out of the house, across the lane and into the pleasure grounds of Rye End Hall. But even here the air felt sultry and still.

Only down by the river did there seem to be a faint breeze stirring the willows. Antonia walked slowly along the river path, yawning and wishing she could sleep.

The moonlight silvered the willow fronds as they flickered in the cooling zephyr and she was suddenly transfixed by the bubbling beauty of the nightingale's song. It was an exquisitely lovely noise, yet melancholy and did nothing to soothe Antonia's heartache.

Ahead, beyond the curve of the river, she heard a splash. Probably fish leaping for the flies that danced over the surface of the water, she mused. What was she about, wandering around at this time of night? Antonia chided herself. All she was achieving was to deepen her gloom. . .on the other hand, just around the bend there was a shelving beach of gravel and a wide pool of water. She could take off her slippers and paddle a little. It would be so cooling.

Silent as a moth, she padded down to the water's edge, cast off her shoes and stepped into the rippling water. Oh, it was so good! Even the soft mud insinuating itself between her toes was cooling. The moon went behind a cloud momentarily, and as it did so she heard another splash, then another.

Alarmed, Antonia peered across the pool, seeing a dark, sleek object appear around the bend. An otter! How wonderful to see the shy animal, she thought, standing very still. Then the moon was unveiled again, the pool suddenly flooded with light, and she saw it was no creature, but a human swimmer, lazily drifting on his back with the current.

Antonia was transfixed with horror at the mortification of being found by one of her tenants, barefooted and unescorted at this time of night. And then the realisation that at any moment she might be confronted by a scarcely clad—even naked—man, sent the colour scalding her cheeks.

She turned to run, but at the same moment the man twisted in the water, his body breaking the surface, and stood up. Antonia's gasp was clearly audible in the still, sultry air. This was no tenant, this was Marcus, water cascading from his sleek dark hair and off the naked planes of his body.

After one startled, horrified, downwards glance Antonia averted her burning face and stood helpless. Moving, saying anything, even running away, were quite beyond her powers.

She was aware of him wading ashore and moving about on the bank, but then to her horror she heard him splashing through the shallows behind her.

'Antonia?' He was close enough to send ripples lapping against her ankles, drenching the hem of her muslin skirts. His breath was warm on her neck and even though he said no more, that one word was full of amusement.

Furious, Antonia spun round, stumbling in the mud,

unheeding of Marcus's state of undress, and found herself confronting him. He had pulled on his breeches and shirt, but the fine white lawn was unfastened and clung to his damp body and his wet hair was slicked back from his forehead.

'Sir. . .I. . .this is not seemly!'

'Indeed it is not. Really, Antonia, you shock me. Do you make a habit of haunting the local bathing pools at night? I was most embarrassed.'

'You! Embarrassed! How dare you imply that I was spying on you!' He was so close that she could see the glitter in his dark eyes, part mockery, part something far more disturbing. His mouth was curved with amusement and a deep sensuality.

'Were you not? Then what were you about out here at this time of night?' He was closer now, his voice husky.

'I was too hot, I went for a walk!' He was overwhelmingly close, his part-clad body disturbingly different, his eyes now openly travelling the length of her frame to where her feet glinted white through the water. Antonia raised both hands in a futile gesture of denial and found her wrists caught lightly in his hands.

Marcus pulled her gently towards him and she went, oblivious to the water splashing to her knees, oblivious to everything in her desperate craving for the touch of his lips. His mouth was burning on hers, his hands cold on her shoulders and the bare skin of his chest wet against the sensitive curves of her breast above her low-cut bodice.

His mouth opened on hers, his tongue gently invading, inciting, tormenting her until she responded, tentatively at first, then with growing abandon, the shock of the intimate intrusion rousing feelings of desire she was not aware she was capable of.

Marcus's strong arms enfolded her, then he picked her up effortlessly without breaking the kiss. Antonia clung to him, unconcerned that he would drop her, only anxious that he never stop kissing her, possessing her like this. . .

Marcus strode up the beach and laid her gently down on the grass slope of the bank. 'Antonia, darling. . .' he murmured huskily, his hands brushing the soft skin at the edge of the bodice, before reaching up to shrug off the clinging fabric of his shirt.

Antonia, looking up into his face as he bent over her, lifted one tremulous hand and traced her fingers over the cool skin of his chest, gasping as his nipple hardened under her fingertip.

Marcus moaned, deep in his throat and stooped to press his mouth to hers again, the weight of him thrilling against the length of her.

The nightingale whistled a few bars, almost beside them, then Antonia realised it was not the bird, but a human, imitating the song. She gasped and pushed against Marcus's chest, but he responded only by tangling his fingers in her tousled hair.

Then the silence was broken by the sharp crack of a twig on the path and Marcus sat up, his eyes narrowed as he searched the shadows. He stood, pushing Antonia behind him and called sharply, 'Who is there?'

Antonia cast around wildly for a bush to hide behind, found none and prayed that the newcomer would take alarm at the challenge and turn tail. She pulled the edges of her gown up, pushing the hair from her face and tried to still the tumultuous beating of her heart.

'I am Jeremy Blake of Rye End Hall! And who the

devil might you be, sir, on my uncle's lands?' came the
sharp response as Jeremy stepped out of the shadows
cast by a willow onto the cropped grass of the little bay.
'Allington! Damn it, man, you gave me a start! I thought
you were a poacher after my uncle's trout.'

'Blake, yes, indeed, it is I. I came down for a swim,
it is so infernally hot. I had not looked to see anyone
else about at this hour. Are you also intending to swim?
It is a good safe bottom here, if you are.' His lordship
spoke easily. Antonia admired his sang-froid and the way
in which he resisted any temptation to glance behind him
to where she stood.

'No, I. . .er. . .' Jeremy faltered. In truth he had woken
and, hearing the nightingale, had decided to stroll along
the river bank to find out if any more were about. He
had a keen interest in matters ornithological, but felt
his lordship would consider it an unmanly occupation.
However, he was conscious that he sounded evasive in
the extreme and was about to say something about seeing
how the fish were rising when he caught a glimpse of
something pale beyond Marcus's shoulder.

So that was what had brought his lordship out at this
time of night. Mr Blake was not sure he approved of
liaisons with village maidens, but neither did he feel that
now was the time to take a moral stand. 'Allington!
You should have said I was intruding. I will bid you
good night!'

Antonia saw him turn to go and stepped forward to
Marcus's side in relief, only to freeze in horror. Just as
she stepped into the moonlight Jeremy turned again. 'You
may rely on my discretion, my lord. . . Good God!
Antonia!'

Chapter Eleven

'Antonia?' Jeremy Blake said again on a note of rising disbelief. Antonia saw herself through his eyes; hair tousled, gown damp about her ankles, her bodice awry. She felt ready to sink through the ground with the sheer mortification of being found in such an embarrassing position.

'Jeremy,' she began, imploringly, desperate to explain to her friend how she came to be so deeply compromised.

Mr Blake, hearing the anguish in her voice, seeing the deep distress on Antonia's face, leapt at once to the conclusion that Lord Allington was hell bent on a course of seduction and the ruination of an innocent young woman. Of course—this explained it all; he had sensed Antonia's attraction to his lordship, yet her unhappiness could only be attributed to cynical attempts in the past by his lordship to seduce her!

Jeremy's hands clenched instinctively at his side, but his natural good sense kept him from a rash demand for a duel. To call his lordship out, as his chivalrous instincts demanded, would be fatal to Antonia's reputation, for it could never be kept quiet. He took a step forward, held out a hand to her and said, in a voice of thunder, 'Sir, I demand to know what you are doing here with my fiancée.'

Marcus's face showed astonishment, swiftly turning to dark anger as he swung round towards Antonia. 'So that was what you were doing here and why Blake was so reticent in his explanations. A tryst, by God! And it appears there are no lengths you would not go to to hide the fact from me, madam. You were most convincing, but no doubt in a few moments you would have discovered a headache and run away home. A pity your lover is less inventive.'

'Marcus. . . I. . .'

'I bid you both good night. I wish you well of your union—it will, I am certain, bring joy to your friends.'

Pausing only to snatch up the rest of his clothing from the river bank, Marcus strode haughtily out of their sight.

There was a moment of stunned silence. Antonia stared blankly at Jeremy who now wore an expression compounded of sheepishness and defiance.

'How dare you!' she stormed, consumed by so many roiling emotions she hit out regardless of who suffered. 'How could you say such a thing. . .to imply that you and I are to be married! Where does that leave me now?'

'In better case than you were in five minutes ago!' he retorted hotly, as confused as she. 'You should look to your reputation, Miss Dane, and consider yourself fortunate it was I who discovered you with his lordship. Your name will be better protected as my wife than as Marcus Allington's mistress!'

They glared at each other in the moonlight, then he saw her underlip was quivering and one tear was rolling down her cheek. His hurt pride melted as he realised she was too upset to think clearly. 'Really, Antonia, what would you have had me do? I had to think quickly, and it was that or hit the man on the jaw. If I could have managed it,' he added with rueful honesty.

'I wish you had,' Antonia responded mutinously. Suddenly she felt very, very tired and sat down with an unladylike thump on the river bank.

'No, you do not,' Jeremy said firmly, sitting down beside her and putting one arm round her shoulders in a comradely manner. 'Fist fights are bloody, unpleasant and rarely achieve anything. Now, tell me what this is all about so we can find a solution to this coil.'

'This is not a legal problem you can resolve by consulting a few dusty tomes,' Antonia snapped, then relented immediately. 'Oh, Jeremy, I am sorry, you are a good friend to tolerate my vapours.' She twisted round to meet his eyes. 'I did wonder if you had a partiality for me, at first. But you have not, have you? I am right?' she questioned anxiously.

Jeremy smiled. 'Mmm. . .there was a time when I felt fairly sure I was going to fall in love with you. But there is nothing quite as dampening as the discovery that the object of one's interest has her affections fixed firmly elsewhere. That said,' he added firmly, 'it is no reason why we should not deal very well together, you and I.'

Antonia kissed his cheek with real affection. 'You are a dear, Jeremy. But I cannot. I love him, you see.'

'Then why do you not marry the man, then?' Mr Blake asked with a touch of impatience. 'Has he not asked you? He is obviously deeply attracted to you.'

Antonia smiled wryly. 'Oh, he has asked me to be his wife. But then I discovered that his lordship is a man who is attracted to many women. In my case, the attraction is embellished by the thought of getting his hands on Rye End Hall and its lands.'

Jeremy understood enough of women to ignore the jibe about lands and to focus on the real heart of the matter. 'I assume you are referring to one woman in particular?' He recalled the expensively gowned figure, the sharply provocative little face, as Claudia Reed lounged at the picnic. 'I can quite see her attraction,' he added mischievously.

'Mutton dressed as lamb!' Antonia responded indignantly. 'You are as bad as he is! I wonder what she looks like first thing in the morning. . .'

'Mmm. . .' Mr Blake said speculatively.

'. . .before her maid and her hairdresser and goodness knows what cosmetics have come to her aid.' She looked at Jeremy sharply. 'You are teasing me.'

'Of course I am teasing you! Women like that are commonplace in London. She is doubtless an entertaining and compliant mistress—my bet is that there is an elderly complaisant husband somewhere; there usually is. A gentleman like Allington is going to expect his entertainment—he is, after all, not a monk.' He paused and cast her a doubtful glance. 'You must forgive me being so free spoken, Antonia, I will say no more if I am offending you.'

'No, dear friend, you are telling me nothing that I had not already fathomed for myself: I have had London Seasons, after all. But how could he continue the liaison while he paid court to me?'

'Er. . .' Jeremy searched for a tactful way of expressing himself, but Antonia swiftly interrupted him.

'Oh, I know that in arranged marriages these things happen. But I truly believed he had at least respect and affection for me. And to flaunt his mistress so openly. . .I could not marry a man who was so careless of my feelings.'

'Then marry me. I can assure you I would never be careless of how you felt. I can offer you the respect, affection and the companionship you deserve in a marriage which would maintain you in a fitting manner.'

'But not love, Jeremy,' she said wistfully.

'It will grow. I have the greatest admiration for love matches—after all, look at the example of my aunt and uncle. But very few people begin their married life with such strong feelings. . .'

'And what would happen if you found the woman for whom you could feel such emotions after we were married?'

'I would not look,' he teased, squeezing her shoulder.

'All men look, it is your nature!' Antonia retorted, laughing, feeling surprisingly cheered. 'No, Jeremy, I like you too much to marry you. Now come, admit it, I am not breaking your heart, am I?'

'Madam, it is in pieces at your feet.' He assumed an expression of anguish. 'It will be noon tomorrow, at the very earliest before I have recovered.'

'Mountebank! Help me to my feet, we cannot sit out here all night and I am suddenly fatigued. Goodness knows what hour it is.'

As they strolled through the silent night, Jeremy asked sombrely, 'This is all very well, but what will you do now? You are sure to encounter his lordship again.'

'I shall pretend none of this happened. After all, he can say nothing without casting himself in a most unfavourable light. If an engagement between you and me is not announced, he will just see it for what it was, a device to get over the awkwardness of the moment.'

They had finally arrived at the back door of the Dower House. Antonia retrieved the big key from under a flower pot and unlocked the door. She turned back to Jeremy. 'Good night, dear friend. I am sorry I have embroiled you in such a coil.'

Jeremy smiled, then bent to drop a brotherly kiss on her cheek. 'Do not give it another thought, my dear. . .'

'Antonia!' Miss Donaldson's cry of outrage rent the still air. Both Antonia and Jeremy started, presenting a picture of perfect guilt to the quivering figure of the chaperon.

Miss Donaldson, hair in curl papers, her thin body encased in a flannel wrapper of hideous design, stood brandishing the poker she had snatched from the kitchen range on her way to investigate the stealthy footsteps she had heard approaching the house.

'Libertine! Blaggard! Rest assured your uncle shall hear of this you. . .you. . .whitened sepulchre, you!' she quavered.

'Donna, please put that poker down and stop abusing poor Mr Blake! He has done nothing to warrant your wrath—he was merely seeing me safely home after my walk.'

'Your walk! At three in the morning! A tryst, more like!'

Mr Blake passed his hand wearily over his brow. 'Miss Donaldson, madam, I can assure you. . .'

But Miss Donaldson was well into her stride and was not to be deflected. 'And I can assure you, sir, that you will marry this poor child at the earliest moment it may be accomplished without scandal.'

'Jeremy—go!' Antonia pushed her much put-upon

friend in the direction of the back gate. 'Donna, let us go inside and I will explain all before the entire household is awakened.' She wrested the poker from Donna's grasp and pushed her down on a chair before the flickering light of the kitchen range.

'That it should come to this! I only thank Heaven your poor mother is not alive to see this day,' Miss Donaldson was wailing.

'Oh, do be quiet, Donna!' Antonia snapped. 'Poor Mr Blake met me quite by chance by the riverbank. I went for a walk because I could not sleep and he was listening to the nightingales. I had a fright because of. . .something I thought I saw in the undergrowth and Mr Blake came to my rescue. . .'

'That's as may be!' Miss Donaldson said, pursing her thin lips. 'But he took advantage of you—I saw him kiss you!'

'If I had a brother living, he could not have kissed me more chastely, Donna.' Seeing doubt on Miss Donaldson's face, she pressed on, 'He is my good friend—and only a friend!'

To her alarm and utter astonishment, Donna responded to these bracing words by bursting into tears.

'What is it?' Antonia fell on her knees beside the chair. 'Were you very frightened because you thought we were burglars?' She took the thin hands in hers and chafed them gently. 'You were very brave.'

'But we thought, we hoped, you were going to marry him!' Donna lamented.

'Who? Who is "we"? You wanted me to marry Mr Blake? Then why make such a hue and cry? Oh, I am so tired I cannot think!'

'Dear Lady Finch and I had such hopes of you and

Mr Blake, such a suitable match. And then to think that he was just another heartless philanderer and then to discover you do not wish to marry him, after all!'

'Go to bed, Donna,' Antonia said wearily. 'We have both had an over-exciting night.'

The next morning, both ladies were distinctly heavy eyed and the atmosphere was awkward with remembered embarrassment. Antonia escaped to the drawing-room to con the post. Her interest in a pamphlet on the manuring of roses sent by Sir Josiah waned, however, in competition with the memory of Marcus's hard body, cold from the river, urgent against hers.

She shivered despite the heat, recalling the feel of wet hair crisping under her fingertips as she had entwined her arms around his neck.

With an effort Antonia pulled herself together and opened the next package, which proved to contain a very sprightly missive from Great-Aunt Honoria.

'I find this new doctor most invigorating, my dear,' the old lady had written. 'He advised changing from that lowering diet to one including red meat, game and Bordeaux and I feel not a day over fifty again! Your cousin Hewitt keeps urging me to rest—sometimes I think he wishes me to remain an invalid—but I find I am enjoying myself too much. And, I confess my dear, that new wife of your cousin Clarence's is such a little peahen that I find myself quite rejuvenated by dislike for her! I know you are much engaged putting the Dower House to rights, but please come and see me soon now that I am returned to my own house. Town is short of company now, but you and I were always able to find some diversion to amuse us. . .'

Antonia, delighted that her beloved great-aunt was so much better, was indulging in a daydream of escaping from all the heartaches of home to a few weeks in London when the crunch of gravel under carriage wheels penetrated her musings.

'Lady Meredith, Miss Antonia,' Anna announced, making her start in her seat and drop the pamphlet on the Turkey rug at her feet.

As Miss Dane sprang up to greet her with a welcoming smile, Anne Meredith's shrewd glance took in the dark shadows under the young woman's eyes and decided that the slim figure was, if anything, even more slender than when she had seen her last.

And as for her brother, stalking around Brightshill like a bear with a sore head with a smile only for the children—why, he was in as bad a case. Oh, she could bang their heads together, really she could!

None of this showed on her calm features as she sank gracefully into a proffered chair and accepted the suggestion of a glass of lemonade with gratitude.

Anne Meredith decided not to beat about the bush. 'I will come straight to the point, Miss Dane: this is not a social call. I am in sore need of your help.'

'My help?' Antonia looked startled. 'Why, of course, any service I can offer I will gladly perform. Is it the children?'

'You are most kind. I am happy to say the children are thriving, for they love the freedom of Brightshill after London. No, it is a certain social awkwardness. . .' She took a strategic sip of her lemonade. 'I felt Lady Reed was not happy: pining for her husband, Sir George, I thought. After all, he has been down at Brighton—doing whatever one does with troops—for months.' There was a slight pause before she resumed. 'Naturally, I assumed that, if I were to invite him to Brightshill to join our houseparty, this would lift Lady Reed's spirits.'

'A natural, and most thoughtful assumption,' Antonia said, straightfaced, commendably concealing her bitter amusement at the thought of Claudia pining for anyone but Marcus.

'Well, I thought so! So I wrote to him. But my brother seems most put out. . .'

'I wonder why.'

'I cannot conceive.' Both ladies sipped their lemonade thoughtfully. 'And as for Claudia, why, she was positively petulant! And the wretched man is arriving tomorrow and Lord Meredith is no help whatsoever, just keeps saying that he cannot see what the problem is!'

'But how can I help?' Antonia queried. This reported reaction only confirmed her belief that Marcus was still hopelessly entangled in Claudia's lures. The husband would be a complication he did not want. Poor man, serving his King and country in the army while behind his back his wife. . . She shut the picture from her mind.

Lady Meredith smoothed her skirts. 'The first dinner will be a very awkward affair, I fear, and I thought to myself, how could I dilute the mood? I felt I could confide in you: you know everyone, and are such delightful company. . .I know it is a lot to ask, but if you could just help me smooth the path. Sir John and Mr Leigh were only saying over breakfast how long it seemed since you were last at Brightshill. . .' She broke off, regarding Antonia with a ruefully apologetic smile.

If she were correct in her suspicions, Antonia would desire nothing more than to see Claudia Reed safely under her husband's eye, but equally, Miss Dane was no fool—she must be very careful not to overegg this pudding.

Quite unaware that her guest had any ulterior motive, Antonia was prey to conflicting emotions. She wanted to see Marcus, be with him, yet she knew it would be painful and humiliating to see him anywhere near that horrible woman. On the other hand, an ignoble spirit of revenge prompted her to witness the lovers' discomfiture when Sir George arrived. And, setting all other considerations aside, she liked Marcus's sister and wanted to help her.

'My dear Lady Meredith, of course, I will help in any way I can. When do you expect Sir George to arrive?'

'Late this afternoon,' Anne confessed. 'That is probably why Marcus is so cross with me—I did rather spring it upon him. Oh, and I do hope Miss Donaldson will be able to join us.'

'I am afraid she will not, for I know she is already engaged this evening at Rye End Hall at a small whist party. Sir Josiah and Lady Finch have an elderly relative staying who is most addicted to the game and Donna is to make up the four.'

'What a pity. Never mind, shall I send the carriage for you at seven o'clock?'

Antonia dressed for the evening with great care, knowing that in a display of feminine charms Claudia Reed would win hands down, possessing as she did a wardrobe created expressly to exhibit her lures. Instead, Antonia sought to appear elegant and cool. She chose her newest gown in a shimmering celadon green silk, cut with total simplicity, and ornamented only with a gauze scarf of silver thread that matched her slippers.

Donna, fussing that Antonia was attending a party without her, helped secure her profusion of dark curls high on her head with pearl pins so that the tendrils just brushed the tops of her ears.

'Do not forget your fan.' Donna hurried after her down the stairs, for the carriage was waiting at the door. 'It is so very close, I fear we will have a storm later tonight.' At the front door she admonished, low-voiced, 'And do make certain you are never alone with that wicked man!'

Brightshill shone eerily in the purplish light of the approaching storm, lightning already forking through the sky far off over the Vale. The carriage horses shifted uneasily as the coachman reined in at the front steps and steadied them while the footman let down the steps to help Antonia alight.

Her heart beat nervously as she stepped into the hall to be greeted by Mead the butler, but as he opened the double doors and she walked into the brightly lit salon, she felt her apprehension start to dissipate. She supposed, greeting her hostess and Lord Meredith, that it was like soldiers going into battle—once committed to action, it was strangely calming.

Antonia moved gracefully through the salon, exchanging smiles and greetings with Sir John and Mr Leigh, stopping to exchange a few words with Miss Fitch, who blushed prettily at the attention.

At length, her circuit of the room brought her face to face with Marcus, who was standing before the empty grate, one foot on the brass fender rail. He straightened as she approached and bowed over her hand, but not fast enough for Antonia to miss the gleam of appreciation in his dark eyes as he took in the cool elegance of her appearance.

'You are in great beauty tonight, Miss Dane,' he observed dispassionately, but not dispassionately enough for Lady Reed sitting nearby, whose eyes narrowed at the overheard compliment.

Antonia looked into his eyes and caught her breath with a shock of love and longing. She wanted to reach out and touch his hair, smooth out the tension that only she could discern in the taut skin over his high cheek-bones and caress the lips that had kissed her so thrillingly only the night before.

Instead, she looked at Claudia Reed and hardened her heart. No, she would not let herself be hurt by a man who continued his liaison with such a woman, so blatantly, so cruelly.

'Is Mr Blake not with you?' Marcus's voice recalled her attention.

'Mr Blake? Why, no, were you expecting him?'

'I expected you to be accompanied by your fiancé.'

'My fiancé? Why, my lord, I am not engaged to be married to anyone.' She widened her eyes innocently. 'You must have dreamed it—the moonlight has such a strange effect, do you not find?'

Marcus's lips narrowed and his eyes blazed with a sudden fire. Antonia found her wrist gripped none too gently as he pulled her closer to his side. 'Do not toy with me, Antonia. Are you telling me Blake lied to me last night?'

'Last night? I cannot imagine to what you refer, my lord. I was in bed last night. . .'

She gasped as his fingers tightened and he bent his head so close to hers that she felt his breath on her mouth.

'Last night, madam, you were in my arms on the river-bank and, if that fool Blake had not blundered in, I would have made you mine.' His eyes glittered and Antonia was seized with the wild thought that he would take her in his arms, stride out into the night and complete his seduction there and then.

'Marcus, do not monopolise Miss Dane, you have all evening to talk to her.' Anne Meredith advanced across the Chinese carpet towards them, 'And here is Sir George just come down. Antonia, allow me to make him known to you.'

Colonel Sir George Reed was a sad disappointment to Antonia who had imagined a distinguished military man of impeccable bearing, nobly sacrificing hearth and home for duty. Instead, the man who took her hand in his damp grasp reminded her of no one more than the Duke of York. Portly, the red veins of his cheeks competing with the scarlet of his dress uniform jacket, and with a lecherous eye to match that of the Prince Regent's brother, he bent over her hand.

For a moment, as he held fast to her fingers, Antonia felt a stab of sympathy for Claudia. Faced with such a husband, who would not turn to another man for consolation—especially if the other man was one such as Marcus?

Sir George's corsets creaked as he straightened up from planting a kiss on Antonia's gloved hand and she had a struggle to repress a giggle. To her alarm, he tucked her hand under his arm and announced, 'Now, my dear, you must allow me to take a little promenade up and down the room while I learn all about you.'

Antonia shot a glance of startled entreaty towards Lord Allington, which he met with a stony gaze. Claudia, on the other hand, smiled vixen-like from her chaise-longue as her elderly husband, perspiring profusely from the combination of tight stays and the intense heat, passed by.

'Now, do not allow Miss Dane to tire you, Georgie darling,' she called sweetly, bringing a flush to Antonia's cheeks.

But Antonia was far more exercised preventing 'Georgie darling's straying fingers from inching any further up her arm towards the swell of her breast. It took all her social grace not to shake him off and slap his face. Instead, she drew herself up stiffly and away from him, enquiring in a voice of frigid formality if the drive from Brighton had been free of incident.

'Tiresome, tiresome, my dear, but nothing which cannot be forgotten in the face of your beauty!' he wheezed enthusiastically. Mercifully, Anne Meredith appeared and begged Sir George to permit her to bear Miss Dane off to admire the new hangings in the study.

The two ladies shut the door of the study behind themselves and gazed at each other. It was difficult to tell which was the more horrified, and almost together they said, 'Beastly man. . .'

'My dear Miss Dane, I cannot apologise enough. . . Had I but known what he was like! No wonder Marcus was so angry with me! And the Reeds obviously loathe one another. . . My dear, you must not leave my side for an instant; fortunately he has shown not the slightest interest in dear Sophia—far too young, thank goodness.' Lady Meredith subsided into a chair and unfurled her fan to cool her heated cheeks.

'What is the seating plan for dinner?' Antonia asked, seized with a sudden alarming thought.

'Oh, my heavens!' Lady Meredith jumped up. 'I must see Mead at once, for I fear I have placed Sir George next to you. . .' She hastened from the room, leaving

Antonia to divert her thoughts by admiring the handsome cut-velvet draperies at the windows. They changed the aspect of the room somewhat from that cool day in March when she had been dragged unceremoniously into Marcus's presence, accused of poaching.

She ran her fingers over the arm of the carved chair in which she had been sitting when he had kissed her for the first time. Her reverie was rudely interrupted by a kiss of a very different kind: the pressure of wet, rubbery lips on her bare shoulder.

Antonia spun round with a small shriek of outrage to find herself pinned against the desk by the rotund and lascivious figure of Colonel Sir George Reed. 'Alone at last!' he announced with undisguised lust.

'No, leave me be!' Antonia gasped, wriggling away.

'No need to pretend now. My wife told me you were a bit of a goer, a game pullet!' He opened his arms as if to envelop her. 'Good of our hostess to make this room available, what? Thought she was a bit starched up at first, but I was wrong. . .'

'Sir George, I believe your wife is looking for you.' Marcus's voice dripped ice. Antonia, glimpsing his set face over the gold braid of the Colonel's shoulder, thought she had never been so glad to see him.

Sir George swung round with an oath, failing to read the danger signals in his host's face. 'Damn it, my boy, no need to spoil sport! After all, you've got Claudia to amuse you. . .'

'Sir, if you cannot take a hint, I may be forced to make my meaning more plain. I do not wish to embarrass Lady Reed, a guest in my house, by calling out her husband, but if you persist in annoying Miss Dane, you leave me no choice.'

Sir George's face purpled, but he straightened his scarlet coat and barged out of the room without a word.

'Nauseating man!' Antonia felt sick with reaction. 'He is really quite beyond the pale!'

'Then why were you foolish enough to permit yourself to be alone with him in here?' Marcus demanded curtly.

Antonia was taken aback by this attack. 'I did not invite him here, I came in here to escape from his lecherous pawings, but it appears that his beloved wife had told him that I might welcome his repellent advances!' She stamped her foot with anger. 'And if you had been half the man I thought you were, you *would* have called him out! But oh, no! That might embarrass dear Claudia, and we would not want to embarrass her, would we? Tell me, Marcus, just what lengths would he have to go to for you to challenge him?'

Marcus's face was cold, with all the old arrogance back in his eyes. 'The man is old enough to be my father, and a guest under my roof. . .'

'. . .and his wife is your mistress! And we do not want to upset him, do we? He might stop being quite so complaisant and take her away! You disgust me, the three of you!' Antonia turned her hot face away, wishing she could bury it in the velvet drapes and burst into tears.

'There you both are!' Lady Meredith swept into the room, beaming to see them both together. Her smile froze on her amiable features as she saw the glittering anger in her brother's eyes and the rigid set of Miss Dane's shoulders. 'I came to tell you that Mead has announced dinner. Marcus, will you take Miss Dane in?' She met his eyes, daring him to refuse, but instead he said politely,

'Miss Dane?' Antonia, gaze averted, took his proffered

arm and allowed herself to be escorted into the glittering dining-room.

Lady Meredith, deprived of a fifth lady by Donna's absence and forced to rearrange her table hastily by Sir George's behaviour, had none the less managed a reasonable disposition of her guests.

Marcus, at the head of the long board, faced his sister, who was flanked by Sir George and Sir John Ollard. With Mr Leigh on Sir George's right, Anne felt she had safely isolated the Colonel from both his wife and Antonia. Miss Fitch had brightened considerably at finding herself opposite her beloved Mr Leigh and next to the paternal Lord Meredith.

Anne, despite some qualms, felt a certain malicious pleasure at seating Antonia and Claudia either side of her brother. They made a striking trio: her brother in the centre flanked by the two women, one so dark and vital, the other so voluptuosly languid. It was about time Marcus decided where his heart lay, his sister resolved.

Marcus met Anne's eye down the length of the gleaming table, heavy with plate and crystal, and raised his glass in an ironic salute to her. She smiled back, reflecting that her brother was never a poor loser and could be relied upon to rise to a challenge.

Antonia sipped the champagne Mead poured for her, relishing its coolness, the burst of bubbles in her mouth. Normally she would make one glass of wine last all evening, but tonight she scarcely noticed that her glass was being refilled again, and then again as the fish dishes were removed with entrées and roasts.

The long windows had been thrown open to the warm evening air and the scent of beeswax, perfumes and food mingled headily. Marcus was being meticulous in his behaviour towards Claudia, maintaining a polite dialogue about trivialities and showing none of the ennui he would normally display at such chatter. But however attentive, he was not flirting and seemed impervious to her coquettish looks and teasing jibes.

It was obvious to Claudia, if not to Antonia, that his attention was equally fixed on her rival. Antonia chatted easily with Lord Meredith, but when he turned politely to engage Miss Fitch in conversation, she found it difficult to talk to, or even to look at Marcus. She was acutely aware of him, of the Russian Leather cologne he used, of his long fingers as they played on the stem of his glass. She wanted them running up and down her throat, caressing her nape. . .

Antonia pulled herself together with a start and took a long mouthful of wine. The effect made her blink with the horrified recognition that she had drunk rather too much.

'Lord Allington. . .' Claudia managed to make the formal title sound like the most intimate endearment. 'Please will you help me to just the tiniest morsel more of that lobster; it is so delicious.'

'And matches your dress so perfectly,' Antonia observed, then giggled, immediately putting her hand over her mouth to suppress the sound.

Marcus bit his lip as he struggled to serve Claudia without bursting into laughter at the sight of her cheeks, flushed with anger, as pink as the boiled crustacean.

Claudia, stung, responded acidly, 'How brave of you, Miss Dane, to wear such a very trying shade of green. One so rarely sees it without feeling depressed, although Lady Jersey, I suppose, has the style to carry it off. . .'

'Well, I wear it a good deal, but I can quite see that

on an older woman with a faded complexion it could be difficult to carry off.' Antonia took another sip of wine and continued smoothly, 'Unless, of course, she used a lot of rouge.'

Anne, pausing to send a worried glance down the table, wondered what was being said to amuse Marcus so much. She would swear, if she knew no better, that he was hiding a broad grin behind his napkin.

Claudia had gone so pale with anger that her rouge stood out in circles on her cheeks. She took a deep breath, knowing how it enhanced the spectacular uplift of her breasts in the low-cut gown and reflected that Miss Dane, for all her pert charms, had not the advantage of being Marcus's mistress. Although, as he had not once come to her all the time she had been at Brightshill, she was beginning to panic.

Damn his discretion! In London, she had sensed his attention was wandering after the first few tumultuous weeks of their liaison. That was why she had invited herself down, playing on his sister's good nature to inveigle herself into the houseparty. But Claudia soon discovered that Marcus would not tolerate loose behaviour in his own household with his sister acting as hostess.

Well, she had waited long enough for him to come to her room—tonight she would go to his. Meanwhile, she could give him a gentle reminder of what he had been ignoring. She put her hand lightly on his thigh, her long nails scoring the fine fabric, feeling the hard muscles tense in response.

Marcus turned his head sharply to meet Claudia's hooded gaze as her fingertips ran down, and then dangerously up, his thigh. As they insinuated themselves down between his legs, he grasped her wrist in none-too-gentle fingers and with great deliberation moved her hand back to her own lap.

Antonia saw the edge of the tablecloth move and had no difficulty interpreting the movement of Marcus's arm. Anger and determination ran through her veins like fire. She was tired of behaving like the well-bred virgin she was. If she wanted Marcus—and with the champagne coursing through her, she knew she wanted nothing more in the world—then she would have to fight for him.

Chapter Twelve

At the end of what seemed to the harrassed hostess to be an interminable meal, Lady Meredith at last stood up, gathering the attention of her female guests with a smile. 'Ladies, shall we leave the gentlemen to their port?'

As she got somewhat unsteadily to her feet, Antonia bent and whispered in Marcus's ear, 'Meet me in the conservatory as soon as may be.'

Neither the gesture, nor Marcus's rapidly controlled reaction, was lost on Claudia, whose eyes narrowed in speculation as she swept past Sophia Fitch and into the salon. What was that little provincial miss about? Well, it scarcely made a difference—tonight she would go to Marcus and obliterate everything but the knowing caress of her fingers from his mind.

Claudia sank down on the chaise with a scarcely concealed sigh. Oh, lord! Yet another interminable evening. She gazed at Anne Meredith with dislike; God, she was plain and such a bore, always prating on about the Whigs. And she was responsible for George being here. At least *he* knew better than to come to her bedroom. . .

Seeing Sophia Fitch perching nervously at the other

end of the chaise, Claudia decided to amuse herself by patronising the little mouse. 'Tell me, Miss Fitch, when are you going to announce your engagement to Mr Leigh? Such a. . .worthy young man, I am sure. Does he have a patron? I suppose, coming from such an obscure family, he will need one.'

Sophia, normally paralysed when addressed by the exotic Lady Reed, rallied at this attack on her beloved Richard. Her little figure quivered with indignation but her voice was steady as she replied, 'Mr Leigh is one of the Hampshire Leighs, and as such need look no further than his uncle the Bishop for advancement. He is going as private secretary to Lord Seymour at the War Office, but hopes before long to stand for Parliament.'

'Oh. . .' Claudia laid one small white hand on her forehead in a weary gesture '. . .do not talk to me of politics, it is so tedious.'

'Well, in that case,' Sophia snapped, 'I will not bore you any longer.' Slightly staggered at her own temerity, she rose to her feet, walked across the room to the piano and began to pick out a new ballad.

Claudia shifted her attention to the other two women. Antonia, to her experienced eye, had had rather too much to drink, although she doubted if Anne Meredith had noticed. What was that minx up to? She was plotting something with Marcus, and now she was shifting uneasily in her chair, glancing every few moments at the ormulu clock on the mantelshelf.

Antonia, unable to bear sitting still any longer, bent and whispered in Anne's ear.

'Oh yes, my dear,' her hostess whispered back. 'Down the corridor on the left, the third door. Marcus has had

one of Mr Bramah's flushing water closets installed—
such a benefit.'

Antonia admired the new-fangled sanitary arrangements, wondering how much it would cost to replace the
old earth closets at the Dower House. She glanced in the
mirror on the wash stand, tweaking her hair into order
and wishing she had a little rice powder to calm her
hectic cheeks. That last glass of wine sang in her veins,
making her feel quite unaccustomedly reckless. Never
mind, it would give her the courage to do what she had
to do and drive Claudia out of Marcus's mind for ever.

The conservatory was filled with a damp heat and the
heady scent of lilies underlaid with wet moss and earth.
A few candelabra had been set on columns amongst the
plant stands and beds of ferns, casting mysterious pools
of shadow. Moths fluttered in through the open doors,
fatally drawn by the voluptuous smell of the hothouse
plants towards the candle flames.

Antonia strolled up and down the tiled floor, her gown
swishing in the stillness. Would he come to her after that
angry scene in the study? She walked on, biting her lip
in growing anxiety as the wine-induced courage began
to ebb away. No, he was not coming, she had lost. . .

'Antonia.' His voice was husky and very close.
Antonia's heart leapt in her bosom, but she turned slowly
to face Marcus, the man she loved.

The moonlight burnished his hair, casting strong
shadows across his face, veiling his eyes. But she could
see his mouth curling with a sensual tenderness and the
rise and fall of his shirt, gleaming white against the dark
blue cloth of his coat, showed that he was not entirely
master of his emotions.

'You wanted to speak to me?'

'No, what I wanted was this.' Antonia stepped straight up to him, wound her arms sinuously around his neck and, pulling his head down, fastened her lips full on his.

There was the merest hint of hesitation: she had taken him by surprise, acted as no well-bred young woman would ever dream of acting. But then his instincts took command and Marcus pulled her tighter against his body, deepened the kiss, opening and exploring the softness of her mouth, the scent of her filling his nostrils, sending his senses reeling, even against the backdrop of the lilies.

Without freeing her mouth, he swept her into his arms and carried her effortlessly to where a bench had been set in a bower of fragrant stephanotis. Antonia found herself nestling on his lap, the strength of his thighs supporting her, his arms holding her fast against his chest.

The kiss went on and on druggingly, sweeping away all reason and sensibility. Antonia had prepared a little speech, all about how she was prepared to forgive him if he renounced Claudia, but even if she had been able to free her mouth, she could hardly recollect what she had intended to say.

At last his mouth left hers and she gave a little moan of protest which became a whimper of sheer sensual pleasure as his teeth nibbled gently down her throat, his tongue-tip tracing the sensitive line of her jaw before his lips found the swell of her breast.

His lips were so hot on the satiny cool curves, they seemed to burn where they touched. Antonia's hands pushed under the edges of his coat, her fingers caressing and tasting the firm flesh beneath the fine lawn of his shirt.

Her fingertips found the waistband of his breeches, tugging his shirt free so she could press her palm against the smooth muscled back. Marcus groaned deep in his throat and cupped the swell of her breast in one hand in an answering caress. His thumb stroked against the silk of the bodice, sending such a sensual shock coursing through her that Antonia gasped.

Concerned, he raised his head and gazed into her eyes. For a long moment their eyes held in a wordless communication, then Antonia saw his eyes flicker as his attention was caught by something behind her.

To Antonia's shock she found herself deposited unceremoniously onto the cold ironwork of the bench as Marcus got to his feet, tugging his waistcoat straight over the chaos she had wrought with his shirt. 'Marcus. . .' she protested softly.

'Shh!' he hissed, hard eyes staring into the dark foliage. Leaving her breathless on the bench, he stepped out into a patch of moonlight. 'Claudia!' His voice was heavy with sensuality. 'So, this is where you are. I was looking for you.' He took another long stride; Antonia, peering through the tangle of foliage, saw him reach the side of Claudia Reed, bend his head and claim her lips with a hard kiss.

Antonia was too shocked even to gasp, then too humiliated to risk being seen by the other woman, who was greedily kissing Marcus, her knowing body curving into his.

'Later, Claudia, later,' Marcus murmured, leading her towards the door. 'We must rejoin the others, or it will cause comment.'

White-faced in the moonlight, all intoxication burned away by anger and humiliation, Antonia stared at a moth scorching its wings in the candle flame. Just like me, she thought in desolation, scorched by my passion for Marcus.

She should have known he was not a forgiving man: she had refused his suit, she had tricked him on the riverbank with Jeremy, putting him at a disadvantage in front of the other man. She had let her satisfaction at the trick show too plainly this evening and he had wreaked a terrible revenge on her, guaranteeing she would never dare cross swords with him again.

Bereft, humiliated, stricken to immobility by misery, she sat on, unheeding of time, until Anne Meredith sought her out, concern on her face.

'Antonia, my dear, are you unwell?' Who could doubt it, looking at the pretty face so pinched and pale, the elegant fingers cramped in the folds of her gown?

'No. . .yes.' Words seemed to come from a long way away; it was an enormous effort to squeeze them past her stiff lips. 'I think I have caught a chill. . .forgive me, but I must go home. May I have the carriage?'

'But, of course, my dear.' Lady Meredith hurried out, returning some minutes later with Antonia's cloak and reticule. 'Let me put this round your shoulders—why, your hands are quite frozen! Mead is sending for the carriage, it will not be long. Would you like me to accompany you back to the Dower House? Miss Donaldson may not have returned. . .'

'No, no, thank you. You are very kind, but I shall be better by myself. I am so sorry.'

'It is I who am sorry,' Anne Meredith replied grimly as she helped Antonia to the front door, cursing the stupidity of all men, and her brother in particular. Not for a moment did she believe Antonia's story. When a young girl is found alone in a conservatory in a distressed state and another woman is almost crowing with triumph, it did not take a genius to understand what had passed.

Anne stood looking after the disappearing carriage, anxiety on her face, fury in her heart. She would speak to her brother tonight. What was he about, she fumed as she re-entered the salon, trifling with a lovely young girl who was worth a hundred of that Reed strumpet? To her frustration, Marcus had ordered the card tables to be set up, foiling her desire to get him alone.

Marcus caught his sister's eye as she swept into the room, guessing from the sounds of carriage wheels on gravel that she had just handed Miss Dane into the conveyance to take her home. His mouth set in a grim line, he continued to play, determined to give Anne no opportunity to speak to him that evening. Beside him, Claudia pressed her thigh against his, her breast brushing his arm whenever she leaned across to examine his cards. No, he needed to avoid Anne tonight, he had other plans.

One o'clock was striking as he dismissed his valet from his bedchamber. 'I will undress myself, thank you, Dale. And if you see my sister as you leave, tell her I have already retired.'

'Very well, my lord.' The valet, used to Marcus's ways, bowed himself out, leaving his master staring rather grimly at the big bed.

Marcus shrugged out of his swallow-tailed coat and waistcoat, removed his cravat and pulled on a light silk dressing-gown. He had no doubt that his solitude would soon be interrupted by Claudia, lured by the promise of his kiss in the conservatory. He could not have given her a much clearer signal that the weeks of denial were over—and that tonight he wanted her in his bedchamber.

Restlessly he tugged aside the heavy curtain and looked out over the pleasure grounds, then his focus changed and he found himself regarding his own reflection as though in a looking glass. 'You damn fool,' he addressed his image dispassionately. 'What a coil.'

He was still at the window when the door opened quietly and Claudia slipped in. He watched her without turning as she tiptoed across the carpet, her negligee of gold silk gauze moulding her voluptuous body. She pressed her palms flat against his shoulder blades, then ran them insinuatingly down the planes of his back until she reached his waist.

Marcus turned then, catching her wrists in his hard grasp, arresting their knowing progress. 'Darling,' she pouted, 'you are so masterful.' She shivered and looked into his face, her tongue-tip running lasciviously round the full curve of her lips. 'It has been so long, Marcus. . . come to bed now.'

She started to back towards the fourposter, only to be pulled up short and none too gently by Marcus's immobility. 'Mmm. . .' She smiled wickedly at him. 'So you want to do it here?'

'No, Claudia, I do not. And I do not want to take you to my bed, now or in the future. It is over.'

Looking into his hard face she could not doubt it, but ever a fighter, she was unwilling to concede defeat. 'I do not believe you! The way you kissed me tonight tells me you do not mean it!'

'I had to make sure you would come to me: there is nowhere else in the house we can be certain of being alone.'

Ready tears started in the lovely blue eyes. 'Marcus, how can you be so cruel? You know you love me, and I have been faithful to you, only to you. . .'

'Faithful to my fortune, my dear Claudia. I have never had any doubt that you would remain faithful to that while you had any hopes of presents—or until a bigger, richer, fish swam by.'

The tears slid decoratively over the pink cheeks, but a hardening anger was forming in the depths of her eyes. 'How could you be so cruel? Inviting me down here only to spurn me when I have done nothing to incur your displeasure. Come, darling, come to bed. You are tired and cross, let Claudia make it better. . .' She wriggled seductively, sending the gauzy fabric sliding from her shoulders. Only the fact that he was still holding her wrists prevented the entire garment slipping to the floor.

'Yes, Claudia, I could go to bed with you. You are a very beautiful woman. But that beauty is only skin deep; it took me but a few weeks to realise that. You knew it was over, you knew I did not want you here, yet somehow you cozened my sister into inviting you down. Since you arrived, I have done nothing to encourage you, yet you persist.'

'But I love you, Marcus,' she wheedled.

'You love only yourself. You are vain, self-absorbed, cruel and dismissive of others' feelings. You are redeemed only by your beauty—for so long as that lasts, my lovely. Do not frown so, Claudia, frown lines are so very ageing.'

'That did not concern you when you were in my bed taking your pleasure of me,' she hissed, two hot spots of colour mottling her cheek bones.

Marcus dropped her wrists and stared down at the spiteful little face that tonight, despite the artful maquillage, had lost every iota of its freshness and appeal. 'But then you managed to hide those characteristics from me so well, did you not?'

Claudia reached up one long-nailed finger and ran it scoringly down his chest, exposed by the open shirt neck. 'I hid nothing from you, remember. . .?'

Marcus did, vividly. Then he had been consumed by passion for the sophisticated, available—oh, so very available—Lady Reed. The burning desire had been short-lived; now he felt only distaste that he had surrendered so easily to her lures. A reflection of his thoughts must have shown on his countenance.

Claudia, her wheedling smile vanishing in a second, struck like an adder, the flat of her hand cracking across his face so hard his head snapped back. Beyond touching the stinging weal with his fingertips, Marcus did nothing, but his eyes burned with a cold fire that stopped Claudia's breath. With a sob which was half-petulance, half-apprehension, she ran from the room, her negligee swirling in disorder around her.

Marcus stalked across the room and shut the heavy panelled door behind her, then slumped down into a wing chair before the empty grate. He stuck his legs out, easing the tension from his long frame, then ran his hands through his hair.

Egad, that had been unpleasant! He blamed himself for having become entangled with Claudia in the first place. At first he had admired her spirits and beauty, the courage with which she coped with an empty life married to a corrupt man old enough to be her father.

Society was full of grass widows, game for a fling with any gentleman who was willing. As long as everyone concerned was discreet, no one turned a hair, even when there were some aristocratic households where all a man

could be certain of was that his first-born son and heir
was his own.

But that sort of life had palled, Marcus realised. It was
no longer enough to have passion without attachment—
not since he had met Antonia.

A great weariness suddenly overcame him. Marcus
shrugged out of his clothes and climbed into the great
fourposter. His last thought before he fell asleep was that
he must ride over and see Antonia as soon as maybe in
the morning. He knew how much he must have hurt her
in the conservatory, but he would explain how he had
needed to shield her from Claudia's venom, and her
vicious, gossiping tongue.

His next conscious act was to blink in the full glare of
the morning sunlight as Dale pulled back the drapes at
the long casements with their view east over the park.
'Another fine morning, my lord. I trust you slept well,
my lord. Shall I direct them to send up your bathwater
immediately?'

Dale, an immaculately trained valet, was well used to
carrying on a one-sided conversation with his master,
who was never talkative much before eleven in the morning. Encouraged by a grunt, he ushered in footmen
carrying hot-water cans and began gathering up his lordship's discarded clothing from the day before.

So well schooled was he and so discreet that Dale
had been known to retrieve intimate articles of feminine
apparel and return them to the wearer's lady's maid perfectly laundered and without even a quirk of an eyebrow.

This morning's tumbled linen revealed no such embar-
rassments, however, somewhat to Dale's surprise: there
was very little in an aristocratic household that escaped

the notice of the upper servants. And later, when he noticed the faint bruise on his lordship's cheek, he did not comment, beyond wielding the cutthroat razor with extra care.

Lady Meredith, sweeping downstairs an hour later with every intention of bearding her brother, encountered him in the hall, dressed for riding and pulling on his gloves as he gave orders to Saye, his head groom.

'And tell Welling to come with us, you can both ride over to Sir George Dover's and collect that bay gelding I bought off him last week. It is unbroken and will need both of you to bring it home.' Seeing his sister, he paused. 'Good morning, Anne. I trust you slept well?'

'Marcus, must you go out now? I particularly wished to speak to you.' It was a demand rather than a request.

'I shall be back later, my dear.' Marcus bowed over her hand, avoiding her gimlet eye. He had no doubt she intended to lecture him on the subject of Antonia; well, by the time he returned, her lecture would be redundant, and she would be too pleased with his news to scold him.

Anne, fulminating over her brother's escape, was even less pleased at the discovery that her sole breakfast companion was Sir George Reed, making a hearty meal of sirloin, ham and porter.

Marcus, meanwhile, giving the horse its head on the fine cropped downland grass, was in the best of spirits as he cut across the parkland to the Dower House. The sound of the church clock striking ten reached him faintly over the pounding of three sets of hooves. The sun, though warm, was still tempered by the fresh early morning air and the prospect of bringing the smile back to Antonia's face lent urgency to the ride.

The old, twisted chimneys of the Dower House came into view behind a stand of trees and Marcus reined the mount in slightly, slowing him as he entered the lane that ran along the front of the property. At the gate he turned in the saddle. 'Wait here, Saye.' What instinct prompted him to keep the two grooms he could not say; something perhaps about the unwonted stillness of the normally bustling house.

Surely they were not still abed, he thought, as the heavy knocker dropped from his hand onto the old oak door. Anna appeared and dropped him a curtsy, her cheeks even pinker than normal.

'Good morning, your lordship.'

'Good morning, Anna. Is Miss Dane at home?'

Anna's pretty country complexion grew more rosy. 'No, my lord.'

'Well, may I speak to Miss Donaldson?' So Antonia was angry with him still. That was not to be wondered at.

'Miss Donaldson is not at home, my lord,' Anna recited with the air of a child repeating a lesson.

Marcus's lips tightened. 'Do you mean,' he enquired with dangerous civility, 'that the ladies are not here, or that they are not at home to me?'

This threw the maid servant into even more confusion than he might have expected. 'Yes. . .no. . .that is. . .' She took a deep breath and said desperately, 'Miss Donaldson said as I was to say, that they aren't at home, your lordship.'

For a moment Anna thought his lordship was going to shoulder her aside and stride into the house, there was such a flare of anger in the dark eyes. But instead he nodded curtly, turned on his heel and vaulted into the saddle. Outside in the lane, the waiting grooms were startled to see their master urge his horse into a gallop away from the house.

'What are we supposed to do now?' Welling demanded. 'Follow him or go for the gelding?'

Saye, well used to his lordship's sudden starts, dug his heels into the side of his hack. 'Follow him—at least, until he rides off that temper.'

After the first quarter of a mile, Marcus reined back to a more temperate pace, smiling grimly at his own mood. He was not used to being thwarted, and he was uneasily aware of how hurt Antonia must be feeling, but storming around the Hertfordshire countryside was no remedy. He would go back and write her a note.

He pulled up where the lane crossed the Berkhamsted road and watched the approaching grooms. If he sent the note with Josh Saye, who was courting young Anna, there was a good chance it would reach Antonia, more so than if he took it himself.

The men had just reached him under the shade of the chestnuts when a gig came bowling round the bend from the direction of the town. It was driven by young Jem, whose cheerful demeanour changed into a look of alarm tinged with shiftiness the moment he saw who was at the crossroads.

A sudden suspicion made Marcus snap, 'Stop that gig,' and the two grooms moved their mounts into the road.

Jem tugged his forelock and shifted uneasily on the bench seat. Marcus, still unsure why he had stopped him, urged his mount alongside the gig, then saw a beribboned hat box on the floor.

'Where have you been, boy?' he demanded sharply.

'Nowhere, sir,' Jem responded sullenly.

'You speak proper to his lordship—' Saye lifted

a hand threateningly '—or I'll thicken your ear.'

'Do not bully the lad,' Marcus intervened. 'What is your name, boy?'

'Jem. . .your lordship.' Still he would not look up.

'Jem, ah, yes. You work for Miss Dane, do you not?'

'Yessir.'

'And have you been driving Miss Dane this morning?'

'Couldn't say, sir. . .my lord.' Jem's face was almost crimson.

'That is all right, Jem, you do not have to tell us anything you do not wish to. What a pity Miss Dane forgot her hat box,' Marcus said sympathetically.

'No, she didn't forget it, she said there weren't no room in the ch—' He broke off appalled, one hand clapping itself to his mouth.

'No room in the chaise?' Marcus finished gently. 'So your mistress has hired a chaise, has she? And where is she bound?'

Saye advanced to the side of the gig. 'You speak up when his lordship asks you a question, boy, or I'll have your ears off.'

'You can boil me in oil and I won't tell you nuffin about Miss Dane,' stammered Jem, almost in tears now.

'Stop bullying the lad. He is only being loyal to his mistress and no doubt following her instructions. Here, lad.' Marcus fished in his waistcoat pocket and sent a half sovereign spinning through the air to the startled boy. 'Do not worry, Jem, you have kept your silence well, now be off back to the Dower House.'

The lad needed no urging and was off down the road as fast as the elderly horse could go. Marcus used his spurs and sent his mount cantering off towards Berkhamsted.

'What the blazes?' Welling demanded.

'You hold your tongue and follow,' Saye growled. He urged his own hack after his master, adding under his breath, 'Never seen his lordship in such a taking over a woman before, and that's the truth.'

The King's Arms was the only hostelry in the town that hired out carriages, but enquiries there were met with little information. Yes, Miss Dane had hired a chaise and four with two postillions, but no, neither the landlord nor the ostlers could say which direction she had taken.

'We've been very busy, my lord,' the landlord explained apologetically, wiping his hands on his apron. 'Market day, you see.'

Marcus was standing in the inn yard, fists on hips, sizing up the possibilities: east for London or west for Aylesbury, when Mr Todd the curate walked through the arch.

'Oh, good morning, my lord,' he beamed, bowing obsequiously. 'Why, all local Society seems to be abroad in Berkhamsted today. I was gratified to see Miss Dane earlier. Such a charming young lady, such an ornament to our Society. . .'

'Mr Todd, good morning to you, I trust I find you well.' Marcus regarded his curate with a speculative eye. 'Splendid sermon last Sunday, I hope you intend to stimulate us again this week.' Marcus had, in fact, dozed through most of Mr Todd's interminable prosing on the subject of the Ephesians, but he did not want to cause gossip by pouncing too readily on the subject of Miss Dane.

'Thank you, my lord, you are too kind. I was, in fact,

intending to enlarge upon the theme of the dangers of heathen imagery. . .'

Marcus allowed him to prate on until he drew breath at last, then slipped in a remark.

'I am glad to hear Miss Dane succeeded in finding a suitable chaise. Now, where was it she was going. . . London, I think. . .?'

'Oh no, my lord,' said Mr Todd brightly. 'She took the Chesham road.'

Chesham, Marcus ruminated, why would she go south to Chesham? Unless she had some intention of disguising her destination, for once along that road she could turn off for either London or Aylesbury. Mr Todd was prattling again, but his lordship excused himself brusquely and strode back to his horse, leaving the curate to worry that he had somehow given offence to his patron.

'Saye, you and Welling take the Chesham road until you find which way Miss Dane's chaise has gone. When you are sure, send Welling back to me and you follow until Miss Dane reaches her destination, then send me word. Here——' he tossed a leather purse to the head groom '——this should cover your expenses.'

Not waiting to see the two men follow his instructions, Marcus turned back towards Brightshill, a thoughtful expression on his face. He had come to expect spirited behaviour from Antonia, but even by her standards, setting off alone in a hired chaise was extraordinarily daring. When he discovered where she had gone—and London or Bath seemed the most obvious destinations—he would follow. Still, for once in his life Marcus Allington was discovering that events were not following his desires.

*   *   *

This impression was reinforced when, no sooner had he set foot over his own threshold, his sister pounced on him and marched him with scant ceremony into his study.

'Well?' Anne demanded. 'Have you been over to speak to Miss Dane?'

Marcus sank into a deep chair and crossed his booted legs negligently. 'Yes.'

'And? What did she say? Marcus, I do wish you would not sprawl like that!'

'She said nothing.' Marcus continued to sprawl, although his rather grim expression showed no desire to tease his sister.

'Nothing? What can you mean? Marcus, you are going about this very badly—did she refuse to speak to you? Although it is not to be wondered at, with that minx Claudia Reed all over you at table last night—'

'Antonia has gone,' Marcus stated baldly, cutting his sister off in mid flow.

'Gone! Gone where?' Anne sat down abruptly in the chair opposite.

'I have no idea, although I would hazard either Bath or London.'

His sister's colour was high, rising to match her temper. 'So you have thrown away the one chance you have of marrying someone who would suit you to perfection—and hurt a sweet girl into the bargain!'

'I offered for her before our first dinner party here, and she turned me down.' This was compressing events somewhat, and made no mention of Claudia's role in it all, but Anne was not to be deflected.

'I suppose you thought she would fall into your arms for the asking?' she demanded hotly. 'After all, everything else does, does it not, Marcus?'

Startled by this attack, he pulled himself up in the chair and stared at her. 'What can you mean?'

'Ever since you were a boy, you have been admired and fêted, for your rank and your fortune and your looks. You have never had to be accountable to anyone for anything, which is no doubt why that sweet girl has refused your suit. No, hear me out,' she held up a hand as he opened his mouth to protest.

'You are a good brother and uncle and an excellent employer, but you are aloof, sometimes haughty. I am assuming you love Antonia? Have you told her so, or have you just presumed that the honour of being courted by the great Marcus Allington is sufficient?'

Marcus returned her angry look with one that was thoughtful, weighing what Anne had said, but before he could respond there was a discreet tap at the door and Mead entered apologetically.

'My lord, I regret the intrusion, but Welling is here, saying you required immediate speech with him.'

Marcus rose swiftly. 'Tell him to wait, Mead, I will be with him directly.' Turning to his sister, he added, 'Will you be so good as to direct Dale to pack a valise for me; this will be news of Miss Dane and I intend to follow her.' He kissed Anne's hot cheek. 'Do not fret, my dear, I have taken your strictures to heart. What you say may be true, but I do not despair of rescuing the situation.'

In the hall he waited only for three words from Welling, 'London, my lord,' before ordering the man to bring round his high-perch phaeton within the half-hour.

Lady Meredith hurried out on to the steps as Dale was stowing the valise under the seat of the carriage and preparing to climb up beside his lordship. 'Marcus!'

'Give my apologies to our guests, my dear, and tell them I have called away to Town by urgent business.'

'So she is in London, then?' Anne asked, keeping her voice low as she looked up into his serious face. 'How will you find her?'

Marcus bent down to touch her cheek. 'Saye is hot on her trail, he will mark where she is staying and then await me at the town house. I will find her, never fear.'

Anne, watching the sporting vehicle sway dangerously round the curve of the drive, prayed that Marcus would not only find Miss Dane, but that having found her, could prevail upon her to receive him.

As she walked slowly back into the hallway, Anne mused that once she would have been glad to see her haughty brother brought low by love; now all she wanted was for him to be happy. With any other unmarried girl Lady Meredith would have had no fears, but Miss Dane was no ordinary debutante: she had a mind of her own and spirits to match.

Chapter Thirteen

The carriage jolted over the London cobblestones, jerking Antonia's mind back from the miserable circles it had been running round all day. Even in a swift chaise, with no money spared in hiring postillions and making changes whenever the horses faltered, the journey had seemed interminable.

In the country it would still be light at eight o'clock, but here, with tall buildings crowding all around and the press of humanity on the streets, the evening seemed well drawn in.

Antonia had directed the postillions to Half Moon Street, hoping that her great-aunt had suffered no relapse and was therefore at her own home and not at Cousin Hewitt's. To her relief, the knocker was still on the door, a sure sign that her ladyship was in residence, and lights glowed from the windows.

As soon as the carriage steps were let down, Antonia hurried up to the front door, which opened as she reached it as if in greeting. But it was not for her—Hodge, her great-aunt's long-serving butler, was in the process of bowing out a portly young gentleman. Antonia would have recognised her cousin Hewitt Granger anywhere by the expression of smug self-satisfaction playing on his fleshy lips and took some pleasure in seeing his face change at the sight of her.

They had never enjoyed a happy relationship: Hewitt was deeply suspicious of Antonia's position in his grandmother's affections and had been only too pleased to see her depart to Hertfordshire. But at the same time she was uncomfortably aware that Hewitt Granger found her attractive. He never lost the opportunity to touch her, squeeze her hand or stare blatantly at her figure in a manner that left her feeling somehow soiled.

Even as he regarded her now with suspicion and dislike in his pale eyes, Hewitt's tongue ran wetly over his full red lips.

'Antonia! What are you doing here? We did not look to see you in London again. Perhaps you sent a missive which has gone astray?' One gingery brow rose haughtily in an attempt at superiority.

'Good evening, Hewitt.' Antonia dismissed him—and his questions—coldly, turning to the elderly butler with warmth. 'Good evening, Hodge. I trust I find you well? How is the lumbago? Better, no doubt, in this warm weather.'

The old man beamed back, for she had always been a favourite with him and he had missed her sorely these last months. 'Much better, thank you, Miss Antonia. And may I say what a pl—'

'Now look here,' Hewitt interrupted rudely. 'I do not know what you think you are about, Antonia, but you cannot go in there.' He moved to block her entrance with his bulky body. 'Grandmother has been very ill, she cannot possibly see you and certainly not at this hour. You must go to an hotel.'

Antonia glimpsed the expression on Hodge's face, the almost imperceptible shake of his head. 'Fiddlesticks, Hewitt! I am here at Great-Aunt's invitation. Now do step aside and let me past. You have grown so stout since we last met; I cannot but feel it will do you no good, especially in this warm weather.' She regarded his empurpling face with cloying sympathy. 'You really look rather hot and agitated—quite puce, in fact. Goodnight, I will not detain you any longer.'

Hodge curbed the smile that was beginning to dawn on his face and said urbanely, 'Your usual chamber is prepared, Miss Antonia. And Cook has your favourite supper all ready.'

Antonia, even knowing this was untrue, could detect no falsity in the butler's tone. With a sweet smile at Hewitt, who was gobbling like a turkey cock, she slipped neatly into the hall. Her cousin was further discommoded by two footmen running down the steps to collect Antonia's luggage from the chaise. Thus comprehensively ignored by everyone, he clapped his hat on his head and strode off towards Piccadilly.

Hodge beamed at Antonia. 'I will ring for Mrs Hodge and have your chamber prepared directly, Miss Antonia. Do you wish to go in directly to her ladyship?'

Antonia twinkled at him. 'You said just now that my room was already prepared, Hodge. Was that an untruth?'

'Merely a slip of the tongue, Miss Antonia,' the butler replied blandly. 'Her ladyship will be delighted to see you, if I may make so bold. She is in the blue parlour; shall I show you up?'

'Thank you, no, Hodge. I know the way.' Antonia

whisked upstairs, happy to be back in the reassuring
familiarity of her old home. It only lacked Donna to be
quite like the old days, but her companion, when Antonia
had announced her intention of fleeing to London, had
reluctantly agreed to remain behind and supervise the
Dower House.

Antonia paused, one hand raised to tap on her great-
aunt's door. She remembered the uncharacteristic blaze
of fury on Donna's face when she realised the exigencies
to which Lord Allington had driven her beloved girl.
Antonia had left in the gig with Miss Donaldson's furious
instructions to Anna ringing in her ears: 'That man is
never—*never*—to be permitted to cross this threshold
again! Do you understand?'

Antonia tapped firmly on the door, for Great-Aunt's
hearing was not what it was, and peeped round the edge,
somewhat concerned that she might give Lady Granger
a shock, for the old lady was in her eighties and her
health was uncertain, despite the recent improvement.

All that was visible was the top of a most elaborate
lace cap showing over the back of a heavily brocaded
wing chair. A small fire flickered in the grate despite the
warmth of the evening and an embroidery stand and a
basket of silks had been pushed to one side.

'Is that you, Hodge?' Lady Granger's voice was still
as strong and commanding as it always had been. 'Has
that fool of a grandson of mine gone? Thinks I do not
know why he comes round! Sits there prattling on and
all the time measuring me for my coffin with those wishy-
washy eyes and wondering about my will! Pshaw! Does
he think I am a fool?'

Antonia smiled to herself. The old lady was as out-
spoken as many of her contemporaries brought up in the

more robust manners of the reign of the second George. She was quite likely to use intemperate language and could be open in her admiration for a comely young man in a way that caused blushes and giggles amongst younger women.

Antonia adored her great-aunt and was about to call her name when the old lady demanded, 'And bring me my brandy, Hodge! Take away the taste of that bloodless sherry wine Hewitt pressed upon me.'

Her niece picked up the tray from the side table and carried it round, carefully placing it before her aunt.

'Good Gad! Antonia, my child, is it really you?' Lady Granger held out her arms and Antonia went into them, enveloped in a cloud of rose scent, rice face powder and lace. 'It does my heart good to see you.'

'I am sorry to come with no warning. I hope it is not a shock, Great-Aunt.' Antonia sat on a footstool beside Lady Granger and took her hand. She was shocked at how thin and papery the skin felt, but under her fingers the pulse beat strongly and the old eyes were bright and shrewd.

'Reading your letter, I was so happy that you are feel-ing better, that I wanted to take up your invitation immediately.' It sounded false even to her own ears and Lady Granger was not fooled.

'Now tell me the real reason you are here,' she demanded. She tipped up Antonia's chin with a bony fingertip and peered into her face. 'Some man has made those shadows under your eyes, I suppose. Who is he?'

Even used as she was to her great-aunt, Antonia was taken aback by her directness and answered honestly, 'Marcus Allington.'

At that moment Mrs Hodge entered to enquire whether

Antonia wished to eat her supper with Lady Granger and, receiving an affirmative answer, gathered up Antonia's pelisse and bonnet and bustled out.

'Allington, eh?' A mischievous glint lit Lady Granger's eyes. 'And is he as handsome a dog as his grandfather, I wonder? Now there was a man with a fine leg in a pair of satin knee breeches. A man with a true damn-your-eyes attitude to life!' She cackled reminiscently. 'I nearly married him, but he was too much a rakehell, even for me.'

'He is handsome, right enough,' Antonia admitted ruefully. 'And arrogant, and a rake. . .'

'And you love him, I suppose?'

'Yes.' Antonia raised her face to her great aunt, tears starting in her eyes and her lip trembling.

The old lady held up an admonishing finger. 'Do not dare cry, girl! Remember who you are and keep your pride. They arc none of them worth a single tear, and I should know.'

Antonia bit her lip until the tears stopped and began to believe the rumours she had heard about her great-aunt: that she had been a great beauty, the mistress of powerful men—even, it was hinted, one of the highest in the land.

The bright eyes suddenly froze on her face. 'Why have you run away, girl? Has he been playing fast and loose with you? Have you permitted him any liberties?' She remembered Edmund Allington and his winning ways with the ladies. If his grandson had seduced her Antonia, he would find himself down the aisle before the week was out, if she had to take a shotgun to him herself.

'No,' Antonia denied, blushing hotly, remembering how close she had come to yielding to the urging of his hard body on the riverbank that night, remembering her responses to his mouth on hers in the conservatory.

'Indeed, miss!' Great-Aunt took a sip of her brandy and fell silent as Mrs Hodge brought in a light collation, laid the table and departed with a neat curtsy.

She brooded quietly as her great-niece ate hungrily, then, when Antonia finally pushed away the plate, asked, 'What is the matter then, that you have come to me?'

'He does not love me and I cannot bear to be near him and his mistress a moment longer,' Antonia burst out, getting to her feet and crossing to the window to look out on the street below. It was full dark now, except for the lanterns at each doorway, and she failed to notice the wiry figure in riding clothes standing in the shadows regarding the house. After a few moments, Saye detached himself from the darkness and hurried away in the direction of Grosvenor Square.

'Keeping a mistress, is he? Clumsy fool to let you know! Young men these days are losing their finesse— his grandfather would never have paraded his fancy piece in front of a girl he was courting. Has he made you any sort of declaration?'

'He has proposed marriage and I have refused.'

'Glad to hear you have that much spirit, girl! And I am glad you had the sense to come to me although, with the Season over, Town is thin of company.' Lady Granger mused on the available men who might take Antonia's mind off her broken heart. Marcus Allington was very eligible, she sighed to herself. She doubted her niece would ever make such a good catch again, but the important thing was that the child be happy.

'Come back and sit by me, child. You may stay as long as you wish, we will be comfortable together.' Antonia put her head in the old lady's lap and felt her hair being gently stroked. She shut her eyes and let the wise old voice wash over her. 'You will forget him in time, child. You are young and beautiful and there are plenty more fish in the sea.'

The following morning brought Hewitt and his younger brother Clarence, accompanied by his wife of a few months who, Antonia decided, after the briefest of acquaintances, was a total ninny.

The ladies had scarce finished their breakfast when the knocker sounded the arrival of the unwelcome party. Lady Granger was not pleased at the early interruption. 'What I have done to deserve such fools for grandsons I do not know,' she confided to Antonia, not bothering to keep her voice down. 'Neither of them has a thought in his head, but that does not stop them sticking their beaks into my business at every turn.'

The unbecoming mottling of Hewitt's complexion showed he had heard at least part of this condemnation, but he swallowed his anger, bustling forward to kiss his grandmother's hand and enquire condescendingly after her health. Clarence followed his elder brother. Although two years separated them, they were as alike as twins with their florid complexions and bulky figures.

Clarence turned to his cousin and presented his wife with the air of a man showing off a rare jewel. Emilia Granger was at least ten years younger than her husband. She was blonde and fluffy and simpered up at Clarence, who swelled with pride at the blatant adoration in the shallow blue eyes.

Antonia marvelled that any woman could regard her cousin with adoration until Mrs Granger opened her mouth. 'Have you been in London before, Miss Dane. . .

oh, yes, silly me, I quite forgot. . . Clarence told me you used to live here. Oh, dear, I am a goose!' She giggled inanely, a noise not unlike a guinea fowl at its most irritating, and prattled on. 'We are just a little early, are we not? But dear brother Hewitt was so set on visiting. He said last night. . .'

Even a woman as stupid as she could not fail to recognise the fury with which her brother-in-law was regarding her. Emilia flushed unbecomingly and subsided into silence. Hewitt glowered at her until he was certain she would prattle no more and turned his attention once more to Antonia.

Gad! His cousin was a handsome woman! Perhaps her complexion had caught the sun too much for fashion, but with her dark hair and flashing eyes it gave her an exotic look. Hewitt's mind drifted to a dark beauty he had encountered the other night in Vauxhall Gardens and the pleasures that had followed after the exchange of more guineas than he normally expended.

Antonia, catching his eye, shifted uncomfortably and moved closer to her great aunt, who was snapping at her visitors, 'Sit down, sit down! Do not hover about like a flock of pigeons! What do you want, Hewitt? You were only here last evening.'

Emilia, scared out of her remaining wits by this terrifying old lady, squeaked and dropped her reticule. The contents fell out and she scrabbled at her feet to pick them up, her cheeks scarlet. The two men sat firmly, one at each end of the sofa opposite their grandmother.

'Ha! Like a pair of bookends!' And with no sense between them. Lady Granger snorted, wondering how her stolid but reliable son had produced two such as these. But then, that well-bred goose he had married. . .

A moment of silence followed. Clarence finally broke it by clearing his throat. 'Well, Grandmama—' he fiddled with his neck cloth '—sensible as we all are of your weakened condition and mindful that your doctor has prescribed rest. . .'

'Poppycock! I have dismissed the old fool, as well you know. Young Dr Hardcastle—does me good just to see his handsome face—stands for none of that nonsense.'

'Be that as it may, Grandmama,' Clarence continued gamely, 'we were concerned that our cousin's presence might fatigue you. So we have come to offer her accommodation with us. For the week or two you are in London, coz,' he added, turning to Antonia.

'She stays here,' the old lady snapped, causing another spasm of fright to course through Emilia's thin frame.

'And I intend to stay for quite some time—months, in fact. So, of course, I could not possibly impose on you in Wimpole Street.' Antonia smiled sweetly at Emilia. 'And I could not possibly intrude into the household of a newly married couple.' Mrs Granger, thus addressed, was so discommoded that she dropped her reticule again.

'Fool of a woman,' Great-Aunt muttered quite audibly, then, raising her voice, added, 'We have all the dress shops to visit—why, Antonia needs a complete change of wardrobe—and I fully intend to buy all the latest novels and volumes of poetry so we may read together. And, of course, we must get out of London soon. Bath, perhaps, or Brighton. What think you, Hewitt? Only a house in the best area, of course, and at this short notice it will no doubt cost a pretty penny. But there, I cannot take it with me, can I?'

Hewitt had raised a hand to cover his eyes and was murmuring gently to himself. Antonia thought she caught the words, 'The money, the money. . .'

Lady Granger tugged the bell-pull at her side. 'Well, you may all remain here if you wish, but we were about to go out. Antonia, did I mention last night that I intend to take my diamond set to Garrard's to be cleaned and reset for you? We can do that on the way to the modiste's.' Having thus completed Hewitt's anguish, she smiled benignly on her grandsons and, leaning on Antonia's arm, crossed the room slowly but steadily.

Antonia was surprised to discover, when they sat down later to luncheon, how effective a good shopping spree was in keeping a broken heart at bay. Her mind still flinched from thinking of Marcus, but her spirits were lighter and she found she could look forward to the next few weeks with pleasant anticipation.

'I must go and lie down for a while, my dear,' Great-Aunt announced. 'No, no, I am not fatigued.' She waved aside Antonia's concern. 'Dr Hardcastle has told me to conserve my energies. Why not take a walk in the park? Or would you prefer one of the grooms to drive you?'

'Thank you, Great-Aunt, but I think I will walk. I have grown used to walking some distances since I have been in Hertfordshire and I confess I miss the exercise.' Antonia dropped a kiss on the dry, papery cheek and went upstairs to put on her bonnet and pelisse.

With one of her great-aunt's maids at her heels, Antonia set off briskly towards Hyde Park. Green Park was closer, but the more open expanses of the larger park beckoned and the afternoon was pleasantly sunny with a light breeze.

Antonia had an enjoyable walk, wandering further than

she had intended. She finally turned for home, much to the relief of Julia the maid, who was not used to lengthy excursions of this sort, when she slipped on a tussock and turned her ankle painfully.

'Oh, Miss Antonia, are you all right, miss?' Julia's face was anxious as Antonia grimaced and rubbed the side of her kid boot.

'Oh! That was a nasty wrench, but I do not think it is sprained.' She placed her foot gingerly to the ground and winced. 'I shall manage well enough if I lean on your arm, Julia.'

The two of them had begun their slow progress homewards when there was the sound of carriage wheels behind them and a cry of, 'Cousin! What has befallen you?' The two young women turned to see Hewitt in a new conveyance pulled by a somewhat showy bay.

'I have turned my ankle, Hewitt, there is no cause for concern.'

Hewitt jumped down from the carriage. 'But you must ride back with me, dear cousin, I insist.'

Antonia's first instinct was to refuse, but the thought of hobbling conspicuously across the Park was not appealing and her ankle was now throbbing.

'Thank you, Hewitt. Is there room for my girl?'

'No!' Hewitt looked appalled at the thought of having a maidservant in his new carriage.

'Very well. Julia, I am afraid you will have to walk—straight back to Half Moon Street, now!'

'Yes, miss.' The girl bobbed a curtsy and watched as the carriage bowled off down the gravelled drive. Humph! She'd rather walk any day than sit squashed up with old frog-face and his wandering hands. And if she hurried there would be time to put her head round the basement door of number twenty and see if Tom the underfootman was about. . .

'Hewitt, do take care,' Antonia remonstrated as Hewitt took a curve so close the carriage rocked. She suspected that he had chosen both horse and curricle for their showy looks rather than quality, and was not entirely certain as to his abilities to control either.

'Well, if you are nervous I will slow down, one would not wish to frighten a lady.' He reined back and leered at Antonia, who placed her parasol firmly on the seat between them.

Antonia averted her gaze from his florid features and began to talk of the magnificence of the shrubberies and the greenness of the grass despite the warm weather.

Her determined horticultural commentary was rudely interrupted by Hewitt's exclamation. 'That's a damn fine bit of horseflesh!'

Antonia turned automatically, but she had no need to follow her cousin's pointing whip. The magnificent black stallion emerging at a controlled walk from one of the side paths was turning all heads in the vicinity. But after one glance, Antonia's attention was riveted not on the horse but on the rider.

Marcus Allington was controlling the spirited animal with one hand, the other at his hat brim acknowledging greetings from many of the passers-by.

'Drive on, Hewitt!' she demanded sharply, but her cousin had reined back almost to a standstill and was not listening. 'Stop gawping, Hewitt, it is only a horse!'

What was Marcus doing here! It was only two days since that disastrous dinner party at Brightshill—now here he was riding through Hyde Park, as cool as a cucumber. One thing was clear—he had not followed her, for how could he know where she had gone after all the precautions she had taken to cover her steps?

Antonia's heart was thudding in her chest so loudly she felt sure it would be audible to her cousin sitting alongside her. She could not take her eyes off Marcus, sitting erect in the saddle. His boots were burnished to the black sheen of the animal beneath him, his riding clothes were immaculate. His hair was caught by the slight breeze as he raised his hat and her fingers clenched against the desire to run her fingers through it.

'It is Lord Allington, is it not?' Hewitt demanded. 'I wonder if he would tell me where he got that animal?'

'Please, Hewitt, take me home, my ankle is painful and I am sure it is swelling.'

'What? Oh, sorry, my dear.' Hewitt, recalled by her sharp voice, started and let his hands drop. The bay, feeling the lack of control, broke into a trot and the carriage lurched. Antonia, thrown off balance, gripped Hewitt's arm with both hands and was still in that position when Marcus saw them.

He urged the stallion forward with the pressure of his knees and came alongside the curricle as Hewitt once more gained control.

Hewitt just managed to doff his hat without dropping either it or the reins. 'My lord.'

'You have the advantage of me, sir, no doubt Miss Dane will introduce us. Miss Dane, your servant, ma'am.' He replaced his tall hat and raised one eyebrow. 'I had not looked to find you here, Miss Dane.'

'And indeed, why should you, sir?' Antonia riposted, chin high and leaving one hand resting on her cousin's arm. 'Allow me to make known to you my cousin, Hewitt Granger. Mr Granger, Lord Allington.'

The gentlemen exchanged stiff half-bows. Hewitt was conscious that Antonia's hand was still on his arm. His lordship might be astride the best bit of horseflesh in the Park, but he, Hewitt Granger, was driving the finest-looking woman abroad that day! His chest swelled with self-importance and he patted Antonia's hand proprietorially.

Marcus's face showed nothing but the bland amiability of a gentleman introduced to a new acquaintance but Antonia, knowing him so well, was aware of a watchfulness in his eyes. Some devil in her made her lay her free hand on top of Hewitt's. 'You will forgive us, Lord Allington; we have been out some time and I am fatigued. Hewitt dear, take me home now.'

Marcus's lip curved in an unpleasantly satirical smile. He did not believe a word of that, and Antonia knew it. 'In that case, ma'am, I would not detain you.' To her chagrin Marcus tipped his hat once more and cantered off without asking for her direction. Not that she would have given it to him anyway!

Hewitt, meanwhile, was recovering from the shock of finding Antonia so affectionate, given that usually she was at best dismissive to him. He had just enough sense not to press matters in the Park, but resolved to call at Half Moon Street the following day and pursue his advantage.

As they bowled along Piccadilly, he reflected that matters could not have fallen better. Antonia's reappearance had been a severe shock to one who had come to regard his grandmother's money as his by right. He knew how highly the old lady valued her niece: now, if Antonia accepted him, he would have it all: the money and the woman. He did not particularly like Antonia, she was too opinionated for him, but he did desire her.

As they turned into Half Moon Street, he resolved to pay a visit to that little actress he had discovered in Covent Garden. A trifle coarse at close quarters, but she bore a startling resemblance to his cousin and his passions were stirred. . .

Antonia was glad to descend from the carriage at her great-aunt's house. The footman helped her down with care and she waved Hewitt goodbye as she limped up the steps on James's arm. To her relief, her cousin showed no desire to accompany her into the house; she had been concerned that she had overdone things in the Park and that he would try and follow up her unexpected warmth. But no, she reassured herself, Hewitt was too stupid to notice.

The following morning her ankle was still stiff. Lady Granger, having failed to persuade her niece to allow her physician to examine it, had insisted that she spend the morning resting with it supported on a footstool. The old lady had driven out to visit an ailing acquaintance, promising to return in time for luncheon.

Antonia obediently settled down to read the latest volume of Lord Byron's work. Many ladies would have considered it far too shocking for an unmarried girl to read, but Lady Granger had thoroughly enjoyed it and had no qualms in passing it to her niece.

Despite the disconcerting tendency of Marcus's face to appear in her imagination every time she read a description of the hero, Antonia was engrossed in 'Manfred' when Hodge threw the door open and announced, 'Mr Granger, miss.'

Antonia groaned inwardly, wishing she had given

instructions to Hodge that she was not at home. But then he would have denied all visitors. . .

Hewitt bustled across the room crying, 'Dear Cousin! How is your afflicted, er. . .' he boggled at naming part of a lady's anatomy and finished lamely '. . .injury?'

'Much better, thank you, Cousin,' Antonia replied coolly. Why was he here? 'Please, sit down and allow me to ring for some refreshment.' Hewitt showed no inclination to sit, instead striking an attitude which displayed an inordinate amount of crimson silk waistcoat. 'What a striking waistcoat,' Antonia said weakly, eyeing the garment with horrid fascination. In combination with trousers in an assertive shade of canary yellow the whole ensemble this early in the morning made her feel quite bilious.

'I knew you would admire it,' he beamed. 'I thought to myself, a woman of taste such as my cousin Antonia will admire this garment. In fact, I would go so far as to say I donned it especially for you.' His expression was doubtless supposed to be a roguish twinkle, but it emerged more like a leer.

'Really?' Antonia was lost for words. She was beginning to feel increasingly uncomfortable and wished she could reach the bell-pull to summon Hodge.

Eyeing her even more warmly, Hewitt crashed to her side on one knee and seized her right hand in his fleshy paw. 'Miss Dane! Cousin! Antonia! Be mine, I beseech you! Say you will consent to be Mrs Hewitt Granger!'

Antonia stared down appalled at the thinning crown of his head bent over her hand, then struggled to her feet with a painful lurch, attempting at the same time to extricate her hand. Hewitt, misinterpreting her gesture, staggered to his feet and seized her in his arms manfully.

'No!' she cried as his lips descended inexorably towards her face, but the sound was muffled by Hewitt's ample chest.

There was a discreet cough behind them and Hodge's voice announced, 'Lord Allington, Miss Dane.'

Antonia, scarlet with mortification, attempted to free herself, but Hewitt clung to her hand until she freed it with a sharp jerk. 'My lord, good morning. Please sit down.' She was amazed at how calm her voice sounded, for inside she was trembling and, in truth, felt a little queasy. Her ankle throbbed, but that was nothing compared to her utter revulsion at Hewitt's embraces.

Steeling herself, she raised her eyes to Marcus's face, hoping to see some sign of jealousy, some sign that finding her in the arms of another man was painful to him.

Lord Allington stared back, his face a polite mask. Not by one whit did he betray surprise, dismay or the slightest sign of jealousy in finding the woman to whom he had recently proposed in the arms of another man.

'How kind of you to call, my lord,' Antonia continued desperately. 'May I offer you some refreshment? Hewitt, please ring the bell before you sit down.'

'Thank you, Miss Dane.' Marcus sat back and crossed his legs, smiling politely at both the cousins. 'How pleasant to see you again, Mr Granger. I was wondering where you had acquired the striking animal you were driving yesterday.'

So you can avoid the same dealer, no doubt, Antonia thought sourly. She was hoping that Hewitt would leave, but at such flattering attention her cousin settled himself comfortably and began to prose on about his search for the perfect driving horse.

Marcus caught Antonia's eye and allowed one eyelid

to drop into an unmistakable wink. Antonia, despite everything, could hardly contain the laugh that bubbled up her throat. Marcus could have asked nothing better calculated to encourage Hewitt into a display of pompous conceit—and now Marcus was inviting her to enjoy it with him.

With a struggle she controlled her expression. Beside her Hewitt, conscious for the first time that his lordship's attention was not solely on him, ground to a halt. Antonia spoke hurriedly in the sudden silence. 'How did you know my direction, my lord?'

'Your direction? Why, I had not come to see you, Miss Dane, but Lady Granger.' Marcus smiled. 'No, this is merely a pleasant coincidence—did you know, Mr Granger, that Miss Dane and I are neighbours in Hertfordshire?'

'No, I was not aware of that,' Hewitt answered rather shortly. 'I was also not aware that you were acquainted with my grandmother.' He disliked the thought that any of his most wealthy relative's business was not known to him.

'I have never had the pleasure of meeting her ladyship, but she and my grandfather were great friends. When I heard she had risen from her sickbed and was receiving once again, I naturally hastened to pay my respects. I would not have wished to, shall we say, leave it too late.'

'I can assure you, my lord,' Antonia snapped, 'that my great-aunt is in the best of health. Touching though your concern is, there was no need to hasten to her side as though she were on her death bed.'

'But she is very frail,' Hewitt added hastily, as if to reassure himself.

At that moment the lady herself entered, looking not

a day over sixty in a mauve silk creation that combined the latest fashion with great dignity. Both men leapt to their feet, but she ignored her grandson completely, fixing Marcus with a gimlet stare before allowing him her hand.

'Well, well—there was no need for Hodge to tell me who my caller was! Just like your grandfather, another handsome dog. Sit down, can't stand people hovering about! What are you still doing here, Hewitt? Every day you are cluttering the place up, every day. Go to your club, why don't you, if you can't stand to go home to that simpering peahen your brother married.'

Hewitt, deciding that being belittled by his grandmother in front of Lord Allington was detrimental to his dignity, smiled at Marcus as though to indicate that the old lady was ga-ga and bowed himself out with a meaningful stare at Antonia.

Marcus sat under the penetrating stare and smiled back, apparently at his ease, but inwardly reflecting that he had never met such a terrifying old woman in his life. The grey eyes regarded him shrewdly but not unkindly, and the wreck of the very great beauty his grandfather had once described was still there in the fine bones of her face and the spirit that still burned strong.

'So you think I am like my grandfather, ma'am?' he enquired.

'Cut from the same cloth: I would have known you anywhere as an Allington.'

'And I would have recognised you, ma'am, from his description.'

'Get away with you, boy!' Lady Granger waved a hand dismissively but Antonia could tell she was pleased.

'I'll wager he did not tell you everything about our acquaintance.'

Antonia blushed at the improper implication, but Marcus laughed. 'Enough to make me envious, ma'am.'

The two settled into a conversation that subtly excluded Antonia. She sat to one side, watching Marcus's face, the play of expression, the movement of his hands, listening to the laugh in his voice. She loved him, wanted nothing more than to run across the room to him, bury her face in his chest and hear his heart beat under her ear.

It was so painful to see him here in her old home, talking to her great-aunt but to know that nothing had changed, nor could it. Ruthlessly she reminded herself that she could not ally herself with a man so unprincipled he would flaunt his mistress before her. And if that meant she had to live out her life in spinsterhood, well, so be it. If she could not have Marcus Allington, she did not want second best.

Not that she any longer had the choice. He had made it quite clear that he was not here to see her and his reaction to Hewitt had been one of total indifference.

Antonia became aware that Marcus was on his feet taking his leave. As he bowed over Lady Granger's hand once more, Antonia saw her great-aunt give a decisive little nod as though she had reached a conclusion to a difficult puzzle.

Antonia curtsied slightly. 'Good day, Lord Allington.' And goodbye for ever, she whispered to herself.

Chapter Fourteen

Antonia discovered, as she dressed for Almack's that evening, that deciding on a life of spinsterhood did not diminish her pleasure in putting on her newest gown. The confection of silver cobweb gauze over a deep jade green underskirt was outrageously becoming, especially when worn with her great-aunt's diamond set, newly returned from the jeweller.

As she waited for the carriage to come round, Great-Aunt Honoria regarded her critically and observed, 'You look very beautiful tonight, my dear: that simple Grecian hairstyle becomes you. But you are not in spirits, are you? It is Allington, is it not?' Antonia nodded silently. 'Well, I can see why you have fallen for him. Can you not forgive him? Men are but fallible creatures.'

'No, never!' Antonia said emphatically. 'He flaunted his mistress before me—and besides, he does not love me.'

Further conversation was curtailed by the arrival of the carriage with the Granger party. Reluctant as she was to accept Emilia's chaperonage, Antonia knew she had little choice, for Great-Aunt Honoria could not be expected to attend every evening party with her niece.

Emilia thoroughly enjoyed being able to patronise her husband's alarming cousin. Mrs Granger sensed that Antonia was not only more beautiful and better bred than she, but also far more intelligent and at ease in Society.

As soon as Antonia took her place in the carriage, Emilia scanned her appearance, noting with dismay how both her husband and her brother-in-law stared openly at the gentle swell of Miss Dane's breasts in the low-cut gown. What was the old lady about, to let an unmarried girl flaunt herself in such a gown? Something like her own modestly cut bodice would have been more appropriate. Emilia arranged her own lace complacently across her thin chest and basked in an unaccustomed feeling of superiority.

As soon as they reached the exclusive establishment, Antonia accepted an invitation to dance and was not displeased at the end of the measure to find herself on the far side of the room from her relations. She was pleased to see the family of Sir George Dover, another Hertfordshire neighbour, and was soon in conversation with his two pretty daughters.

Miss Kitty fell silent in the middle of a description of the most ravishing silk warehouse she had visited the day before '. . .and two dress lengths for scarcely more than you would expect to pay for one. . .' and blushed.

Antonia, turning to follow her gaze, saw Marcus Allington enter the room. Few men could carry off the severe evening wear insisted upon by the Patronesses of Almack's to such advantage. Antonia's heart beat wildly and she fanned herself, lest her cheeks were as flushed as Miss Kitty's.

'Is he not the most handsome man in the room, Miss

Dane?' Kitty Dover whispered in Antonia's ear. 'In fact, I do declare him the most handsome man in Town.'

Antonia could only stare dumbly across the dance floor, lost in hopeless love for Marcus. A lump in her throat prevented her from answering Miss Dover and she could only hope her feelings were not written plain on her face.

'Oh! He is coming over here! Why, I shall just die if he asks me to dance,' exclaimed Kitty's younger sister Amanda.

Marcus strode across the floor as the next set was forming. Antonia was aware that many pairs of female eyes followed his elegant progress, and when he stopped before the three young women, bowed and then addressed her, she was conscious of several dagger-like looks.

'Miss Dane, Miss Dover, Miss Amanda. Good evening to you. Miss Dane, will you do me the honour of standing up with me for this cotillion?'

'You must forgive me, my lord, I have a headache and cannot dance. Excuse me.' Without a backward glance, Antonia pulled back a curtain and stepped into one of the small retiring rooms.

The room was deserted, without even the presence of the maidservant who was normally in attendance armed with smelling salts, a pincushion and other essentials for rescuing ladies at a disadvantage.

Antonia laid one hand on her breast in a vain attempt to steady her hectic breathing. It was so foolish to respond so—after all, she told herself with an attempt at lightness, if she came to the most fashionable resort in Town she must expect to find Marcus there. She must accustom herself to the sight of him. . .

A footfall behind her sent her whirling around.

'Marcus!' she gasped. 'You should not be in here, it is most improper. Were we to be seen. . .people might believe. . .assume. . .'

'Then they would be correct,' he remarked calmly, taking her in his arms in a manner which brooked no argument.

Nevertheless, Antonia tried to break free, but his arms were strong around her waist and when his lips neared hers she stopped struggling. All propriety, all thought of what was correct flew from her mind the moment his teeth nibbled delicately along the sensitive curve of her upper lip.

Antonia gave herself up to the sensation of being kissed by the only man she would ever love and when he deepened the kiss she responded in kind, kissing him so fiercely that she felt rather than heard his answering groan.

At length he freed her mouth, although his arms continued to support her. That, Antonia acknowledged shakily to herself, was a good thing, for her legs were too tremulous to hold her up.

Marcus's eyes as they smiled down into hers were dark with desire, yet sparkling with mischief. 'Now confess—that preposterous cousin of yours does not kiss you like that.'

Antonia freed herself with an angry shake. 'So that was what prompted your kiss, was it? A desire, not for me, but to best my cousin Hewitt? Well, for your information, sir, I have never permitted Mr Granger to embrace me, nor will I ever do so!'

Marcus looked down into the angry eyes, sparkling magnificently in the indignant face, saw the rise and fall of Antonia's bosom and judged the time was right to do what he had intended ever since he came to Town in pursuit of her.

'But you permit me to embrace you. Come, madam, let us end this foolish charade: say you will be my wife and have done with it.'

'It is no charade, sir. When I give my hand, it will be to a man whom I can love and respect, not to one seemingly prompted by an unwarranted possessiveness.'

'Antonia, enough! Stop behaving like an outraged old maid. After all, you have not always shown such delicacy.' Marcus groaned inwardly as soon as the words were out, for there was hurt as well as anger now in her face. Even so, he was not prepared for the stinging rebuttal that followed as her palm met his cheek.

With a sob, Antonia whisked out of the retiring room, carried onto the dance floor by the speed of her exit. A stately measure was in progress with complicated sets moving slowly the length of the ballroom. Her intrusion set several couples out of rhythm, but they were even more discommoded when Marcus strode to her side, seized her hands and forced her into the line.

'What do you think you are doing?' Antonia hissed, sending apologetic glances to the couples on either side.

'I had not finished with you,' Marcus ground out, the social smile on his lips at variance with his tone. 'And if the only way to stop you boxing my ears again is to converse on the dance floor, then so be it.'

They had reached the head of the set. To her horror, this brought them directly under the scrutiny of Lady Jersey. From her raised brows, Antonia gathered that their irregular entrance had not escaped the Patroness's notice. Beside her, Marcus directed a charming smile at her ladyship and was rewarded by a relaxing of her adamantine gaze.

He whirled Antonia around and they took their place in the centre of the circle, Antonia convinced that every eye in the hall was on them. She curtsied and began the complex sequence of steps with her partner while the other couples circled around them. Miss Kitty, brown curls bouncing, was agog with excitement at Miss Dane's unconventional behaviour.

'Will you stop this nonsense and say yes?' Marcus demanded, in an almost conversational tone that was surely audible to those around.

Antonia's cheeks flamed. 'Shh!' The steps took them apart and then together again.

'I mean it, Antonia!'

'You cannot force me!' she flashed back, still in a whisper.

Now they were hand in hand, sidestepping down the long row. 'You will stay on this dance floor until you give me an answer.' Marcus's eyes were hard with determination.

Antonia was conscious that heads were turning and amongst the watchers some women were whispering behind their fans. She half-turned, looking to flee through the throng, but Marcus was too swift for her, seizing her wrists and keeping her to the measure.

'Marry me, Antonia, you know it was meant to be,' he insisted as they whirled around.

'Never! Nothing you can do or say will induce me to marry you, Marcus Allington!' The words fell into a sudden silence as the band came to a halt in a flurry of strings.

Aghast, staring wildly about her, Antonia realised her

words had been audible in every corner of the room. The floor failing to open up and swallow her, she picked up her skirts and fled, the crowd parting before her.

Outside, careless of cloak or bonnet, she hailed a passing hackney carriage. The driver seemed startled to find a lone gentlewoman hailing him outside Almack's, but he was polite enough when she stammered out the direction.

Hodge, with the licence of an old family retainer, was frankly scandalised to find her alone. 'Miss Antonia! Where's Mrs Clarence? And your cloak. . .and your bonnet! What is amiss?'

'Oh, never mind! Please pay the driver and send my maid up to me.'

Antonia managed to maintain her sang-froid until the maid had helped her into her nightgown, then hastened to dismiss the girl. 'Thank you, that will be all. Please make sure Lady Granger knows I am returned, but tell her I have a headache and will see her at breakfast.'

Antonia sank down on the bed, put her head in her hands and despaired. Under her fingers her temples throbbed and she could still feel the heat of humiliation burning her cheeks.

The whole of Society would know by tomorrow that she had made an indecorous exhibition of herself at Almack's and humiliatingly rejected Lord Allington into the bargain. He would never forgive her for that very public rebuff, even though it was he who had been to blame.

Antonia groaned. To think she had come to London for sanctuary! Now she would have to retreat once more into Hertfordshire and rusticate until some other scandal arose to titillate Society and she was once more forgotten.

And Great-Aunt would never forgive her, broadminded though she was.

At that moment the knocker thudded, audible even through her closed door. Hewitt, no doubt, with Emilia squeaking in his wake, ensuring that no sordid detail of her disgrace remained untold. There were footsteps on the landing and her great-aunt's sitting-room door opened and closed, but strain as she could, Antonia could not hear voices.

The visit lasted half an hour. When carriage wheels rumbled away in the street outside, Antonia sat tensely, awaiting the summons to account for herself. It never came and eventually she fell asleep.

Nervously, Antonia entered the breakfast parlour the next morning to be met by a benign smile from Lady Granger. 'Good morning, my dear. I trust you had a pleasant evening last night.'

'No, Aunt, I did not.' Antonia sat down, gazing miserably at her plate. 'Surely you have heard. . .surely Hewitt told you last night when he came?'

'Oh, Hewitt! I never pay any attention to what he says.' Lady Granger fell silent as a footman brought in a fresh jug of chocolate. As he left, she remarked, 'I suppose you will be wanting to go out of Town for a while?'

Antonia raised troubled eyes and the old lady saw with a pang the depths of her misery. But years of experience had taught her how to keep her thoughts from her countenance and she merely added, 'You may take my travelling carriage and Blake my coachman will, of course, drive you into Hertfordshire.'

Antonia accepted gratefully. She was a little surprised

that her great-aunt had not offered one of the maids to accompany her, but concluded that, despite her calm, the old lady was displeased with her and so she did not care to ask the favour.

It was only a few hours later that Antonia found herself driving out of London, feeling not unlike an unwanted package being returned to its sender. Great-Aunt Honoria had been affectionate, but somehow distracted. Antonia concluded miserably that the old lady was concerned with limiting the damage to the family's reputation and did not press her to talk.

Blake was a middle-aged man used to driving an elderly lady and so progress was steady and smooth. Arriving at last in the late afternoon at the Saracen's Head in King's Langley for the last change of horses, Antonia declined the landlady's offer of refreshment in a private parlour and sighed to see the coachman lumber down from the box and stride into the taproom.

Antonia picked up a book, resigned to wait at least half an hour, but scarcely had she found her place than she saw the skirts of his great coat as he once more mounted the box. Soon they were bowling through the green countryside with surprising speed. The new horses must have been an excellent pair but, even so, Blake's driving had acquired a verve and flair he had not demonstrated in the previous miles.

She thought little of it, however, grateful to be making such good progress and hopeful of being back at the Dower House by nightfall. Blake made the correct turning in Berkhamsted, wheeled left by the castle and began the long steady climb to the Common. Antonia dozed fitfully, but was woken with a start as the carriage lurched.

Strange, she did not remember the road being quite so rough. Puzzled, Antonia looked out and realised she had no idea where they were. Blake must be lost, and she had given him such careful instructions before they set out from Half Moon Street!

Irritated, she knocked briskly on the carriage roof with the handle of her parasol, but Blake took no notice, nor did the conveyance slow. Antonia's annoyance increased. Was the man deaf? They could end up miles out of their way and the shadows were lengthening. She dropped the window and, clutching her hat firmly, leant out.

'Blake! Stop the carriage. You are going the wrong way!' To her relief she felt the pace ease off and saw a clearing ahead with a barn beside it. At least he could turn the carriage there.

As they drew up, she opened the door without waiting for him to descend and jumped down on to the grass. 'Really, Blake, this will not do! Heavens knows where we are.'

He had turned and was climbing down from the box. Antonia waited impatiently. 'There is no need to get down. Just turn the carriage. . .' The rest of the sentence died on her lips as the man reached the ground and turned to face her. 'Marcus! What are you doing?'

Lord Allington shrugged off the heavy greatcoat and tossed the battered beaver hat up on to the coachman's seat. 'Why, I am abducting you, of course.' His manner was so matter of fact he might have been offering her a cup of tea.

Antonia stood amazed, robbed of speech and movement by the shock of his outrageous words. Marcus led the horses over to the barn and began to unbuckle the harness. 'Will you come and hold their heads for a moment while I drop the shafts?'

Mutely Antonia complied, wondering if it were he or she who had lost their senses. At length Marcus loosed the animals into a nearby meadow. Taking Antonia by the hand, he led her unresisting into the barn.

It was a small building as barns went, but clean and dry and smelling of hay. The floor was swept clean to the beaten earth and pitchforks were propped against the walls. Only a small pile of hay remained, and that was incongruously heaped with rugs and pillows.

Even more astounding was the sight of a table and two chairs, the board set with a white cloth and various covered dishes laid out. Marcus crossed and struck flint to light the candles which, in their fine candelabra, added the final touch of unreality to the scene.

Antonia put one hand to her brow and pushed back the curls. 'Are you run mad? What can you hope to achieve by this?'

Marcus came and untied the ribbons of her bonnet and took it from her head. He undid the buttons of her pelisse and handed her into the nearest chair, then reached for a bottle of wine.

'Here, you must be in sore need of something to eat and drink.'

Antonia took a reviving sip of wine and demanded again, 'What do you mean to do with me?'

'Why, ruin you, of course.' Marcus raised his glass in a toast and drank.

Antonia put down the glass sharply, sending the red liquid splashing on to the white cloth. 'Can you be so vindictive, sir? I have thought many things of you over these past months, but not that you would seek revenge for a humiliation last night that was at least as much your fault as mine.'

Marcus smiled. His teeth gleamed white, and almost menacing in the shadows. 'I can assure you, revenge does not come into it. Admittedly, I do not relish having to apologise to Lady Jersey, and many mamas have had their opinion of me as a rakehell confirmed. On the other hand, the odds on our marriage have shortened in most of the betting books of the clubs: I am glad I placed my bet when I did. . .'

'You. . .you. . .you are no gentleman, sir, to bet on such a thing, to bandy my name. . .' She was on her feet now, heading for the door. If she had to walk to Berkhamsted—whichever direction it lay in—she would do so, whatever the risk.

'Come back, Antonia. Where do you think you are going? It is nearly dark. I was only teasing—I have never so much as whispered your name in my club or any other. I cannot resist seeing your eyes flash so, it is most piquant.'

Antonia hesitated. Indeed, it was dark out there, and the woods were pressing in on all sides. She turned from the door and found he had taken off his jacket, tugged his neckcloth loose and was lounging easily in his chair, his long legs stretched out in front of him. The candlelight glanced gold from his hair and shadowed the dangerous, mocking mouth. But his eyes were warm on her; when he stretched out a hand, she walked uncertainly towards him.

As she reached her chair, he caught her hand and pulled her on to his lap, settling her comfortably in the crook of his arm. Knowing the certain outcome of struggling, Antonia yielded to the temptation to sit quietly.

'You do not really intend to ruin me, do you?' she asked, afraid to hear the answer.

'You are ruined, anyway, by the very act of being alone with me, here, all night. Come, Antonia, let us be hanged for the sheep, not the lamb.' As he spoke he stood up, lifting her easily in his arms and walked slowly to the hay bed. Antonia found herself laid gently on a rug.

Marcus loomed above her. He seemed very large and all the humour had fled from the dark eyes. 'Antonia? One word from you and I will take a rug to the far side of this barn and stay there all night. But, as a result of this night you are ruined in the sight of Society. You must marry me, you have no choice.'

She understood him well enough, and believed him. If she told him to, he would take himself off and not trouble her. But she loved him, and if she were never to see him again for the rest of her life, she would at least have this night.

Wordlessly Antonia held up her arms to him and he sank on to the soft bed beside her. Marcus's fingers ran through her hair, tossing aside pins, fanning out the lustrous curls against the blanket. 'You are so beautiful, you take my breath away,' he murmured, his voice curiously husky. His finger traced the line of her jaw then moved to map the curve of her full upper lip.

Antonia shivered in delicious anticipation, shot through with apprehension. Instinctively her teeth fastened on his fingertip and she saw his eyes close momentarily. Antonia began to unbutton his shirt and, smoothing the linen aside, ran her palms flat across the planes of his chest. The heat of him shocked her, but even more shocking was the realisation of the power that her touch gave her over him.

Her fingers moved, tugging and smoothing until she could push the shirt from his shoulders. It was silent in the barn except for his ragged breathing. To her surprise, he did not kiss her, seemingly willing to let her set the pace.

Exploring, giving way entirely to instinct, Antonia let her mouth trail kisses down his muscular shoulder before hesitating for only a heart beat as her lips moved across to his chest. They fastened on his nipple and she heard him gasp as her tongue flicked out and over the sensitive tip.

Startled by her own temerity and the effect she was having on him, Antonia stopped in confusion, hiding her hot face in his neck. Marcus caressed her neck, then neatly unfastened the row of pearl buttons securing her bodice at the back. The gauzy muslin seemed to float from her shoulders and she felt her naked breast against his bare chest, cool against the hot, muscular planes.

He rolled her gently over on to her back, deftly freeing the rest of the dress from her limbs, leaving her clad only in her stockings and chemise. He got to his feet and Antonia closed her eyes, hearing the rest of his clothes fall to the bed beside her.

Antonia ventured to open her eyes again as she felt his weight dip the hay beside her and found herself looking into his intent, serious face. 'Antonia, my darling, are you sure?' For the first time she saw uncertainty in his face.

Apprehension filled her, but was overwhelmed by longing and her love for him. 'Yes,' she whispered, 'but kiss me.'

He needed no further bidding, his mouth possessing hers, his tongue invading sweetly so that she was scarcely aware at first of his weight upon her. When that other, totally intimate invasion came, she cried out against his mouth, but then she was carried on a tide of sensation with him. The pleasure alarmed her even more than the momentary pain, but she gave herself up to it, trusting him to guide her.

Then came a moment when he became still above her, his body rigid as he groaned deep in his throat and then he cried out, a shout of triumph as she too arched against him, her cry of ecstasy muffled against his hard shoulder.

Marcus pulled her into the curve of his shoulder as he fell back on to the bed and she let him hold her, holding on to him in turn as though she would never let him go. They slept wrapped in each other's arms, oblivious to the noises of the night.

They awoke at dawn, Antonia blissfully becoming aware of the movement of Marcus's mouth on the swell of her breast.

'Mmm,' she murmured, sleepily, rolling over to wrap her arms and legs possessively around his naked body. This time it was she who set the pace, urgent in her need for him, revelling in his strength, his power.

At length he propped himself up on one elbow and gazed down at her flushed face. 'And how do you feel this morning, my beauty?' he enquired softly.

'Quite, quite ruined,' she confessed, praying that he would not say the words that would destroy this dream of happiness. But it was a futile hope.

'And how long are you going to make me wait until we marry?' Marcus asked, getting up and reaching for his shirt.

Antonia was struck silent by seeing him standing there,

naked, so close, so real, so very masculine. Then she too reached for her chemise; somehow she felt the need for clothes before she could continue this.

'I am not going to marry you,' she said bluntly as she stood, her back to him for Marcus to fasten the buttons of her bodice.

His lips grazed down her nape. 'Tease.'

'No, I mean it.' She stepped away and turned to face him. 'I never said I would marry you.'

'But you have no choice!' He gestured to the rumpled hay bed with its eloquent impression of two bodies.

'I will not marry you. If anyone realises that we have been here all night, then yes, I am ruined. But I will have to live with that.'

'And if you are with child?' he demanded brutally.

Antonia felt herself grow pale. The thought had never entered her mind, she had been so swept along by her love for him. Her nails bit into her palms as she regained her self-control: she almost capitulated then, but at no time had he told her that he loved her, needed her, could not live without her and she would not marry him without that declaration of love.

All his words of tenderness were occasioned by their lovemaking; none of them had spoken of a shared future. 'If that is the case, I shall raise the child myself, as others have done before me.'

Suddenly he was in front of her, holding her by the shoulders, impelling her to meet his gaze. But he was not angry as she had thought. His face was curiously gentle as was his voice when he asked her, 'Just why, in the face of all this, will you not be my wife?'

Antonia could not meet his eyes or he would see the

way she felt about him. She could not bear for him to pretend to love her out of pity.

'This is not about Claudia, is it?' he demanded. 'Nor about your feelings for Jeremy Blake, let alone your ludicrous cousin Hewitt?'

She shook her head mutely, her eyes still averted from his.

'You told me there was nothing I could do or say to make you agree to marry me. Well, I have done all I can, but I have not said all I should.'

Antonia did look at him then; something in the tone of his voice was different, more tender even than it had been last night. She held her breath, waiting.

'I have never told you I love you, Antonia, but I do. I love you, heart and soul and body—and for ever. I have never loved another woman, and I never will. So if you do not marry me, I shall never marry—for no one could ever take your place.'

Antonia gave a little sob and threw herself into his arms, too overcome even to kiss him. All she could do was hold on to him, feeling his heart beat against her cheek, knowing his strength and his love were hers for ever.

'Well?' he murmured into her hair. 'Will you marry me?'

'Yes, Marcus, my love, of course I will.'

They stood there, holding each other as the rising sun sent a shaft of sunlight spilling across the floor of the barn. At last Antonia freed herself. 'We cannot stand here all day, we must have some breakfast and go home. Thank goodness Donna is not expecting me.'

As she spoke, she moved to the table and began to sort through the hamper with hands that trembled. 'Look, here is bread and ham and a flask of ale. Marcus, how did you manage to contrive all this? And what have you done to my great-aunt's unfortunate coachman?' Somehow the calm domesticity of preparing food with this man convinced her that this was real, and forever.

He moved to her side and began to cut bread. 'He is on his way back to London, having hired a hack as his mistress instructed him.'

Antonia stared at him. 'You mean, you and she. . .that you plotted it and she knew. . .and permitted it? Last night. . .' Antonia could not help but blush.

'I had to ask her permission.' He laughed at Antonia as he reached for the ham. 'When you said there was nothing I could do, I knew I would have to take desperate measures. I could sense Lady Granger approved of me. . .'

'She remembered your grandfather!' Antonia riposted, but she was smiling.

'I went to her direct from Almack's. She told me to behave like a red-blooded man and all would be well. Then I remembered my sister's advice.'

'Anne was in this plot, too?' Now Antonia really was incredulous.

'She told me, when you left for London, that I was arrogant, that I had never felt the need to explain myself or my actions to anyone. I realised I had never told you I loved you, never realised that I needed to. I should have known you would never marry for anything less.'

Antonia reached up and kissed him. 'And when did you realise you loved me?'

'When I saw you in Pethybridge's office. I knew what it must have cost a gentlewoman to undertake business like that. And despite the reverse you had obviously suffered, you were brave and defiant. Although I was still angry with you about your poachers, yet in that moment all I wanted to do was to protect you.'

She stepped into the shelter of his arms. 'And now you can,' she said softly.

Marcus kissed her gently, all the love he had never spoken until now evident in the embrace. Eventually he released her, with a sigh. 'I could stay here for ever, but I suppose we should eat and then make our way home.'

When they left, he handed her up onto the seat of the carriage next to him. 'Come, ride here beside me until we get closer to the village, there will be no one about at this hour to see you.'

Antonia linked her arm through his as he gathered up the reins and asked, in a mock-severe tone, 'And you can tell me all about Lady Reed.'

Marcus looked down into her laughing face and knew he had never been so happy. 'Lady who?'

Historical Romance™

Coming next month

A LORD FOR MISS LARKIN
Carola Dunn

Alison Larkin thought the most romantic thing in the
world would be to have a lord falling at her feet and
pledging eternal love.

With the arrival of her recently widowed and wealthy
aunt, Alison's dream could become a reality. She was
granted a Season and would be introduced to the
crème of the ton.

How vexing that the first eligible gentleman she was to
meet was a plain *Mr* Philip Trevelyan who had a way of
making Alison forget that it was her dearest wish to marry
a lord.

THE IMPOSSIBLE EARL
Sarah Westleigh

Leonora wanted him to leave: having been reduced to
working as a governess, she was left her uncle's fortune
and fine town house in Bath. But she also inherited Blaise,
Earl of Kelsey!

Blaise refused to go: her uncle had leased the ground floor
to Blaise, where he ran a gentlemen's club.

Leonora's hopes for a respectable life in Society and the
possibility of marriage would come to nought without a
compromise, particularly when the Earl was so clearly *not*
a candidate in the marriage mart.

FREE!

FOUR FREE
specially selected
Historical Romance™ novels
<u>PLUS</u> a FREE Mystery Gift
when you return this page...

Return this coupon and we'll send you 4 Historical Romance novels and a mystery gift absolutely FREE! We'll even pay the postage and packing for you.

We're making you this offer to introduce you to the benefits of the Reader Service™– FREE home delivery of brand-new Historical Romance novels, at least a month before they are available in the shops, FREE gifts and a monthly Newsletter packed with information, competitions, author profiles and lots more...

Accepting these FREE books and gift places you under no obligation to buy, you may cancel at any time, even after receiving just your free shipment. Simply complete the coupon below and send it to:

MILLS & BOON READER SERVICE, FREEPOST, CROYDON, SURREY, CR9 3WZ.

READERS IN EIRE PLEASE SEND COUPON TO PO BOX 4546, DUBLIN 24

NO STAMP NEEDED

Yes, please send me 4 free Historical Romance novels and a mystery gift. I understand that unless you hear from me, I will receive 4 superb new titles every month for just £2.99* each, postage and packing free. I am under no obligation to purchase any books and I may cancel or suspend my subscription at any time, but the free books and gift will be mine to keep in any case. (I am over 18 years of age)

H7YE

Ms/Mrs/Miss/Mr_____
BLOCK CAPS PLEASE

Address_____

_____

_____

_____ Postcode _____

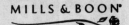

MILLS & BOON

Christmas Treats

A sparkling new anthology —the perfect Christmas gift!

Celebrate the season with a taste of love in this delightful collection of brand-new short stories combining the pleasures of food and love.

Figgy Pudding
by PENNY JORDAN
All the Trimmings
by LINDSAY ARMSTRONG
A Man For All Seasonings
by DAY LECLAIRE

And, as an extra treat, we've included the authors' own recipe ideas in this collection—because no yuletide would be complete without...Christmas Dinner!